Escape

Book Two of the Kahidon Mountain Series

Alyce Everton

Table of Contents

Prologue:

Jess fastened the last button on her black pants and then pulled on her black shirt as she stood alone in the empty bedroom. The room had only a single bed, and a mirror that hung on the wall. There was enough light shining in from the window that allowed her to see without the use of a candle. She checked that her dagger was secure in its sheath that was attached to her belt that lay on the bed. Next she fastened her belt securely around her waist. Then she looked up and saw her reflection looking back. The black dragon tattooed on her arm seemed to fit perfectly with her new black clothes. She looked just like a Black Dragon, which was exactly what she wanted. She saw the one streak of black hair that had appeared hours earlier, it seemed to be out of place amongst her long blonde hair.

As she looked at her reflection in the mirror she pondered on the events that had led her to where she was now. From the event that started everything up until that very moment. The first moment in the forbidden forest near Morganstin when Erika and herself found the red and silver drawstring bag. The bag contained a magical golden brown fur cloak which ended up giving Erika the ability to control the weather and natural elements. Also inside the bag was a prophecy book which was given to Linder, the man whom Jess wanted to marry, whom they met along their way to return the items they had found in the bag to a man name Kedar Ainsley. Along their way to Kedar's castle a few people helped shelter them from the Black Dragons who were hunting them because they possessed the talismans from the bag. On their travels they learned that magic was real and the Black Dragons were trying to take control of the world by using black magic. They would be willing to kill many people in their process to find all four talismans. This would give Karlsen Soldum, the leader of the Black Dragons power to control every aspect of life and could control anyone's thoughts and actions.

Jess thought about how she met Linder, Marcus, and Jusdan. Jusdan taught them about many terrible black magic creatures. This was useful because they ended up fighting them several times on their way to Kedar's castle. She thought about how much she hated Therion's, the werewolf like creatures that could change into the form of their last victim, usually humans. They would trick their prey into their lair until night when it would change into its true form and tear the person apart with its sharp fangs.

Jess also thought about Ksoldums. The terrible firefly like creatures that lived in Spirit Tunnel. They have fangs and a poisonous bite, and whom also produce voices that sound like someone you have heard before that they use to lure you towards them. They sound like someone calling for help, or a child crying or family members scolding you for not coming to them for help. All of which are just tricks to get people to come close to them until they bite your skin and kill you almost instantly. She contemplated about the many times she thought that her and her best friend Erika along with their new friends were going to die from the black magic creatures. She also thought about how Linder saved her after being shot in the stomach with an arrow and took her safely to Kedar's castle.

Once she was healed by the use of magic she learned all about the magical talismans and the history of ancient wizards. She learned what the talismans represented and the task she would undertake if she accepted the calling of wizard that came along with the talismans. She shook her head as she looked at herself in the mirror as she remembered accepting the responsibilities and the impossible task to defeat the Black Dragons and rid the world of black magic. She also thought about the gold chain necklace with a small gold hollow heart hanging from the end of it that she wore around her neck. The necklace used to give her the power of empathy. She could feel others feelings and manipulate them as well. Making others feel whatever she wanted them to feel. The necklace did her no good now but she still kept it around her neck. She picked up the gold heart that hung at the end of the chain in between her fingers and looked at it for a long moment then put it under her shirt.

It didn't matter anymore. She thought to herself. After looking at her new self once more in the mirror she glanced out the window. The sun was starting to set, it would be dusk soon.

Changing her thoughts to the upcoming events that the night would bring, she left the room and closed the door behind herself.

Many Weeks Earlier…

Chapter One- Leaving Kedar's Castle

"What is that?" Erika asked with curiosity and apprehension in her voice as the large beast lowered itself from the sky onto the ground in front of them. This caused everyone except Kedar to step back many steps in fear, as they tried to put as much distance as they could between them and the beast. As soon as the beast put its four large lion paws onto the ground it walked right up next to Kedar. To everyone's surprise it bowed its eagle shaped head then lowered its big tan colored lion body onto the ground, tucking its large dark brown eagle wings next to its body. It then rested its eagle's head that was covered with brown feathers, with black starring eyes, and long hooked black beak onto its big tan front lion paws as it waited for Kedar to respond.

Kedar wore dark tan trousers, a very loose and flowing dark green shirt with a leather belt that ran across his stomach. He wore a simple well worn brown cloak with the hood down exposing his shoulder length brown and gray hair that was tied back with a small piece of thread. He bowed then outstretched his hand and touched the great beast's fur. "Thank you for coming. Arise my friend." Kedar said then removed his hand from the beast. The beast stood up on its four paws and stretched its long furry neck to its full height. It then pointed his eagle head down and looked at everyone who was several steps away. Brian gasped at the size of the beast. Its lion's body stood much taller than a man with its total height with its long furry neck and eagle head the beast easily stood ten feet taller than a man, and its large furry and muscular stature was very intimidating.

"Kedar, where did you find that? They are supposedly extinct." Jusdan asked amazement in his voice as he stared at the beast in front of him. "How did you earn its trust?" Annabella asked bewildered while holding onto Jusdan's hand. Hannah stood staring at it unsure what to do or say. Everyone still kept their distance.

"What is it?" Erika asked once more. "This, my friends, is a griffin." Kedar replied waving his hand out towards the beast in introduction. As if the griffin understood, it bowed its head down and then up again. "Well don't just stand there, come and introduce yourselves." Kedar instructed. Everyone stood nervously in their same spots eyeing the Griffin. "He won't hurt you. I promise." Kedar reassured. "Tell me how you earned its trust first." Annabella insisted. "I saved him." Kedar answered bluntly. "Saved him from what?" Jusdan asked. "Well from a Therion of course." Kedar replied like he was stating the obvious. "A Therion!" Linder exclaimed, speaking up for the first time since the griffin had landed.

With Linder's exclamation the griffin lets out a loud screeching sound. "Well yes indirectly I saved him from a Therion; if I wouldn't have helped him heal faster a Therion would have been able to catch him and certainly would have killed him. I found him injured in the woods one day while going for a stroll. I don't know how long he had been injured but he kept crying out in long painful screeching cries. Somehow he injured one of his wings and was unable to fly. I almost got my head pecked off from that peak of his in my attempt to help but in the end I was able to put a healing spell onto his injured wing. I watched him for many hours until the sun was well on the other side of the sky, during that time that I spent with him I kept an eye out for any predators that might be around also.

Nothing dangerous came but with the sky slowly getting darker I knew my chances of getting back to my castle safely were dwindling away with the passing time. Finally I decided that I had to start heading back and I hoped that the griffin would be alright. You see during the time that I watched it, it never once tried to fly away it just paced back and forth and when it wasn't pacing it was sitting on the ground watching me. I hoped that it would try to fly away when I left. I wasn't sure how well my healing spell had worked on it and I needed to be going to make it back to my castle before dark so I stood up from the fallen tree I was sitting on, and for some reason I felt the need to say something to it before I left so I spoke to it. "I wish you a safe night and farewell." I said. With that the beast outstretched its wing, rose to the air and then flew out of sight. I watched it leave until it was blocked by the tree tops and then I headed home.

The next morning I heard a strange high pitched screeching noise that sound like it was right outside of my bedroom wall. I looked out my bedroom window and to my great surprise the griffin was flying in circles next to my window. I quickly got dressed then went outside. The griffin spotted me and landed on the ground next to me. I introduced myself and told it good morning like I was speaking to an old friend. The griffin lowered its body down to the ground and I placed my hand on its fur like I just did when he arrived. I wasn't sure what was going to happen if I touched it but I had to try.

After I touched its fur it rose to his full height; I then noticed he had something wooden in his beak. I reached my hand up to take it from him and he opened his beak and dropped it into my hand. It was a whistle. I looked at the whistle closely and saw nothing abnormal about it so I put the thin wooden whistle to my lips and blew, the sound continued even after I had stopped blowing. I noticed that the griffin's head lifted to the sky, watching. I looked up also and to my astonishment within moments out of the forest above the tree tops flew two more griffins flying towards my castle. I knew from that moment on I had earned the trust of the griffins.

I have used the whistle only a small number of times, each time I did the griffins came. I earned their trust more and more. Griffins are very intelligent creatures that can't be tamed like a household pet but you can earn their trust if you prove yourself worthy to them. During those times I talked to them, I fed them and I studied them." "How come I never saw them?" Annabella interjected. "You were always busy teaching your children or cooking. With all the time I have spent with them I know he won't hurt anyone, he trusts me and I trust him. Come introduce yourselves." Kedar replied gesturing with his hand for everyone to come forward.

Jusdan and Annabella each holding the others hand moved towards the griffin first. Brian and Hannah, followed their parents closely behind and slowly stepped the few steps closer the griffin. "I am Jusdan and this is my wife Annabella, and these are our two children, Hannah and Brian." Jusdan said and pointed to each in turn.

"We are Kedar's family." Jusdan continued. The griffin looked at each in turn then turned its eagle head and looked at Kedar then back to Jusdan then it bowed its head in acknowledgment. Marcus, Erika, Linder and Jess all took turns introducing themselves to the griffin, which in turn bowed its head after each one. "Well now that the formalities are over let's get down to business. I believe that these magnificent creatures aren't restrained to just this mountain, I have seen them fly higher than anything I have ever seen before and I believe that they can travel wherever they please, if I am correct and if they would be willing, I think you could ride on them over the mountains and if they aren't restrained to this mountain by any magic then they could fly you all the way back to Morganstin, which would cut your traveling time down by an incredible amount of time and we all know that right now time is against us." Kedar explained.

"That's a lot of ifs." Marcus interjected. "How are we going know if they would be willing to help us?" Linder asked, while looking up towards the Griffin's head. "Just ask." Kedar replied. "They are very intelligent creatures and I believe they understand our language. Just ask, and see what kind of response you get from him." Kedar insisted. Jess nervously let go of Linder's hand and moved to stand directly under the Griffin.

Looking up at the Griffins black eyes, which were staring back at her, she placed one hand onto its soft furry body and trying not to show her nervousness for the Griffin she bravely asked it directly. "Can you fly us over these mountains safely to Morganstin so we can do what is necessary to defeat the black magic that is invading our world?" Everyone held their breath in anticipation of the Griffin's response.

The Griffin stared down into Jess's eyes for a long moment and without any warning it outstretched it long brown wings, beat them up and down then rose into the sky and quick as lighting flew into the trees of the surrounding forest. Jess lowered her hand from where it had been resting on the Griffin and turned to face all of the people that were watching her. "I guess not." She replied to the silence, discouraged and dejected by the occurrence. "It will be alright." Linder reassured her taking her hand. "I truly thought that they would help us." Kedar answered solemnly shaking his head in surprise. "Well…I guess that's that. I suppose we go back to our original plan of traveling by foot. We don't have much time to spare if we want to keep ahead of Karlsen Soldum." Marcus indicated. "You're right. We need to leave soon." Linder acknowledged.

"Well this is good bye then." Erika said to Annabella, Jusdan and their two children, Hannah and Brian, who were standing closest to her. "Good bye" Hannah replied. "Bye" Brian said. "Safe journey to you all and after you succeed at defeating Karlsen Soldum we will meet again. Remember to keep practicing your powers, they will come in use when the time is right and keep each other safe. You will face many obstacles and dangers along your way and the task ahead may seem daunting but if you rely on each other's knowledge to help, along with each of your abilities, and your bravery and determination then you will succeed and rid this world of the black magic plague. When that day comes it will be a momentous occasion which we will all celebrate together. Why am I standing around telling things you already know? You must be going now. Good luck, and farewell" Kedar imparted.

"Stay safe, all of you." Annabella instructed. "Keep your wits about you, and when the time is right we will meet again." Jusdan imparted. "We will do our best." Linder answered. Jess picked up her pack from the ground and threw it on her shoulder. "Thanks, we will see you all again someday." She replied then took Linder's hand into her own once more. Marcus and Erika said their goodbyes and then they turned to leave. Facing the Kahidon forest with fear in their minds, hope in their hearts, and determination to overcome the many impossible tasks ahead and with a little magic to help, Linder, Jess, Marcus and Erika took their first steps on their new adventure.

Together they traveled a slightly worn dirt path farther into the forest; their goal was to reach the Spirit Tunnel before night fall. Jusdan had written down the directions for which tunnels to take during their travels through the tunnel on a piece of parchment and had given it to Linder. Jess was dreading going through the Spirit Tunnel again, but it was the quickest way to get to the other side of the Kahidon Mountains. She still had nightmares from going through the tunnel the first time and the voices from the Ksoldums that mimicked her family crying out in pain and yelling in anger at her were still fresh in her mind. Jess knew the voices weren't really her family but the pain of the voices and the tantalizing need to go and help them was almost too overwhelming. If she were to leave the main path to follow the voices the Ksoldums, who were making the voices, they would kill her with their poisonous bites.

"Jess are you alright?" Linder asked her softly as they traveled farther into the forest. "Yes, I was just thinking about the Spirit Tunnel." "I will keep you safe. You'll see we will make it through there without any problems." Linder commented gripping her hand tighter in reassurance. She believed him about keeping her safe, but getting through Spirit Tunnel without any problems was a harder concept to believe than the previous. She knew he was trying to comfort her but it didn't help much. "As long as we don't encounter any Therion's on our way there then I think we will be doing pretty well, don't you?" Marcus replied with a small laugh as if he was making a joke but due to the real seriousness of the issue Jess couldn't laugh along. As if Marcus's comment were a reminder of the dangers around them everyone then walked in silent vigilance for a time being.

The farther they traveled into the forest the darker the sky became, not because of the time of day but because how of tight knit the tree branches entwined together near the top of the canopies, almost forming one continues blanket of branches and leaves, which allowed little sunlight to shine through to the ground. Erika readjusted her sword belt on her waist to make it easier to walk. Marcus led the way farther into the forest with Erika beside him while Jess and Linder held hands followed closely behind. They all listened and watched diligently for any dangers ahead.

After traveling for a few hours this way, Marcus suggested that they rest for a quick lunch. Not seeing or hearing any danger the whole time in the forest so far, they decided that a quick lunch would be good for them. They needed the nourishment for strength and energy to continue on and having some food in the stomachs might lighten their spirits.

They ate a lunch of roasted quail, a loaf of white bread smothered in a blackberry jam which was a special treat Annabella made. She had given it to Erika before they left. They also enjoyed a variety of raw fruits and vegetables. Once done eating they packed away the remaining foods into their packs and set off once more. Not more than thirty minutes after they had eaten Erika started looking around the surrounding forest and back towards the way they had come wearily as if searching for something amiss. "What is it?" Jess asked her. "I thought I heard something, but I'm not sure, it was so quite, it could have just been the wind." Erika replied. "There is no wind. What did you hear?" Marcus asked his full attention towards her as they all slowed to a stop. "I thought I heard something moving through the bushes." Everyone looked around, searching for anything out of place in the dark foreboding forest. "I don't see or hear anything." Linder answered. "Neither do I." Jess replied.

Marcus had a look of intense concentration come across his face then replied. "That's just it. There is no noise, and no movement of any kind, except us. So if Erika heard something besides us it must have been scared away. Let's keep going, keep an extra watch out though. I don't want to be surprised by something jumping out at us, again." Marcus stated emphasizing the last word. Erika tilted her head as trying to listen to something far away and from the side. "There." She said. Everyone listened. After a moment of silence Jess replied. "I don't hear anything." Not wanting to imply that she didn't believe Erika, she said. "Sorry, I just don't hear anything." "I don't either." Marcus said then rubbed the black stubble on his dark chin. Linder strained to hear anything.

"Oh wait, I think I do hear something but it's very faint. It does sound like something moving through the forest. I'm not sure though it's too far away or it's something small that is too quiet to hear." He admitted. "Is it coming our direction?" Marcus asked. "I don't know." Erika confided as she listened to the forest for the noise. "Let's keep moving then, I don't want to find out what it is or whether or not it is coming this way." Jess stated. They all start walking again, in silence listening for the unknown noise. Just then a large black crow flew through the canopy of branches and landed on the ground in front of them, almost as if bouncing up and down on his claws it squawked very loudly towards them. Surprised by the crow and unsure what to do everyone stopped. The crow flapped it wings while cawing then turned its beak towards the forest in front of them, cawed once more then flew into the trees towards the direction they were traveling.

"That was the oddest behaving crow I have ever seen. What do think it was doing?" Linder asked looking at the others. Before anyone could answer there came a loud cawing noise followed by a sound they all dreaded hearing. The sound was a loud guttural ferocious roar which belonged to only one thing, a Therion. The crow's caw and the roar of the Therion came from a short distance in front of them. Linder had his sword pulled from his sheath, along with Marcus before the second roar vibrated through the air. "That crow must have been warning us about the Therion ahead." Erika stated as if that was the obvious answer to the crows actions. "We wouldn't have known it was there until we came upon it, now we know it's there and can be prepared." She continued, and then the realization hit her with fear.

There was Therion just ahead of them. The thought hit her like a brick wall. Her face went white and her eyes became large with fear as the thought sunk in. The crow cawed once more then with incredible speed flew through the trees to where they were and sped over their heads and flew past them into the forest the way they had already come. The Therion's roar drew closer and closer. "Get your swords out and hide behind those trees! If we have to fight we will!" Linder commanded. Jess and Erika quickly drew their swords from their sheaths on the weapons belts and they all ran off the path, each hid behind nearby trees. They kept crouched down to the ground, hoping to keep hidden from the oncoming beast. Within seconds a massive furry beast, which is twice the size of a man, with sharp claws, blunt snout, snapping teeth and glowing red eyes charged past, its earsplitting cry ringed deep, savage, and ferocious once more in the air as he rampaged right past where Jess and the others were hiding, as if determined to catch the crow.

Linder was the first to move from his hiding spot. "Let's go while it's distracted." He said keeping his sword tightly gripped in his right hand. With their hearts racing they hurriedly made their way farther into the forest and closer to Spirit Tunnel. With a few hours left until they should reach Spirit Tunnel, and over an hour's since the Therion incident, they thought it safe to slow their pace and began speaking to each other once more. "One thing that perplexes me is I thought Therion's only took their true form at night. I thought they took the shape of a human during the day and then at night change back. Why was that Therion in its true form?" Marcus asked voicing his thoughts out loud.

"That is strange" Jess replied, perplexed by the thought. "I wonder…" Linder began. "The crow!" Erika stated as if she were having the same thought as Linder. "Yes. I wonder if the sound we originally heard was the Therion, in its human form and the crow was trying to warn us about the danger ahead. Then the crow did something to make the Therion mad and forced it to change into its real form and go after it, leaving the way open for us to pass safely. I know it sounds farfetched, but that's the only explanation I can think of." Linder explained as they all gave him a bewildered look.

"That doesn't seem too farfetched. Actually that answers most of what happened. What I still don't understand is why a crow would warn us. Crows don't typically act like that. It's just a crow, right?" Jess asked. "I hope so; I don't want to think about what it could really be, if not a crow." Erika replied as they traveled through the dark forest, which seemed to be void of all animal life. Jess requested that they eat supper sometime soon. Agreeing about being hungry, Erika's stomach growled. Marcus suggested that they travel to the mouth of Spirit Tunnel before they eat supper. Linder agreed with Marcus, and then Jess and Erika also agreed. Marcus estimated that they have another hour and a half until they would reach the tunnel. A snapping noise jolted all their heads towards the forest behind them.

They all stopped walking as soon as they saw what was coming out of a dense part of the trees. Out of the trees stepped a woman. The woman looked too clean and regal to be in this forest, well any forest for that fact. Jess thought to herself. She didn't have a speck of dirt on her. Marcus caught his breath from looking at the raw beauty of the woman. Her skin was a perfectly smooth pale brown; her eyes looked as if they couldn't decide whether to be a light brown or a light green, so they combined both colors together. Her lips were a light pink, while her dark brown hair flowed voluptuously down her half exposed back all the way to the end of her back. She was wearing an overly exposing long black and red gown that flowed down to her ankles. The dress was tight fitting on the top including a low cut front which was exposing the top of her cleavage. The back of the dress looked to have been specially made for her the way it form fitted her body, with the top of her back exposed. She was wearing an exquisite diamond necklace, where around the entire necklace diamonds hung by small chains which were connected to the chain that went around her neck.

Linder glanced between the woman approaching and at Jess then back to the woman. Jess seemed to be the only one that noticed that the woman wasn't wearing any shoes and from what Jess could tell from her pale brown feet didn't look dirty, or bruised from walking on the rough forest ground without any shoes. It looked as if the woman might have just taken off her shoes the moment before coming out the trees, Jess thought to herself. It only took a few seconds for the woman to catch up to where all of them had stopped.

"Hello, my name is Adaze. I seem to be lost. I was traveling with some guards that were escorting me to Taharan and I seem to have lost them. Do you think it will be alright if I travel with you and maybe you can possibly help me find my guards?" the woman asked in a smooth and entrancing tone. "Yes!" Marcus blurted out. "I mean, we will gladly help you." he corrected his face flushing red which was hard to tell with his dark skin but still visible none the less. "I am at your service." Linder replied and took a step closer to the woman. Erika glanced at Jess, whose eyes had grown wide with a look of disbelief on her face. Jess couldn't believe it, Linder said he loved her, and she loved him and he said they were meant to be together and then the minute a beautiful woman asked for his help he just forgets all about her.

Erika nudged Jess's arm to get her attention. Jess looked over at Erika who had a questioning look on her face and nodded her head towards Linder. Jess shrugged as if she didn't know what was going on. "I am at your service also; I will do anything for you." Marcus responded. "I am so pleased." Adaze replied smoothly. "Where are you headed if you don't mind me asking?" she asked in an alluring tone. Jess spoke up before anyone else could. "We were going to stop to eat supper shortly." She said in a straight forward tone and a determined look on her face deliberately leaving out the location of where they were headed. There was something about Adaze that Jess didn't like. When Jess answered, Adaze didn't look at her, she kept her eyes on the two men, as if Jess and Erika weren't there.

"I am famished; my guards were carrying all my food. Would it be alright if I joined you for supper? I found a clearing a short distance away that we could go to enjoy each other's company and eat supper together, would you like me to show you where it is?" Adaze proposed so smoothly and tantalizing, Jess was starting to feel the need to obey anything she said, almost. Something about her isn't right. Jess thought to herself. "That would be wonderful. Please lead the way." Marcus answered, swoon by this stranger. "Yes please do." Linder replied keeping his eyes fixed to her. Jess nudged Erika, and was just about to say something to her. Erika shook her head, as if she were confused about something then looked at Jess. Her eyes showed a mix of feelings in them, confusion, curiosity, and then anger. She looked away from Jess and then replied to Adaze. "I would love to go with you." Jess didn't understand what was happening.

"Linder, I thought we had a plan, remember?" Jess asked. "Yeah, we will do that later." He nonchalantly replied without looking at her. Had they all gone crazy? Jess thought. "The clearing is this way." Adaze soothed and then turned around to face the direction she had just come from and began walking away. Instantly Linder, Marcus, and Erika followed. Jess stood momentarily befuddled by what was happening. She watched as Adaze walked over rocks, sticks, pine needles and other forest debris in bare feet without showing any signs of pain, as if she wasn't feeling any of it. Jess followed behind keeping a watchful eye on Adaze and the others. They traveled for half an hour before reaching large clearing the in the forest. "What do you think?" Adaze cooed. "This will be great." Marcus replied, not even looking around at his surroundings. "I am so famished, could you share your food with me?" she asked Linder drawing herself a lot closer to Linder than Jess would have liked. "Of course." He answered smiling, as if it would be his greatest pleasure in the world to do whatever she asked.

Immediately Erika, Marcus and Linder were all taking off their packs and rummaging through them pulling out different foods. Adaze sat on a fallen tree log nearby one of the edges of the clearing. Jess took off her own pack and pulled out only enough food for herself while the others continuously asked Adaze if she would like many different foods that they offered her. Jess ate a piece of bread, an apple and two dried meat slices while watching the others. Adaze politely declined everything they offered her and told them to eat first and she would eat after they were done. Jess finished eating, as the others just started. Adaze glanced over at Jess and saw that she was watching her. She smiled a knowing smile then turned her attention towards the others.

As soon as everyone else was finished eating, they offered their foods to Adaze once more and she declined again. For someone who said she was famished, she was sure is picky eater. Jess thought to herself. Just then the large black crow flew right over their heads and flew past them. Jess watched it as it flew past. There came a deep low growl from somewhere close. Jess turned her attention away from the direction the crow had flown and looked around trying to see where the growl had come from. "Did you hear that?" Jess asked to no one in particular. No one answered. The crow flew back into the clearing and right over Adaze, who to Jess's surprise growled, a deep low growl with a look a pure hatred on her face that she directed towards the crow. The crow turned itself around and flew out of the clearing the way it had just came in from. Jess stared at Adaze. No one else seemed to notice any of what had happened. They were all still looking at Adaze as if she were the most perfect thing in the world. There is something really wrong here. Jess thought to herself.

Adaze stood up and walked over to where Jess was sitting and then kneeled down beside her. Taking Jess's hand she said. "Jess, I am very afraid of crows will you please go and kill that one for me? It would make me feel so much better." Jess suddenly had the urge to do exactly what Adaze instructed but could feel something pulling at her telling her that this was wrong.

"Sure" Jess answered then stood up, retrieving her bow and quiver from on top of her pack that lay on the ground then headed into the forest following the direction where the crow went. Adaze stood, starring at Jess until she was out of the clearing.

As soon as Jess left the clearing her mind went instantly clear, as if there were a layer of fog clouding her thoughts before and now she could think clearly. She had to stop for an instant to figure out what she was doing away from the others. Remembering what Adaze had instructed her to do, but now realizing that she didn't want to do that she decided just to go for a short walk instead. That would give her time to try to figure out what was going on. Continuing to follow a straight path away from the others so she wouldn't get lost, Jess walked at a leisurely pace but still cautious about her surroundings. After walking for ten minutes or more, there came a small pecking sound just around the next tree in front of her. She paused listening, the pecking sound was constant so she quietly knocked an arrow in her bow and made her way to the tree. Slowly peering around it, she found the large black crow pecking at the tree. Pointing the arrow at the crow, it stopped and looked at her. She held its gaze for an instant and then lowered her bow.

"I'm not going to hurt you." She told the crow, even though she knew the crow wouldn't understand. She placed the arrow back into the quiver and tossed the bow back over her shoulder. The crow hopped to the next tree farther away and began pecking at it. Jess decided to follow, when she looked at where on the tree where the bird was pecking she saw large claw marks dug into the bark. She backed up a few steps. The crow flew to another tree, Jess followed. This tree also had large claw marks dug into the bark. The crow flew on once more but this time landed on the ground and started pecking at something on the ground. Jess reached the spot and put her hand on the leafy section where the crow was pecking.

There was something under the leaves shining. The crow moved over as Jess moved the leaves around. Gagging at what she found, she turned her head away. She scrambled away a few paces away, and then sat down on the ground before she would fall down. What does that mean? She thought to herself. It obviously has something to do with Adaze. The crow flew to the nearest tree, pecked at the claw marks then flew back to the gruesome scene that lay hidden under the leaves. Jess thought about what it all meant and then in a sickening rush it all came together in her head as she remembered what Jusdan had said about Therion's. "During the day it takes the shape of a human to lure them into its boundaries of its realm until night, when it changes into its real form and then eats its prey." The claw marks on the trees nearby, the half eaten mutilated head in the leaves and the perfect disguise to get anyone to follow it. Adaze is a Therion. Disguising itself as its last victim, she or it had led them into its realm and that's why she said she was famished and then refused all their food. "She is going to eat them." Jess said unintentionally said out loud. The crow cawed excitedly.

"You helped us before, didn't you?" She asked the crow. "And now you're helping us again. Thank you." Jess nodded to the crow, not caring if it could understand her or not. She then changed her thoughts and knew what she had to do, gathering enough courage she moved the leaves off the head and untangled the exquisite diamond necklace, which held diamonds hung by small chains around the entire necklace which were connected to the chain which was entangled in bone, blood, hair and what brain matter remained of what was left of the girls head that looked exactly like Adaze. Jess wiped off the necklace and her hands on a small pile of damp leaves from nearby to get the blood off, then tucked the necklace into her pocket.

She looked up towards the sky, even though the thick canopy of branches blocked most of the sunlight she could tell that it was getting late and would be dark soon. She didn't have much time; she had to get back to the others before the Therion changed into its true form. If Jess could get to it and kill it before it changed then she would save her friends. "Hopefully it will be easier to kill when it is in human form." Jess said to the crow, which cawed excitedly at that remark. Jess looked down on the crow once more, said thank you and then started running back to where the others were.

She ran as fast as she could, stopping just short of entering the clearing. Looking in from the shadows of the trees she could see that Linder, Marcus, and Erika were sitting around Adaze like they were little puppies waiting to be pat on the head. Jess remembered the fog clearing her mind as soon as she left the clearing so she decided to stay out of there unless she absolutely had to enter. Pulling her bow off her shoulder then knocking an arrow she took a deep breath. She would have to hit Adaze just in the right spot to cause the damage she was hoping for. The shot would be tricky considering how close the others were to her and Jess wasn't a great archer but she had confidence that she would be able to make the shot.

She took another deep breath, no one seeming to notice her and with the one quick motion released the arrow and watched it fly through the air. The target hit its mark. Adaze let out an earsplitting ferocious roar as the arrow hit its heart. Within seconds the once beautiful woman burst into millions of tiny pieces and there twice the size of a man stood a Therion. Its large claws swiping at the air, his blunt nose dripping mucus and its glowing red eyes fixed on Jess. Then it started to move. Erika screamed and backed away as fast as she could. Marcus and Linder seemed to be awoken from a dream, dazed and confused yet aware of the danger they reached for their swords. Jess shot another arrow into the beast as it roared in anger. Hitting the beast in the heart right next to the first arrow, it dropped to the ground. Blood now soaking its fur, thrashing on the ground the Therion roared out in pain and anger. Marcus stabbed it in the heart with his sword and it made one last sound which was a mix between a gurgle and a roar and then went motionless.

"Jess!" Linder called out in desperation, unsure and unable to see where Jess was standing. "I'm here." Jess said as she entered the clearing, the bow still in her hand. Linder rushed over to her and put his arms around her, embracing her. Erika and Marcus looked over at Jess. "What happened?" Linder asked confusion in his voice. "Let's get out of here and then I will explain." Jess answered pulling away from his embrace.

Marcus withdrew his sword from the dead Therion and pulled out Jess's two arrows then wiped the blood off the arrows with a pile of leaves. "Thanks for that." He said as he handed Jess her arrows back. She took the arrows, placed them into her quiver then replied, "You're welcome". "Everyone get your packs, we need to go now." Jess sternly instructed as she went for her own pack. Within a minute they all had their packs on.

"Which way to Spirit Tunnel?" she asked. "We need to go back to the path we were on before and follow that south. I don't even remember leaving it, so I'm not sure which way that path is." Linder admitted. "I don't either" Marcus replied. "I vaguely remember, but it was like walking through fog. I could only see small bits and pieces and nothing made sense then I went into darkness and I don't remember anything after that, except Adaze." Erika said. "I can get us back to that path, follow me and if you see any beautiful women don't follow them." Jess reprimanded. A crow's caw turned Jess's attention from the way she was going to take them. It cawed again, Jess lead the way into the forest to where the crow was waiting on a low hanging branch.

"A crow again? I wouldn't think that crows would typically live in an area such as this." Marcus stated curiously. "Is that the same crow as before?" Erika asked. "Yes. This crow helped me save all of you from the Therion. I believe it's trying to help us." Jess acknowledged. The crow cawed and then flew off farther into the forest. "I think we should follow it." Jess replied. "You saved our lives. If you think this crow is going to help us then by all means let's follow it." Marcus replied. "I agree." said Erika. Linder took Jess's hand into his. Together they led the way followed by Marcus and Erika who were walking together, all of whom were following the crow. Linder leaned in close to Jess's ear as they continued walking and whispered something soft, and sweet. "If I did anything to make you think less of me, I am truly sorry. I love you." Jess turned her face to his and kissed him on the cheek. "Apology accepted. I love you too."

Chapter Two- Sergeant Randy Porter

Sergeant Randy Porter's military training never taught him how to handle anything like what had just happened and it never would have. Nothing like that ever existed where he was from. There were wars and combat but those have strategically planned maneuvers for each circumstance. There were armies versus armies, who have equally equivalent weapons. But there were never men versus evil beasts. With one injured leg and fear driving him on. His main objective now was to put as much distance as he could between him and the beast that attacked the rest of his squad. Keeping to his sworn duty of protecting the princess he must now find the princess, who got lost in the midst of all the confusion and fighting and then he needed to find a way out of this evil forest.

With his left leg bandaged with his own cloak to stop the bleeding from a cut he received while fighting the beast, he kept traveling north as fast as his hurt leg would allow. For many hours he traveled north ever vigilant and wary of what might be hidden in the forest around him. After some time of traveling he felt warm liquid trickling down his leg and noticed that his cut on his leg had started bleeding again, not wanting to stop moving he re-tied his cloak around his leg once more and quickly continued on. He needed to find the princess but was afraid to make any sound such as calling out her name, in fear of one of those horrible beasts hearing him. Without his sword or dagger, which he lost in the fight, he would be helpless and of no aid to the princess. Deciding to just keep a vigilant eye out for her and to continue heading north which was the way they were originally traveling before the nightmarish encounter with the beast. He was hoping he might be able to find her. After many hours his leg began to throb, the cold winter chill bit at his arms, and his exhaustion took over making him stop.

Knowing he couldn't stop for long, he found a cave entrance nearby thinking it would be a safer spot to rest than out in the open and went inside. Almost instantly he knew something was wrong, he saw a cluster of small floating lights coming closer towards him and then he heard the voices calling him. Unsure what to think and scared of what it could be he stumbled out of the caves entrance and with his leg almost unusable now, he limped over to a nearby boulder and placed his back against it and slid down it onto the ground. He hoped and prayed that the floating lights and voices wouldn't be able to find him on the other side of the boulder as well as the beast that had taken the others.

With pain throbbing through his leg, the cold freezing his arms and being at the point of exhaustion with the last bit of adrenalin he had just used getting away from the cave, his body couldn't take anymore and he slumped into unconsciousness. Waking with a start, Sergeant Randy Porter looked around at his surroundings. The sun was on the far side of the sky and it looked as if it would be nightfall within the hour. He didn't even realize that he had gone to sleep and now many hours of the day have passed by. He tried to stand, not remembering his hurt leg which instantly buckled from his weight making him land face first onto the forest floor. He cried out in pain and pulled himself to a sitting position against the boulder. He started to untie the cloak that was wrapped around his leg to see how bad his cut was when he heard voices coming his direction and instantly froze. Not wanting to give away his position he sat motionless, trying not to make any sound.

"Did you hear that?" Erika asked as they made their way towards Spirit Tunnel. "Yes. It's either a trap or someone in trouble. Let's just assume the worst and be prepared." Marcus answered as he pulled his sword free from its sheath. Linder, and Erika followed and both pulled their swords out. Jess decided to use her bow. She loaded an arrow into the bow and knocked the arrow. With weapons at the ready they continued cautiously toward the cave entrance. As they drew closer to a cluster of boulders near the entrance to the cave, Jess put out her arms to stop everyone. "What is it?" Linder asked scanning the area with his eyes looking for danger.

Jess put a finger to her lips, indicating silence and pointed to a lone man sitting on the ground leaning his back against one of the boulders, looking to be injured. His bright red military shirt stood out against the green of the forest. His black pants were torn and covered in dirt. He had shaggy dark brown hair, a tall lean but muscular stature. He looked to be in his mid twenties, he had his red military cloak wrapped around an injury on his leg. The man looked as if he just came out of battle. Besides the wound on his leg, Jess could see the man had claw marks on his arms, and slashes in his clothes and the look of exhaustion on his dirt and blood smeared face. "Shoot him." Marcus whispered. "It could be another trap." Linder answered to Jess's shake of the head and then a smile crept onto her face, the way a person looked when they have something mischievous planned. "Jess, this is no time for games." Erika replied in a serious tone. Jess smiled, and then she told everyone to stay right there and then with her bow loaded she walked away from them and straight towards the man, not giving anyone time to object. It took her only a few moments to reach the man. Keeping her distance she stopped a few yards in front of him. When the man saw her he looked terrified. She would have the same look too if someone was pointing a loaded bow at her.

"What's your name?" she asked in an even tone. "Why should I answer you, you might be one of those creatures in disguise." The man replied with a strained yet strong voice. "What creatures?" Jess asked him as if she didn't know what he was talking about. She knew exactly what creatures the man was talking about but wanted him to keep talking long enough for her to use her powers and feel what his true feelings were. "You would know you're probably one of them. You're just playing with me, trying to make me think you're a real person until you get hungry and tear me apart limb from limb. Well it's not going to work. I will not fall for your games; I will defeat you, find my princess and get out of here." The man declared still sitting on the ground.

Jess lowered her bow and put the arrows away. "It's safe. Linder we need your herbs over here, he is hurt bad." Jess called back to the others. Linder, Marcus and Erika came out of the trees from where they were waiting, re-sheathing their swords on their way and walked up next to the man. Confusion crossed the man's face. Jess bent down next to the man. "I am Jess. I am not a Therion, I will not hurt you. We can help you." She said to the man in a soft smooth tone. The man looked at Jess and then the others with a scrupulous look for a long moment then spoke.

"I am Sergeant Randy Porter. Red squadron, Fifth quarter, in the Northstin Army from Tasintall." "What did you say?" Jess asked, unsure she heard correctly. She thought he had said the Northstin Army. Her last name was Northstin and she had never met anyone else with that last name, except her immediate family. He repeated wearily. Jess, Erika, Linder and Marcus all share a look together, unsure what it could mean. "Did I say something wrong? Please don't hurt me." The man pleaded noticing their reactions. "We're not going to hurt you. I'm Linder. We can help you. Let me see your leg, I have some herbs that will help ease the pain." Randy looked at Linder, trying to decide whether to trust him or not then after a few seconds he decided that Linder's intentions were good and then started to untie his cloak from around his leg.

Linder bent down next to Randy and took the cloak from his hands and finished untying it. Linder was amazed at how the man could even move with as bad as the leg looked. "Well, at least you made it this far. The cut on your leg is bad. It also looks to be getting infected. Jess lets clean it together and give him some relaxing herbs and then see what we can do." Linder instructed. The cut wasn't very long but was incredibly deep and cleaning it with water from their water skins only made it look worse. While Linder and Jess gave Randy some passionflower that will help relax him and clean the wound, Marcus kept watch for any danger. Erika sat on the ground a short distance away from where Randy was sitting.

"Are you hungry?" Erika asked him, noticing that he didn't have anything with him. "I couldn't take food from you ma'am." he responded, smiling yet flinching from the pain of getting his wound cleaned by Jess and Linder. "You wouldn't be taking it; I would be giving it to you. There's a big difference." she replied then reached into her pack and pulled out an apple, a small loaf of bread, a dried meat strip and a piece of cheese. "Here take these." she said as she handed the food to him. "Thank you ma'am, I greatly appreciate it." he replied, taking the food from her, graciously. "You're welcome and call me Erika."

"It will be dark soon, I think we should set up camp here for the night and leave first thing in the morning and we can't leave him here, he will have to come with us." Marcus suggested. "I can't leave here yet, tomorrow I have to find my princess after that then I can leave. I am on an important mission. I can't leave until my mission is complete and that requires finding the princess."Sergeant Randy urgently replied. Jess looked between the others then looked back at Sergeant Randy. Fearing she would already know the answer before she asked him the question that would change his plans.

"What does your princess look like? Maybe we could help you find her?" Jess added with a smile. "Really, that would be wonderful. She has smooth pale brown skin, very long dark hair, she was wearing a black and red gown with a diamond necklace the last time I saw her. Her name is Princess Adaze; she is from the royal family of Tasintall. Would you really be able to help me search for her?" he asked hopefully. Jess's thoughts were right; she did know what the princess looked like and what had happened to her. "I have already seen your princess." Jess stated flatly. A solemn look came across the others faces.

"You have? Where at? Is it far from here? Maybe we can..." he started to say and then noticed the look on the others faces. "What happened? Is she alright?" he asked, concern crossing his face. "She is..."Jess started to say but could see the pain in the man's eyes as he realized what she was saying even before she could finish her sentence. "I am sorry, she is dead. A Therion got her." Jess finished.

"Therion's are the creatures that impersonate humans until night when they change shape into their true nightmarish form and kill and eat anything that it can get its claws on." Marcus explained towards the look of confusion that crossed Randy's face. "I was afraid of that. When she got separated from the rest of us, I was hoping she could get away safely but I guess I was wrong." Randy replied looking down at his sore leg, which was now cleaned, and had herb paste rubbed on it and a clean long sleeved shirt tied around it.

"My squad ran into a few of the beasts on the night before this one. We thought we were helping a lost woman find a way out of the forest. Unnoticing she led us right into its territory. She told us that we should make camp there for the night. Some of my men didn't like the idea but most didn't question and started unpacking their sleeping pads. Princess Adaze turned to me for direction since I was the highest ranking officer and she relied on me to help her to accomplish our mission. I trusted my men's judgment and decided that we should set up camp there. We all became relaxed, and carefree. The sun was starting to set, and with it came the cold so I decided to go off into the forest to collect wood for a fire. I had one other man accompany me.

As soon as we left the rest of the men, it seemed as if a cloud of fog was lifted from my mind and I could think clearly. That is when the screams started. I glanced at the man I was with, and then we ran back to the others. It seemed to take an extremely long time to reach the others; I hadn't realized how far we had gone. The sight we returned to was something far worse than any nightmare. My military instincts took over and I quickly assessed the situation. The other officer went to help a fallen soldiers and that was the last time I saw him. There were bloody body parts strewn all over the area. There was blood everywhere, staining the ground a dark red. There were a few of my men that were using the swords trying to fight off two terrible beasts. They fought bravely but were no match for the beasts and were ripped apart in moments.

I quickly saw that the princess wasn't there and the men that weren't fighting were trying to help the wounded. I asked a man that was lying on the ground near the edge of the clearing that was closest to me if he knew where the princess had gone. My responsibility was to take care of the princess and not seeing her anywhere, I assumed the worse. The man told me that one of the other officers grabbed her arm and they ran into the forest. The man that answered me was wounded bad, knowing I couldn't help him at the moment I started to walk away to help the men fighting the beasts. The dying man grabbed my ankle and with shallow breathing he told me something that ran shivers down my spine. "The woman was the beast. They can be people, or anyone. Don't trust anyone. It was a trap." After that his grip went limp and he died.

Many thoughts were running through my head at that time but I had to help my men first. I drew my sword and ran to help the men that were fighting the beasts. It was so horrible, most of my men didn't have the skills that I do and were cut down easily. I received these scratches while fighting the first beast. With the help of a couple other men, we killed the first beast. That seemed to make the other beast furious because it became even more savage and went on a rampage and started swinging its deadly claws around, slashing through men as it went.

It snarled, showing its massive sharp teeth while snapping at anything close enough. One of my officers was to close and before he could act, the beast snapped its fangs around the man's head and pulled. His body dropped to the ground as the beast spit out the man's head that it bit off. I tried to attack the beast but after losing my sword during the fight with the other beast, all I had left was a dagger. The beast swung its claws at me, I tried to jump out of the way but it got my leg. I lost my dagger when jumping out of the way. I stood but felt an incredibly sharp pain shoot through my leg.

Knowing I couldn't fight like that and with no weapons I decided the best thing I could do for myself and for those who survived was to runaway. If I didn't then I would be dead now. I thought that I could go back for any survivors after I took care of my leg and I needed to find the princess and keep her safe.

As I left the sounds of men screaming in pain and the terrible ear piercing roar that came from the beasts along with the bloody sight of everything was starting to make me feel sick. I was able to get away from the gruesome sight and made my way north. I was hoping to find the princess with the officer that took her away. I kept traveling through the night, but no matter how far away I got, I could still hear the painful screams coming from my men.

My leg throbbed with pain but I knew I couldn't stop. I kept going until a few hours past morning when my hurt leg and exhaustion took over. I found that cave and was going to rest in there but as soon as I went in there, small floating lights and voices came after me and I fled from the cave. I barely remember coming to this boulder and then the next thing I remember was that I heard voices, which woke me up and then I met you." Randy explained. While Randy told everyone of his experience they all retrieved food from their packs and ate while listening to his tale. "How many men were with you?" Marcus asked. "When we started on our mission, there were fifty officers and the princess. By the time we got to this forest there were only around twenty of us left. Many got sick from the cold, others deserted the mission, some got lost in the cities and forests that we traveled through and the ones that were left I fear are all dead now." Randy answered looking at every one in turn.

"You keep talking about a mission. What was your mission?" Linder asked while eating a piece of bread. "Our mission was to find the Northstin Wind and the great prophet and bring them back to Tasintall so the beginning of the great battle can commence. The princess had a message only she knew that she was going to tell them that would convince them to come and help save our people." Jess and Linder shared a look between each other. "Do you know who the Northstin Wind or the great prophet is?" Linder asked. "No, we only knew that a long time ago the Northstin's from long ago traveled to a place and made that their home, we do know that the town was named after one of them. We believed that the place to start looking for them would be in Morganstin. Do you know of it? I have traveled for many weeks trying to get there but I fear I still have a long way to go to get there." Randy answered in-between eating bites of the food Erika had given him.

"Do you still plan to go on with your mission, even without the princess?" Linder asked, looking towards Randy. "Yes. I think I am the people of Tasintall's only hope. The great battle cannot begin without those two people and the place it's foretold to begin is in Tasintall." "What is this great battle?" Marcus interjected. Randy looked surprised. "How can anyone not know of the great battle to come? It's the great battle of good versus evil. The battle of dark versus light. You do not know of this?" Randy asked astonished by the concept that they didn't know what he was talking about. Everyone in his land was taught from the time they were young about the great battle to come and they trained and anticipated for it.

"The great battle to rid the world of the black magic plague." he added. "The prophecy." Linder said quietly, mostly to himself. "I think you're right." Jess replied to Linder, as she placed her hand on his arm. "Could you excuse us for a moment?" Jess asked Randy." He nodded. Jess, Linder, Marcus and Erika all walked far enough away from Sergeant Randy so that he couldn't hear what they were saying. "What do you think it means Jess?" Erika asked as soon as they stopped walking. "I don't know." Jess shrugged then tossed her long blonde braid over her shoulder. "I don't think he means anyone any harm, I think we should take him with us. We can't leave him here or the Therion's will surely devour him before morning." Linder commented.

"He will slow us down, but I think you are right. I think that the great battle that he is talking about it is the battle that we are all part of. Maybe by bringing him with us we can learn more that will help us defeat the black magic." Marcus said. "I agree." Erika replied. "Okay, that's settled, he is coming with us but now do we tell him who we really are or do we wait until we reach Morganstin?" Linder asked. "I want to wait and see how much we can find out about this great battle and what he means by the Northstin Wind." Jess replied. "Okay, now one more thing. How are we going to get him to go through Spirit Tunnel? That's the only way to get to Morganstin and by the looks of it; he got quite a spook when he entered on accident." Linder pointed out.

"Just tell him. He's a soldier I think he will be able to handle it if he has a warning about what lies ahead." Erika stated. "Very well." Linder replied. "Let's get back it will be dark in just a few minutes. We can take turns keeping guard during the night and then first thing in the morning set off into the cave." he continued. Everyone agreed then they walked back to where Sergeant Randy waited.

"Is everything alright?" Randy asked as the others approached. Randy was still sitting in the same spot on the ground with his back against the boulder where they first found him when they returned. "Yes, everything is fine. We have something to tell you. We are actually on our way to Morganstin as well." Linder began to say. "You know how to get to Morganstin." Randy interjected excitedly. "Yes we do and we are headed there. Would you like to travel with us?" Linder asked. "Does that mean you will help me find the Northstin Wind and the prophet? Oh this is wonderful. This means that my people will be saved. We can find the Northstin Wind and the prophet and then I can take them back to Tasintall and then the Great War can commence and the world will finally be rid of the black plague. Oh this is so great. How far is it to Morganstin? How long will it take?" Randy rambled on. "Whoa. Slow down, we said you could travel with us to Morganstin, we didn't say anything about helping you find the people that you are looking for and it will take almost a month to get there. It is on the other side of these mountains and a few weeks traveling on foot farther to get there." Marcus interjected.

"Oh. Sorry I just assumed you would be willing to help." Randy sighed. "Maybe when we get there we will help you find the people you are looking for but for now let's just worry about getting there safely. Once we get there then we can worry about finding the people or not." Jess said softly. Randy nodded in understanding. "I will take the first watch. Everyone get as good of a night's sleep as you can. We will leave at first dawn." Linder instructed. "I will take the second watch." Marcus offered. "I will take the third." Erika replied.

"What? A woman? No ma'am. Women should not have to keep watch at night. That is a man's job. Men are the protectors." Randy protested. "I think I can manage." Erika answered. "I will take her watch." Randy told Linder. "No you won't. You can barely stand, you have no weapon and you need to get as much rest as you can so your leg can heal better. I have more than one weapon, which I am familiar with, and am very capable of keeping watch." Erika defended. Randy looked to Linder and Marcus as if they were going to instruct Erika otherwise. "She's right." Marcus answered shrugging. Randy looked as if he was going to say something but then changed his mind and nodded in acknowledgment. Erika handed Randy an extra wool blanket that she had in her pack for him to use. With the sun setting the cold winter chill reminded them that it was still winter.

The past two weeks spent at Kedar's castle, the temperature was always a nice warm spring temperature and with Erika's new powers she could change the weather to whatever she desired. Before that, the time when they were traveling through forests and making their way to Kedar's castle the temperature was warmer than winter normally would have been. Kedar said that the temperature change were due to the Black Dragons using magic to help them find the magical talismans, which Jess, Linder, Erika and Marcus carried and had the magical powers bestowed onto them. Jess had almost forgotten that it still was winter but the cold chill quickly reminded her. Jess unrolled her bedroll from her pack, as did Erika, Linder and Marcus. Randy thanked Erika for the blanket. Marcus put on another shirt on top of the one he was already wearing to add more warmth to his body and then put is cloak back on. Jess laid down on her bed roll which was located next to Linder's and threw her blanket on herself.

Erika lay down on her bed roll which was on the other side of Jess, and next to Marcus's. Marcus sat on his bed roll, watching the forest around him. They couldn't risk making a fire that would bring unwanted visitors so it was going to be a cold night. "Here Randy, you're going to need this. It's going to be cold and without a cloak to keep you warm this should help." Linder offered holding out one of his long sleeved shirts. Randy took it gratefully, then pulled it over his head and fit it onto his body. He was a slightly larger man than Linder, so the shirt was a tight fit but still added warmth that he desperately wanted. Linder than laid down next on his bedroll next to Jess and put his arm around her. She placed her hand on his that was lying across her body. Randy watched them for a moment and then lay down on the dirt and went to sleep.

The morning came too quickly, when Erika woke him up. Everyone else was awake and had their bedrolls tied to their packs. Erika offered him a slice of bread with jam on it, and half of an apple. He took it and thanked her. Erika sat down beside him on the ground to eat her own piece of bread and the other half of the apple. "Here is your blanket back, thank you for letting me use it." Randy said while handing the blanket towards her. "Thanks. How is your leg feeling?" "Much better thanks but the real test will be when I have to get up and use it all day long." "Linder has more herbs if you need them." "Thanks, I will keep that in mind." "Is everyone ready to go?" Marcus asked while he situated his pack onto his shoulders. Jess and Linder already had their packs on and their weapons belts fastened tightly on their waist. "We're ready." Linder replied answering for him and Jess. "I will be ready in just a minute." Erika answered then put the blanket into her back and stood up, pulling her pack onto her shoulders as she stood.

Randy stood up awkwardly. The pain is his leg was considerably less than it had been but it was still tender and sore and as he begin walking he could tell that he was still favoring it which caused him to limb slightly with every step that he took. "Will you be able to travel?" Linder asked watching Randy. "Yes, I can. I must make it to Morganstin as soon as possible. My injured leg isn't going to stop me. I will keep going until I can't stand anymore." Randy replied. "Good. Then let's go." Marcus replied promptly.

"Here take this. You can keep it. You are going to need a weapon." Linder said directly as he offered his short handled dagger to Randy. "Thank you. You all have done so much for me already, one day I will repay you all for your kindness." Randy remarked. "Don't thank us yet. We still have a long way to go and many dangers ahead of us before we reach Morganstin." Jess replied. "Okay then which direction are we headed?" Randy asked. "That way." Erika pointed towards Spirit Tunnel.

Randy looked confused when he replied. "The only thing over there is that cave with the floating lights and voices in it." "That's where we are headed." Marcus replied without any hint of emotion in his voice. "Alright here is what you need to know. It's not a cave but a tunnel that goes through the mountain to the other side. It is the fasted way to get to Morganstin but it is dangerous, very dangerous. It's a labyrinth of passageways and tunnels. A person could very easily get lost in there. There is only one right course to take and we know which one it is. It will take around six hours to travel through and it is almost completely dark. The worst part is the creatures that you already encountered. The floating lights and the voices you heard are from a terrible creature. They are called Ksoldums. They are much like fireflies, with their glow but they are deadly.

When you hear the voices they could sound like any one you have ever heard in your entire life, whether living or deceased, don't listen to them, it is the Ksoldums trying to lead you away from the main path. They will try anything to get you to follow them. Sometimes they will call for you in a small child's voice to go and play with them, or you will hear a loved one crying and you will want to comfort them, they will also imitate someone screaming in pain and crying to be helped. It can be really difficult to ignore them and keep on the main path. If they lure you away from the main path and get you alone they will bite you on your skin with their small fangs and within minutes you will die.

Do not listen to them and make sure to stay with us. We have all been through the tunnel once so we know what it's like and can help you ignore them and make it safely through to the other side." Linder told Randy, who was wide eyed and flushed faced. "Well let's get going, we don't want to stand around here and improve our chances of more Therion's coming. We were lucky last night that none showed up but you know they will come around sooner than later." Marcus stated and then without waiting for a response started walking towards Spirit Tunnel.

"You're serious! We have to go in there. With those kso...those creatures." Randy anxiously answered, unsure what the name was exactly of the creatures and unsure he was ready to face another evil creature that wanted him dead. "Yes. We do. If you don't want to come with us then stay here, but it is the fastest way to get to Morganstin and that's the direction we are headed. It's up to you whether you go with us or not." Linder answered firmly, then taking Jess's outstretched hand they strode off to follow Marcus. Erika glanced at Randy and without saying anything turned and left him standing alone. "Wait. I'm coming." Randy called to them and followed after them. "Wait." Came a voice that was to eerily familiar from behind them right as they were about to enter the tunnel.

Randy's face light up when he saw who it was while Marcus, Linder, Jess and Erika all had weapons drawn instantly at the sight of who they saw walking their direction. "Please don't harm me." The woman said smoothly. "Don't shoot. That's the princess Adaze. That's my princess. You were wrong, she isn't dead, she is right here. Oh this is wonderful." Randy exclaimed. "It's not her. That is a Therion." Jess proclaimed knocking an arrow in her bow. "I am not. I am Princess Adaze, like he said." Adaze purred as she drew ever nearer. "Stop moving or I will shoot." Linder demanded. Jess and Linder had loaded bows aimed at her, while Erika and Marcus had their swords drawn. Adaze stopped moving.

"You can trust me, come with me and I will prove I am who I say I am. Just follow me." She offered gesturing with her hand for them to come towards her. Randy started to take a step closer. "Randy, don't move or I will shoot her." Jess stated in an angry voice. How many times do I have to kill these beasts? Jess thought to herself. "But..." Randy began to speak. Jess's glare cut him off, while she kept her bow pointed at Adaze. "Oh, but you can trust me. I will show you. Just follow me, everything will be fine." Adaze cooed so soft and luxurious that Jess could tell it was making Marcus and Linder falter. With that thought Jess released the knocked arrow and it hit its target. Just as Jess had predicted, it roared an ear piercing sound that was almost unbearable to hear.

The lovely pale browned skin woman burst into millions of tiny pieces and there in place of the beautiful woman, twice the size of a man stood a Therion. All of the other Therion's that Jess had seen had coarse brown fur but this one had long dirty black fur that seemed blacker than the blackest night. Its large claws swiped at the air, his blunt nose dripping mucus and its glowing red eyes glared at Jess. Just then another arrow hit the beast in the chest, then another hit its head. Dropping to the ground it roared and roared as it writhed in pain on the forest floor. "Thanks." She yelled to Linder over the sound of the roaring from the beast. Marcus grabbed Randy's arm and pulled him away and closer to the tunnel. "Jess look, it's a crow." Erika pointed out as they turned away from the beast. Perched on a tree nearby flapped a large crow, cawing as if trying to get their attention. "Watch him." Linder instructed to Marcus gesturing towards Randy, then taking Jess's hand lead the way over to the tree where the crow was perched. Erika joined them.

The crow flew down to the ground, and pointing its peak the opposite direction from the tunnel started cawing and hopping away. "We have to go this way." Erika said pointing towards the tunnel. The crow shook its head and turned its beak away, cawing once more. Barely hearing the crows caw over the roars that still sounded from the dyeing Therion, Jess understood what the crow wanted. "Jess?" Linder asked. Jess nodded her head and replied, "Let's do it." Marcus watching them understood what happened and led Randy over to where Jess, Linder and Erika waited. Once Marcus and Randy were next to them they headed off farther into the forest, away from the tunnel and followed the crow wherever it was leading them.

Chapter Three- The Unexpected

The roars from the dying Therion grew quieter the farther they traveled. Jess was surprised the beast was still alive for this long. "I thought we had to go through that tunnel?" Randy asked as he glanced back. "We do, but for now we need to go this way. Just go with it." Erika replied as she tucked a piece of her wavy brown hair behind her ear. Randy thought that Erika was beautiful but didn't comment on her beauty, thinking Erika was married, and mentioning her beauty would be out of line towards a married woman. "Okay." Randy responded, trusting in Erika's word. They traveled for thirty minutes following the crow farther away from Spirit Tunnel when all of a sudden the crow flew up in the air and started circling an area a short distance ahead of them. "What is that?" Jess asked as they drew nearer to where the crow circled. There were many broken branches on the ground and some of the leaves had blood on them. There was no way of telling if the blood was human or animal. There was a cluster of trees under where the crow circled. "Jess, Erika and Randy please stay here. Marcus you come with me." Linder instructed as he looked ahead at what awaited. "Why?" Jess asked, her curiosity peaking. "Please just stay here for a minute." Linder responded holding her hand up in his.

"Alright but just for a minute." Jess replied. Without smiling back, he kissed her hand and then let it go. Erika eyed Marcus and Linder suspiciously then agreed to stay back. "I am a Sergeant in the Northstin Army I can handle anything. I am coming with you." Randy stated, not wanting to stay back with the women. Linder and Marcus shared a look between each other then acknowledged that he could join them.

"Be prepared for anything." Marcus instructed. Randy pulled the dagger that Linder had given him free and gripped it tightly in his right hand. Linder and Marcus both drew their swords and walked together to where the crow circled. After stepping through a cluster of trees the sight they saw was one they would never forget. Throughout the cluster of trees were many bloody human body parts strewn all over, in the midst of all of it lay a dead Therion.

"Why would the crow bring us here?" Marcus asked eyeing the surroundings for any danger. As if to answer his question, there came a soft deep moan from somewhere nearby. The three men walked to where the sound originated from and just on the other side of a fallen log laid a man, well a part of a man. The man was missing one leg below the knee, and one arm almost to the shoulder and half of his body parts that were mean to be inside his body was falling out of large gash on his left side. It looked as if his whole left side had been bitten on several times by many large sharp teeth. There was a large puddle of blood that he lay in.

He could have been in his early twenties, but with all the blood it was hard to tell. Linder was glad he made Jess and Erika stay back; he didn't want them to see any of this. "He's still alive." Marcus said quietly and astonished. "Help me." The man whispered. "I think I know who that man is." Randy said with a hint of disgust in his voice. "Officer Hunt? Is that you?" Randy asked cautiously as he drew near. Marcus put out an arm to stop Randy from getting any closer. The man's eyes lit up slightly in recognition. "Sergeant. Lost. Princess. Help me." The man blurted out in an agonized tone, staggering each word. Thinking he would already know the answer Randy asked. "Is there anything we can do to help him?" while looking between Linder and Marcus. "Please" the man on the ground pleaded softly.

"Close your eyes. We will help." Linder said to the dying man. That was not the answer Randy thought they would say. "How?" Randy asked astonished that Linder thought he would be able to help the dying soldier. Linder twisted his sword in his hand. Marcus nodded in acknowledgment. "You're going to..." Randy started to say but Linder cut him off. "I am going to save him the only way we can." Linder replied. Randy looked at Linder then at Marcus then with a sigh of regret that this was the best thing to do he nodded his approval. It didn't matter how many times Randy saw it happen; it was always difficult to see one of his soldiers die and not being able to do anything to save them.

"Please" the man on the ground whispered, so quietly they could barely hear his plea, even in the still quiet battle field. Marcus knelt down closer to the man and whispered "May the gates of heaven open to your arrival and peace enwrap your soul." The man closed his eyes, Linder plunged his sword into the man's heart.

There was only a small visible slacking of the man's muscles to inform Randy, Marcus and Linder that he was dead. Linder pulled his sword from the man, and re-sheathed it onto his belt. There was a moment of silence that filled the air that quickly past when Marcus suggested that they return to Erika and Jess, before the two women decide to come after them. Once they returned to where Erika and Jess waited, the women instantly picked up on the mood the men were in. "What happened? Why is there blood on your pants?" Erika asked worriedly looking at Marcus. "We saved a man." Marcus replied quietly. "Really? I thought you would be happy if you were able to save a man, and if that was the case where is he?" Erika asked incredulously. "He's dead. We saved him from having to deal with a prolonged and painful death. We saved him from the possibility of any other Therion's tearing him apart more than he already was. We saved him and sent his spirit onwards." Marcus replied solemnly looking into Erika's eyes. "Oh I'm sorry." Erika replied and touched Marcus's arm reassuringly. "Did you really have to tell them all of that?" Linder asked Marcus accusingly. "It's alright. Are you okay?" Jess asked Linder taking his hand into hers. "I will be fine. We need to get out of this place before the scent of blood draws near any unwanted creatures and we really don't want to fight any off right now." Linder remarked calmly. "I agree." Randy replied.

They all turned around to start back towards Spirit Tunnel when the crow flew by, cawing and making its intentions known; they followed the crow towards a different direction in the forest. Traveling in silence with a cold winter breeze blowing on the backs they headed east. Some time passed Erika wasn't sure how much, but she did know that she was getting hungry and was hoping that they were going to reach wherever the crow was leading soon. It seemed to be around the middle of the day. No one had spoken during the whole walk; a depressed mood was set over them.

Erika jumped at the sound of a loud shrill high pitched twittering sound coming from somewhere very close ahead of them. It didn't sound like anything from a Therion but was still intimidating. The crow cawed and flapped its wings in encouragement to continue on. Everyone had stopped walking once they heard the sound. Linder had his hand on his sword handle, as did Marcus and Randy was reaching for his dagger. Erika looked at Jess who had an unreadable expression on her face. Speaking first Jess looked between Linder, Marcus, Erika and Randy and silently asked, "What was that?" The crow cawed and flapped its wings again. "It wants us to keep going?" Randy asked.

"Yes, but that is where the sound came from. Do you really want to find out what it was or here is a better question, are you ready to fight another beast with your leg hurt?" Linder remarked. The shrill high pitched sound came again; it wasn't the guttural vicious roar like a Therion it was more like an eagles twittering chatter. Jess's face lit up. "I think I know what it is. Linder come with me, you others stay here until we get back." Jess stated excitedly as she grabbed Linder's hand and pulled him along with her. "You know she is going get herself and Linder into a lot of trouble one of these days by just running head first into these situations." Marcus said to Erika as they waited with Randy as Jess and Linder ran ahead following the crow. "Yeah I know. Luckily they have us to save them." Erika replied smiling at Marcus, glad that the depressed mood had left the group.

Jess and Linder ran ahead of the others pushing their way through snow covered bushes and cluster of trees. Jess was relieved that her instincts were right. There in front of them was a beautiful snow dusted meadow with three large griffins and a crow circling above them. One twittered at another and the other twittered back as if answering the first. The crow cawed and leisurely flew down and then rested on the ground next to one of the large griffins.

"Whoa!" Linder exclaimed. The sound of his voice seemed to draw the attention of all the griffins towards them. The largest of the griffins, the one next to the crow stood up on all fours, tucked its large dark brown eagle wings onto its back then walked up next to Jess and Linder. Jess gripped Linder's hand tighter but showed no fear on her face as they both stood their ground. The griffin towered over them and stood not more than a few feet away. The griffin lowered its eagle head and peered at Jess and Linder in turn with its sharp black eagle eyes. It only took a few seconds but it felt like much longer to Jess as it starred into her eyes seemingly searching for something. The griffin rose to its full height looked down at Jess and Linder then sounded a single shrill high pitched twitter once. For some reason Jess felt comfort in the sound, as if it was telling her not to be afraid. The griffin bowed its long head down as if showing respect to them like it did to Kedar back at the castle. Jess and Linder bowed their heads down like Kedar had told them to do to return the gesture of respect.

Once they raised their heads they saw the two other griffins walking towards them. As soon as the griffins reached them they bowed their heads like the first, Jess and Linder returned the bow. After the formalities were done the two griffins returned to where they had been previously. The largest griffin twittered and gestured its long head towards the other griffins as if offering an invitation for Jess and Linder to join them. "We have three friends waiting back that way a bit, would it be alright if we bring them here?" Jess asked as she pointed towards the direction of where Marcus, Erika, and Randy waited. The griffin looked towards the forest the direction Jess pointed then nodded its long eagle head.

"Thank you, we will go and get them and then return." Jess answered. "Thank you." Linder added. Still holding hands they turned around and walked back to where the others waited. Surprisingly the others still stood in the same spot where they had left them. "So, obviously it's not Therion's up ahead or you wouldn't be back so soon." Marcus pointed out. "We found the Griffins and they want us to join them." Jess stated excitedly. "Really? Join them doing what?" Erika asked with a hint of excitement in her voice. "I don't know but at least we will be safe with them for a while." Jess answered. "Okay, okay what is it really ahead?" Randy asked, thinking they were joking. "There is no such thing as Griffins. What is it?"

"She is telling the truth, there really are three griffins waiting ahead. We have already met one griffin, and they are very much real and when we get there bow your head in respect for them." Linder told Randy straightly. "I have a hard time believing that mystical creatures exist but I will play along with it." Randy replied casually. "Just make sure to show them respect, this is their forest and I don't know what they would do if they were offended." Linder stated. "Okay" Randy replied nonchalantly, not believing them, thinking that the others were just playing a trick on him. He would soon see for himself what really was ahead.

"Well what are we waiting, let's go and see these griffins." He said smoothly. "Randy, please believe them, they are telling the truth." Erika said softly to Randy. "Yeah okay" he replied waving her off. "Well let's go." Marcus instructed. With that Jess and Linder led the way back to the griffins. As soon as the griffins came into sight Randy gasped in fright and astonishment and stumbled backwards. If not for Marcus who was walking right behind him, and catching him as he stumbled he would have fallen to the ground. "We told you so." Jess said to Randy. "I believe you now." He replied. The largest of the griffins stood on all four paws, its large lion body taller than any of the men with eagle head pointed down to look at them and its eagle wings spread out to their full length as it stood regally in all of its glory.

The griffin tucked its wings onto its back and walked over next to the group of people waiting, closing the ten foot distance in a couple strides. Jess, Linder, Marcus and Erika bowed their heads at the griffin. "Bow" Marcus whispered to Randy, who was standing frozen in his steps starring at the griffin. The griffin bowed its head at them then raised it head and drew nearer to Randy. Instinctively Randy reached his hand towards his dagger. "Don't move!" Linder commanded. Randy stopped his hand and held perfectly still. The griffin lowered it eagle head until it was right in front of Randy, inches away from his face the griffin starred into his eyes, unsure what to do Randy held as still as he could. He locked his eyes to the griffins that seemed to be penetrating his soul. He could hear the rhythmic breathing coming from the Griffin so close to him.

Suddenly the Griffin sounded a loud shrill high pitched twitter, startling Randy so bad that it made him fall backwards and land on the ground. The griffin backed up a few steps then bowed its head toward Randy, who was now regaining his posture onto to his feet. Jess couldn't help laughing. The griffin had scared Randy just to tease him. Linder tried to hold back his snickers. Erika and Marcus both had smiles on their faces. Randy looked between Linder, and Jess then the griffin. Realization crossed his face and then he bowed his head towards the griffin. The griffin tilted his head towards the other griffins who were sitting on the ground a short distance away, as if gesturing to go to them. The black crow sat on top of one of the other griffins. "Come on, we will be safe with them. We can eat lunch and rest and then go from there. I think that the crow led us here for a reason so we should at least see if we can figure out why that is." Jess said while tossing her long blonde braid behind her shoulder. "That is fine with me." Marcus replied. Soon they were all walking past the large griffin that still stood before them and headed towards the other two griffins which were smaller than the first, but still much bigger than any man. These two were sitting on the snow a short distance away.

After taking their packs off and setting them on the ground, they all positioned themselves on the ground. The first griffin, the largest of them all, who was the one they had previously met at Kedar's castle, sat on the opposite side of the two other griffins and with their big bodies taking up so much space all three griffins had formed a complete circle around the group of people. "Umm Jess, we are surrounded. Was this part of your plan?" Randy asked nervously as he looked around at the mighty griffins circled around them. Jess glanced around then replied "Well no but we will be fine. Don't worry about them, they won't hurt us. Let's eat lunch, I'm starving." "You're always starving." Erika commented with a smile. Jess shrugged.

They all took out different foods from their packs and ate a mix of dried meats, breads, fruits, vegetables and cinnamon rolls, made by Annabella for dessert. They drank from their water skins when they got thirsty. Everyone shared what they had with Randy, who was ever weary of the large griffins that surrounded them but nonetheless enjoy his lunch. While they ate they talked about their time at Kedar's castle, leaving out the details about the magical talismans and the powers that each one of them held. Linder and Marcus decided that it was wise not to disclose that information with Randy just yet. They talked about Jess and Linder's engagement and the wonderful meals that were cooked by Annabella and her daughter Hannah while they were staying at Kedar's castle. While sitting in the middle of the griffins the cold winter breeze wasn't able to reach them and they felt safe for a short time.

Randy seemed to have a look of concentration on his face for some time while he kept glancing at Erika before he finally got the nerve to ask. "Are you…How long have you been married to Marcus?" he asked changing what he was going to say mid sentence. "What?" Marcus asked surprised. "We're not married. We are just friends." Erika replied, her cheeks turning a slight pink. "Yeah, we are just friends. Erika's a great woman but I don't think about her that way, we are just friends." Marcus answered then smiled at Erika. "Oh, I just got the impression that Jess was married to Linder but now I know that they are just engaged and that you and Marcus were married. Sorry for misunderstanding and if you don't mind then I would like to tell you how beautiful I think you are." Randy said to Erika. "Oh, thank you." she replied as her cheeks turned to bright red now. This brought a smile to everyone's faces. They all finished eating and repacked what remained.

The three griffins sat in the snow occasionally twittering at each other leisurely but never rising from their spots. They didn't even seem to notice the people that were in the middle of them. The black crow sat on the ground watching every person and beast in turn. Once everyone was done eating and packed away the remains they started discussing which direction to go to get to Spirit Tunnel and how long it would take to get there. "I'm not complaining but following this crow has really taken a lot of our time; we do need to get to Morganstin as quickly as possible." Linder remarked.

Suddenly the crow and the griffins rose to attention, the crow flapped its wings raising itself into the air and cawed several times. All three griffins rose to their feet and twittered simultaneously. "What's going on?" Jess asked Linder, who were surprised by the griffins and crows reactions. "I'm not sure." "It must have been something you said." Marcus suggested. Rising to his feet Linder quickly searched through the words he had just spoken to figure out what he had said that cause the griffins to act the way they were. Every else rose to their feet. "Morganstin?" he repeated in an asking tone. The crow and the griffins excitedly cawed and twittered together. "You want us to go to Morganstin?" Erika asked as she stood unintentionally close to Randy.

The largest of the griffins twittered and nodded its eagle head. "Why?" Erika asked. Suddenly the crow flew over to where Linder's pack lay on the ground and started rummaging through it with its beak, then to their surprise it pulled out the prophecy book which contained prophecies from the prophets of old and also any prophecies or visions that Linder's had seen since receiving it from Kedar. Inside the book contained a prophecy which told of four magical talismans and a quest for their owners to defeat the black magic that plagued the world. The owners of the four magical talismans happened to be Linder, Jess, Erika and Marcus. The crow pecked it beak on the cover of the prophecy book.

"The prophecy, is that why you want us to go to Morganstin?" Linder asked. "What prophecy?" Randy inquired as he looked between the crow and the prophecy book to Linder who was holding Jess's hand. The crow cawed excitedly. "You know about the prophecy?" Jess asked. The crow cawed excitedly once more. "What prophecy?" Randy asked again. "The prophecy is the real reason why we are headed to Morganstin. We have special business that needs to be taken care of there that pertains to what is said in the prophecy." Linder replied to Randy. "What does the prophecy say?" Randy asked very interested. Linder picked up the book from the ground then opened the book to a specific page and began reading.

"When north and south meet the prophet, the spark will be lit. The guardian will show them the way. The illusionist will show himself in his truest form. With talismans in hand their journey shall begin, once bestowed with power the platform awaits. Place the talismans on the stone and with this comes their fate. Wizards shall they become, a marriage shall await, free the stolen and misjudged ones, destroy the blackness too, restore the forest to its real form then life will be anew. But beware if all doesn't precede then destruction and darkness will feed. The darkness waits and will attack if all the wizards fail to act."

"What does that mean? It does mention the prophet, like in the prophecy that I follow. Are you searching for the prophet also?" Randy asked excitedly. "Not quite." Linder answered. Randy's eyes seemed to grow ten times larger than normal when he looked between Linder's face and the book that Linder held.

"You! You are the prophet, aren't you?" Randy asked in pure awe. "Yes, I am." Linder replied coolly. "Oh, this is wonderful. Do you know who the Northstin Wind is, because if you do that would be superb, then we wouldn't have to travel to Morganstin, we could just get that person from wherever they are and then we can travel to Tasintall, and you can help get rid of the black plague." Randy said excitedly, but dragging out the last few words as if he just realized something. "The prophecy you just told me said something about the darkness prevailing if all these wizards don't act, didn't it. You have to go to Morganstin don't you, that is one of the things you must do to help defeat the darkness, isn't it? But I don't understand, you're not a wizard, you are a prophet and who are all of the other people spoken about in the prophecy? You have to go to Morganstin to find them so that you can fulfill the prophecy, right? Wait a minute, why are all of you here?" Randy rambled on but was interrupted by Erika.

"Randy, slow down. We can explain everything, if you can stop asking questions for a minute." Erika said in a warm tone. "Sorry" he apologized."It's alright, Jess do you want to explain it?" Erika asked. "Sure, you now know that Linder is the prophet and Erika's last name is South and mine is…" Jess began to say but was interrupted by loud and dangerously close lightning strike with the sound of the thunder echoing off the mountains. Noticing that the sky was quickly turning black with thunder and lightning going off all around them, Jess instantly knew something was terribly wrong. Only moments ago it was partly sunny, cold but partly sunny nonetheless and now within moments there was a terrible dark storm upon them. The sky was getting darker by the second; the cold winter wind was blowing fiercely at them, blowing snow from the trees into their faces. Jess thought it was not natural. "Storms can't appear out of nowhere, unless…" She trailed off.

The griffins twittered in a threatening way towards the sky, as the crow flew frantically in circles right above their heads. "We have to get out of here. Everyone get your gear. They are coming for us." Jess yelled frantically then gathered up her gear as quickly as she could. "Who? Who is coming?" Randy asked with panic in his tone. "The Black Dragons!" Jess yelled frantically. "Come on let's go!" Marcus shouted over the howl of the wind.

Jess froze and held perfectly still, breathing slowly and trying to stay calm she pushed her power outwards and searched for anyone's feelings that weren't right near her. She could feel the panic in Erika, the confusion in Randy, the fear and determination in Marcus and the love for her and the feeling of protection coming from Linder. She pushed her power out stretching it beyond them and out into the darkness of the forest. Every time she had used her power in the past it felt like a warm breeze blowing over her but this time it hit her like a being hit with a large icy rock. Before her connection was separated she felt the feelings of many other people all around her. Jess gasped, "We are surrounded." "I have a plan, follow me." Marcus informed the others then ran towards the griffins.

"Can you fly us out of here?" He shouted in a pleading voice towards the griffins. It was getting harder to see even ten feet in front of their eyes, but in the darkening day all of them were relieved to see the griffins nod their heads. All the griffins lowered their bodies down to the ground, Marcus then climbed on top of the one closest to him. Erika and Randy climbed onto another and Linder and Jess climbed onto the largest one. The griffins spread out the large eagle wings and started to rise from the ground, the crow flapping its wings following. "Erika, put your cloak on and clear us a nice window through the storm to get through." Marcus shouted towards her over the howl of the snow blowing in the wind. "Okay" She replied then while trying to hold on to Randy and the beast so that she didn't fall off the rising beast, she reached behind herself with one hand and took off her pack from her shoulders and moved it onto her lap.

As quickly as she could she reached inside her pack, pulled out a large golden brown wolf fur cloak with silver trimmings with a big fur hood attached to it and put it on herself. While fastening it around her neck, she clumsily dropped her pack from her lap. As she watched it fall towards the ground for a few seconds she realized that there was nothing she could do about it now so she turned her attention towards the storm. Wrapping her left arm around Randy's waist, who was sitting in front of her on the griffin, she raised her right hand into the air and thinking about a clear blue sky she pushed her elemental power outwards and instantly there came sunlight with blue skies shining through a gap in the storms clouds.

"Go!" Erika yelled. All three griffins rose higher into the sky aiming for the gap in the storm. The blue sky started to grow fainter, Erika held out her right hand and pushed her power out harder and extended the gap in the storm clouds larger once more. One after another the griffins and the crow fly through the snow and pushed their way into the blue sky gap in the storm. Once through the gap in the storm, they encountered blue skies all around them. They continued to fly south, glancing back at the magic conjured storm that laid havoc over the spot where they had just been. "Can you fly us to Morganstin?" Linder asked the griffin him and Jess were riding on. The griffin shook its head. "Can you take us as close to Morganstin as you can please?" The griffin nodded then made a loud eagle caw; the two other griffins cawed in reply. All three griffins turned directions slightly and continued to fly on. Higher they rose and farther they flew ever getting closer to the tallest point of the Kahidon Mountains. The air was clear with little clouds in the sky, the sun was moving slowly to the west side of the sky as it drew nearer to sunset. The air was cold, especially as it moved past the griffin's wings as they flew high in the sky. They flew over the top of the tallest point of the Kahidon Mountain range, Jess looked down at the mountains below her. The tall pine trees were covered in snow, the jagged rocks and cliff sides looked even more menacing with snow and ice covering their tops that dropped shear off into caverns of blackness below.

Jess could see the movement of many dark colored furry creatures in the snow below, she instantly knew what they were and was glad that she wasn't on the ground anymore. She did not want to run into any more Therion's, especially as many as she could see spread out below her. Occasionally she saw dark red spots in between the trees that stood out in the contrast of the white snow that covered everything. Her stomach clinched every time she saw one of those. Erika looked down once and saw Therion's below and dark red spots intermixed with the trees, combined with the growing distance away from the ground that they were traveling; she closed her eyes, wrapped her arms around Randy tighter and decided not to look down anymore. She would look ahead or keep her eyes closed from that point on. The Griffins flew over the top of the mountains and started their descent. To Jess's surprise the griffins didn't land though they leveled out their flight right above the tree tops and continued to fly on. One hour later Linder pointed out that he could see the city of Taharan ahead.

The largest of the griffins twittered in its eagles voice then began rising higher into the sky, the other griffins followed. Rising through and above the low hanging clouds they continued to fly south. Randy gasped at how wet he had become when passing through the clouds. He never realized how much water was in clouds. They flew southwards for a few more hours, passing Taharan and on to another mountain range that lay ahead. After a while they descended and landed in a small meadow somewhere in a forest. Linder dismounted off the griffin once it landed and lowered itself to the ground then helped Jess get down. Marcus dismounted as well as Randy who then offered to help Erika dismount. Randy placed his hands around Erika's waist then lifted her off the griffin and set her on the ground. "Thank you." Erika replied with a smile and a small blush on her cheeks. "You are very welcome." Randy replied with a nod of his head.

"Where are we?" Marcus asked looking around at his surroundings. "I'm not sure. But we need to figure out where we are and which direction we need to head before it gets to dark." Linder replied as he looked around as well. "Your right; Well the sun is there, so south would be this way. Let's travel that way and find a spot to set up camp for the night. I don't think this meadow would be a safe place, it's to open and we could be spotted from anyone coming near. I think we need to stay as hidden as possible."Marcus stated as he pointed to the sun and then southwards.

"That sounds like a great plan." Linder replied to Marcus. "What do you think about that?" Linder asked the others. "That's sound good. I agree that we need to stay hidden. I would like to know how they found us back there." Jess said. "Yeah me too. But what about the Griffins? We just can't leave them here alone." Erika answered while pulling her cloak tighter around herself to block the cold winter air from touching her. In response the griffins twittered their high pitched eagle sound and then rose to the sky and flew above the tree tops and out of sight. "Well I guess that solves that problem." Randy replied. "I hope that they will be okay." Erika responded. "They will be." Linder remarked. Behind them came a caw that startled all of them. Sitting on top of a tree branch sat the black crow that had helped them before and had followed the griffins over the mountains and to this spot. Surprisingly the crow had kept in pace with the griffins but with the cloud coverage and darkening sky they couldn't see if the crow was with them or not. The crow flapped its wings and cawed then flew off to the direction that they were just about to travel. "Well let's go then. It is getting late and we need to find a spot to stay the night." Linder instructed.

They traveled through the snow laden ground for almost an hour then found a spot in the trees where they could make a camp for the night. The temperature was dropping as the sun was setting. "No fire tonight. I know it's cold and it's only going to get colder in the night, and with Erika's pack gone our supplies are fewer but I don't want to risk a fire being seen by anyone. We barely got away last time, and we wouldn't have if not for the griffins. We will have to share anything we have to keep each other warm during the night. We cannot get caught especially now that we are so much closer to our destination. We will share what we have for now and if we can we will get more supplies later." Linder informed the others as soon as the all of them were together in the small spot in the trees where they were going to make camp. "I agree with Linder." Jess acknowledged. "Why don't we eat some food and then divide what we have to keep each other warm during the night and plan our watch turns for the night." Marcus answered then scratched the hair that was growing on his black face. "That sounds great." Erika replied.

Marcus, Jess, and Linder took of their packs and divided food amongst them all. They ate rolls, cold meat and potato pies, and a few apples for dinner. Afterwards Linder offered his bedroll to Erika, who graciously accepted. As Erika was laying it on the ground, she placed her hand on the ground and with her power melted the snow and warmed the ground where she placed the bedroll. "How did you do that? You did something like that with the clouds earlier too, didn't you? How are you doing that?" Randy asked surprised and astonished. Erika looked at Randy then towards Jess, who shrugged as if she didn't care whether Erika told Randy about the magic or not.

Looking back at Randy she answered. "I can use magic." "Magic?" Randy exclaimed. "Well only magic that deals with weather and plants. Like I can control the weather and help make plants grow, but only when I where this cloak. I can't do any magic without it." "So it's not you that has magic, it's the cloak." Randy implied.

"For now, yes." Erika replied. "So if I wore the cloak then I could control the weather?" Randy inquired. "Well no, I have been bestowed with the power and it will only work for me." "Bestowed with the power? What does that mean?" Randy asked with a look of confusion growing on his face. "A wizard bestowed the elemental power onto me." "A wizard, a real wizard?" "Yes, he…" Erika began to reply but Jess cut her off abruptly. "Quiet!" Erika gave Jess a worried look. Jess wasn't the kind of person to demand someone to stop talking unless it was really important. Jess stood with her eyes closed, breathing slowly. "What's wrong with her?" Randy asked irritated that she so rudely interrupted Erika. Erika put her hand on Randy's arm and put one of her fingers on her other hand to her lips indicating silence. Jess's eyes flew open and she quietly yet sternly spoke. "We have to go now. Leave the bedrolls, grab the packs, and be quiet." Linder grabbed his pack and hers, Marcus grabbed his pack and then they all followed Jess who was fleeing into the forest. They ran as quietly as they could for some time until Jess slowed to a stop.

Breathing hard she closed her eyes and tried to calm herself and using her power she searched for anyone else's feeling in the area. None was there. She opened her eyes, "We are safe for now." "What was all that about?" Randy asked as he tried to catch his breath from the run. "We weren't alone. There were about ten others in the forest near us, with cruel intentions. Anger, hatred, and killing were all that they were feeling." "How do you know that?" Randy asked. "Magic" she replied forwardly. "Do you all have magical abilities?" he asked looking between all of them. "Yes, we do." Linder answered straightly. "Are you sure we are safe here?" he asked Jess while placing one hand onto her arm. "I don't know about safe but we are alone." "Maybe we shouldn't stop for the night but continue on until we get to the nearest city." Linder offered then handed Jess her pack.

"I don't like traveling in an unknown forest in the dark but I think that you are right. If there really are people after us then stopping wouldn't be very smart." Randy acknowledged. "Let's continue south and keep alert. There's no point in standing around here, we all know what must be done so let's go." Marcus instructed. Acknowledging that they knew it was the best thing to do they continued walking south, hoping to find a town soon. The sun was gone and the moon was full by the time they started seeing small flickering lights through the trees ahead. "Once we find a way into the city, we will have to find a place to stay hidden for the rest of the night. Stay together and try to stay hidden." Marcus instructed. All together they emerged from the forest to find a city sprawled out in front of them.

"That's Hyrum City" Erika whispered. "I know where we can stay, if we can get there." She continued. "Judon" Jess replied as if she had just had the same idea. "That will work." Linder whispered back excitedly. "Who's Judon?" Marcus asked. "The man who made our swords, we can stay with him until morning." Linder replied. Marcus nodded. They silently crept over a fence and into someone's back yard. There was no light coming from the house so the silently crept past the house and onto the cobblestone street. Linder looked around to get his bearings and then pointed to the right.

They followed Linder's silent direction through the city until they came close to the town market, where in the center of the market stood a large fountain. The fountain was shaped like a tree that stood twenty feet high and had many stone leaves carved onto the many branches stretching out towards the market. The fountain sat in the very center of town and when the weather is warm people would use a pump that is nearby which sent water up the tree and made the many branches spray water from their tips. The children of the town would run and play under the water tree. But now that it was winter the tree just looked like a frozen stone tree, which was exactly what it was.

Linder pointed down the street towards a small house, which was the only house with a candle still lit inside it. Just before they reached Judon's house they heard footsteps running towards them. Instead of knocking, Linder quickly turned the door handle and to his surprise the door opened to Judon's house, relieved that it was unlocked they went quickly inside. After Marcus shut and locked the door quickly and quietly he joined the others in the kitchen.

On the table sat a single candle lit with a note written on the table under it. "Blow out the candle and be quiet." Linder blew out the candle and they all held still, following the instruction that was written.

They heard the sound of men running down the street passing Judon's house. No one moved until they heard a small purposeful cough from behind them. Turning to face the inside of the house they could see only a faint outline of a man standing in front of them. He was holding what looked to be a sword in his right hand held out pointed towards them. "State your names!" He sharply and quietly demanded. "Jess Northstin, Erika South, Linder, Marcus and Randy." Jess replied quickly for all of them. "Jess, Erika and Linder, you three have caused some grief around here since the last time you were here. Where's Jusdan and who are these men with you? Do you trust them?" Judon asked while peering through the darkness trying to see the people that were standing in his kitchen. "Yes, we trust them" Linder answered.

Judon came closer while putting his sword away in a sheath around his belt. "Good. I didn't except you to come this early but you're here now so let's get some rest and talk in the morning. You will be safe here for a while. Find a spot on the floor somewhere and I will see you in the morning." Judon instructed then reached for the candle off the table. "Do you have any extra blankets that we could use? We lost some of our supplies earlier." Erika asked. "Yeah, wait here I'll bring you some. How many do you need?" Judon asked in his gruff voice. "Two" Erika replied. "Alright, just minute and I'll bring you some." He replied then left the kitchen, taking the candlestick with him.

"You trust this man?" Marcus asked Linder in a whisper. "Yes" Linder whispered back. "Okay" Judon re-entered the kitchen, "I can't see who is who in this blackness so someone take these blankets. You can sleep here, and there is a little space in the hall but not much. Hopefully you can all fit in here. I am so blasted tired, I am going to bed and we can talk more in the morning." Judon announced while holding out the extra blankets. "Thank you." Erika replied as she took the blankets from him. "Good night and thank you for your hospitality, again." Jess told Judon in a sweet and sincere voice emphasizing the last word. "You're welcome, good night." Judon replied yawning. He turned and walked out of the kitchen and into his bedroom where he then closed the door and silence filled the air.

"Everyone get some sleep, we've had a long day. We will be safe here for the night." Linder instructed as he placed his pack onto the ground and pulled out a blanket from inside it. Erika handed Randy one of the extra blankets. Marcus and Jess took out their own blankets from their packs. They all found a spot to lie down at on the floor. Jess and Linder lay close to each other on one side of the kitchen table; Erika and Randy lay close together on the opposite side of the kitchen table, each using their own blankets. Marcus laid half in the kitchen and half into the hall leading towards Judon's room. The house was much warmer than sleeping out in the forest. "Good night everyone, tomorrow will be a good day, I just know it." Erika said then yawned. Everyone replied and soon the room went silent besides the soft rhythmic breathing of the sleeping people.

Chapter Four- The Black Order

Erika awoke to the smell of fresh baked bread. She slowly opened her eyes and looked around. The smell made her think of home and her family. Standing by the small wood burning stove stood a woman. She was carefully trying to not step on anyone lying on the floor while pulling a loaf of bread out of the oven. Erika didn't recognize the woman. She had long black hair that flowed down her back that was tied into one large braid; Erika thought that the woman looked to be only a few years younger than her. She wore a long ankle length light yellow and blue dress that had a blue ribbon tied in the back, its sleeves went mid way down her arms with small laces sewn around the edges. She was a thin woman and wore what looked to be sturdy boots underneath her dress as he moved. She wore a gray apron on top of her dress that was dusted with flour. Erika rose to a sitting position, causing the floor beneath to creak slightly. The woman turned around to face her.

"I thought you might be the first one up. You're Erika right?" the woman asked quietly after she placed the loaf of bread on the top of the stove. "Yes, how did you know?" Erika asked watching the woman. "From the pictures on the wanted posters and my father told me about you, Jess, and Linder. We have been expecting you." "Your father?" "Oh, Judon is my father." "Oh okay." Erika replied with recognition. "Wait. You were expecting us?" "Yeah for a couple days now but we really didn't know when exactly you would be coming; it was sort of a surprise that you arrived so early. Hold that thought" The woman replied then turned around and took another loaf of bread out of the oven. She took both loaves and carefully stepped over Jess and Linder and placed the two loaves of bread onto the table. Erika watched the woman as she then walked out the back door without saying anything else.

Moments later she returned carrying two glass jars full of ice cold milk. The cold breeze that blew into the house when she returned made Erika shiver. Marcus abruptly sat up and was alerted to his surroundings. "Who are you?" he asked in a stern voice towards the woman who froze in her tracks when Marcus spoke.

"I am Judon's daughter. My name is Lillian." She answered as she stared at Marcus, unsure what to do. Her father hadn't told her about this man so she didn't know if she could trust him or if he was dangerous. Marcus could see that the woman was scared of him, and then he noticed he had his hand onto his sword hilt and he hadn't meant to snap at her. He released his hand and stood. "I'm sorry. I did not mean to scare you. I am Marcushan, you can call me Marcus." He replied and reached out his hand towards her. Her dark brown eyes met his and for an instant they just looked at each other then she reached out and shook his hand.

Everyone else was waking up now. Lillian released Marcus's hand and turned her attention to all those who were waking up now. "Good morning. I am Lillian, my father is Judon. He had to leave early but will be back later this afternoon. I am to help you in any way I can, oh and keep you out of trouble." Lillian told the others. "I made some bread and was going to make some oatmeal and we have cold milk to drink for breakfast. I have to admit you all look worse than I thought you would." She said looking at everyone around the room before anyone had a chance to say anything she spoke.

"I don't need to know who or what's blood is all over you as long as you promise to never wear those clothes again, once you all change. Never mind that, those clothes are going right in the fire." Lillian said as she looked at each visitor in turn. Jess, Linder, Erika, Randy and Marcus all took a look at the clothes they were wearing. All of them had blood stains on their clothes, some of the blood was from killing Therion's, some was from the dying man in the woods, and some was of their own from the fights with the Therion's. None of them had really noticed how bloody, dirty and ragged they were until this moment. Jess's hair wasn't in the nice single braid over her shoulder anymore, some strands were still tied together but most of it lay in clumpy strands around her head with dried blood in it.

Erika's hair with its natural curls was ratted into a mess upon her head. The ride on the griffins must have whipped them around more than Jess thought. Some of their clothes had rips in them and were just plain unsalvageable. "Don't worry about your clothes, I will go to the market and get you all some new ones, plus whatever supplies you will need." Lillian continued on before anyone spoke. "We also have a bath inside the house so you can all clean up, you will have to fill up the bucket a few times from above the sink to fill up the bath but I think you will all enjoy getting clean." "Thank you." Erika responded first. "Yeah no problem, it's the least I can do." Lillian replied. Erika's expression changed, "Wait, you said that you recognized me from the wanted poster. What wanted poster?" "What?" Marcus asked quickly. "Oh, I forgot, you don't know. I will explain everything while we eat breakfast." Lillian replied then pulled out a sack of oats from a drawer.

"Why don't you all put away your blankets while I fix breakfast, then we can eat and talk and I will tell you everything I know?" "That would be great." Jess replied. Lillian went on making breakfast while the others put away their blankets and gathered all their packs and weapons into one pile. Lillian announced that the oatmeal was ready. Erika had folded the blankets that Judon had let them borrow and put them into a pile on the floor then sat down on a chair at the table. Lillian handed out bowls to everyone and told them to help themselves to the oatmeal, bread, and milk. Soon everyone had their food and was sitting around the kitchen table.

"I just realized that we haven't introduced ourselves yet. I am Jess; it's nice to meet you. I didn't know Judon had a daughter." "Yeah, and I have...had a brother." "Had? What happened to him?" Marcus asked in between eating his breakfast. "I don't know. One day he went to the market and never returned. It has been almost a year. We looked and looked but never found him and no one seemed to know anything. Just like my mother." Lillian replied quietly.

"What happened to your mother?" Jess asked. "She and I were at the market one day buying food and fabric. I saw some men wearing dark red cloaks with something on their faces talking to her. The merchant I was buying food from told me how much it would costs for what I held in my hands which drew my attention away from my mother. I quickly paid for the food and turned to face my mother and she was gone, and so were the men. No one seemed to see anything. One minute she was there and the next she was gone. That was right after my brother went missing. I don't think it was coincidence. Right after that my father packed up our belongings and moved us across town and changed our last name. He found a job as a blacksmith and we have been alright until right after your last visit. Well personally we have been okay but every since your last visit there have been many changes around here. First the king has gotten rid of curfew guards and his own king's guards." Lillian began to say.

"That should be good right?" Erika asked in confusion. "No. He made them pick to become part of the Black Order and become men like the ones that I believe took my mother or they could chose the second option, be hung in the town square. As you can imagine they all picked to be part of the Black Order. They all wear dark red cloaks, which look like the dried blood on your clothes and have black dragons tattooed onto their faces." "That is what the men are called. They are Black Dragons. Those are the men we are hiding from. Karlsen Soldum must have gotten to the king. This could be a lot harder than we originally thought." Linder commented as he ate some of the hearty breakfast. "They are stationed all over the town and also in the forests around here and also in the other cities; well that is what I have been told.

The curfew bell rings a lot earlier now and everyone is to stay inside their homes or wherever they are at the time when the curfew bell rings. Members of the Black Order can enter any home and search it, and if anyone refuses they are killed on the spot. They haven't found what or who they are searching for and if anyone questions them they are killed or told that its Black Order business and not any of our concern. They have searched our house three times since they placed that order in affect. They never found what they were looking for so they left.

After the first time it happened my father thought for a long time trying to figure out what had changed or what would be causing all the changes and then he realized that all the changes started right after he met some of you. He knew that there were men after you and that you all had something important that you needed to do. I was staying with my grandmother across town when he first met you and when I returned a few days later he told me of your visit. He knew then that things were about to change and that's why he isn't here right now. He was right; shortly after the Kings Guards and the Curfew Guards joined the Black Order there was a massive increase in weapons demands.

The Black Order men have ordered all the blacksmiths to make them many weapons. There is a certain amount of weapons that have to be made each day and if that number isn't met the Black Order will kill a black smith to make the others work harder. My father leaves early in the morning and usually doesn't get home until right before the curfew bell rings. He works so hard every day and then in the evening he plans our escape and sleeps. He told me that we had to leave Hyrum as soon as we can." Lillian explained. "Where are you going to escape to?" Erika asked then took a bite of the fresh bread. "There's a small town called Morganstin a couple days away from here, we plan on going there. There is a rumor going around that someone important lives there in hiding that might be able to help." Lillian replied. "Who is it? Do you know the person's name?" Jess asked while finishing her last pieces of bread. "No I don't. I just know that it's a woman. Why?"

"Erika and I are from Morganstin and that is where we are headed now." "Maybe we can come with you. How soon are you leaving? I'm not sure if my father is ready to go yet or not. He hasn't told me when exactly we are leaving. He was still making plans the last time I talked to him about it." "How long ago was that?" Marcus asked. "Well the night before we received the letter about all of you, so three nights ago." Lillian replied. "What letter? You said earlier that you were expecting us. Who is the letter from and what does it say?" Linder asked.

"Someone with the initials K.A, I have the letter, you can read it yourselves. It doesn't say much, I will get it for you." Lillian responded then rose from the table and went to one of the drawers in the kitchen and pulled out a letter that was folded in half with a broken wax seal on it. Lillian handed the letter out to Linder. After taking the letter he read it out loud. "Leave a candle lit every night until our friends arrive, help them out. The illusionist will provide a way." "See I told you, it doesn't say much. My father and I both don't know of any illusionists." Lillian remarked as she sat back down at the table. Jess, Linder and Erika turned to face Marcus. "I do. Watch this." Marcus instructed then waved his right hand over the table. Randy and Lillian gasped at the sight. Instead of six bowls sitting on the table there were now twelve, each matching one that had previously been there.

"You are the illusionist!" Lillian stated excitedly as she tried reaching for one of the bowls. "Yes I am." Marcus replied watching as Lillian went to pick up one of the bowls she thought was an illusion and to her surprise was able to pick it up. Confused that she had picked up a real bowl she set it down and picked up another so knew to be an illusion. Turning the bowl in her hand she replied. "That is remarkable! How are you doing that? I can really hold and feel it. It looks and feels real." "Magic." Marcus answered and waved his hands once more and all the extra bowls vanished, including the one Lillian was holding.

"That never gets old" Jess commented as she smiled to Lillian's wide eyes. "Parlor tricks that's all it is." Marcus replied. "So you can help us. Can you make illusions of people?" she asked hopefully. Marcus looked at Lillian then moved his eyes to an empty spot in the small room. Suddenly a full size illusion that looked exactly like Lillian stood before them. "Can you make illusions of people?" the illusion repeated Lillian's words. "Wow!" Randy exclaimed. Even Jess, Erika and Linder were surprised. Marcus hadn't told anyone that he had figured out how to make illusions of people. "That's me!" Lillian stated excitedly. Marcus looked at Lillian, the illusion vanished. "What happened to it?" Lillian asked turning to look at Marcus. "I can't control human illusions for very long yet. But I think that is how I am going to be able to help. If I was able to make it appear that we were somewhere and then we go the other way we might be able to get out of the city unnoticed." Marcus replied.

"If that doesn't work can you make us appear differently, so that we are not as recognizable?" Linder asked. "I'm not sure. I will practice and see what I can do by the time we leave." He answered. "Well nobody is going out there in broad day light. There are wanted posters around for Jess, Linder, and Erika and I am sorry Marcus but...." She paused unsure how to say the next words. "All dark skinned people have been banished from here and Taharan. They were all ordered to go to Delkija. So you won't be going out there either." Lillian said in a rush, embarrassed to say such things.

"I can though. I could help you get the supplies that we will need. No one will suspect anything from me." Randy offered. "You will have to get all cleaned up first." Lillian informed him. "Yes ma'am I will." He replied formally. "Very well, we will stay here and hide while you two go and get supplies. If you have a piece of parchment and some ink and quill I will make a list of what supplies we will need." Linder insisted. "Yes, I will get it for you then I will show Randy where the inside bath is." She said then turned her attention to Randy. "Once you get all cleaned up and changed we can go to the market." "That will be good, except there is one problem. I don't have any extra clothes." Randy admitted. "Oh, my father's would be too big on you." Lillian remarked. "You can use some of mine." Linder offered. "Thank you." Randy replied then stood up leaning to one side, still limping because of his cut on his leg. Lillian looked up and down Randy; her eyes grew big when she saw his pants.

"Your part of that army that came to town a few days ago! Why didn't you tell me! You can't trust him." Lillian yelled. "What? Why not?" Erika asked confused. "He has been with us for the past few days and before that there would be no way he could have been here. There were others dressed like him that came here? What did they do?" Linder asked nerves on edge now. "They said they were from some place far away and that their leaders sent them here to join the Black Order and help spread the word of the good that the Black Order could bring to all the lands. They also said that they were looking for someone called the Northstin Wind and a prophet that are evil wizards that want to stop the Black Order. " Lillian explained. "Do you know any of the men's names?" Randy asked while lifting his dirty bowl off the table. "I don't."

"Let me guess, there were about twenty men and they were led by a large man with red hair and a big scar across his face." Randy asked. "Yeah, how did you know?" Lillian confirmed. "They are the men that disserted the mission that I led. They left our squadron and traveled a different direction. I knew they were going to be trouble from the very beginning. Officer Travis always questioned my orders and one day he and some others decided that they no longer wanted to follow my order and that our mission was a waste of time. They knew that they couldn't return home without the Northstin Wind and the prophet so they decided that they were going to hunt them down and kill them. That way once they were dead they could return home, give the town the bad news and be hero's for trying. It sounds to me like they joined the Black Dragons to get glory and help spread the black plague which would prove that the Northstin Wind and the Prophet were dead." Randy said then limping over placed his bowl into the sink. "But they haven't killed them, and I have a good feeling that they don't even know who the Northstin Wind and the Prophet are." Jess commented then placed her and Linder's bowls into the sink. "I think your right. That could benefit us greatly." Linder acknowledged.

"How do you know that they don't know who those people are and haven't killed them yet? Things have gotten bad lately. Maybe they already have killed them." Lillian remarked. Linder, Jess, Marcus and Erika shared a look between each other then Linder spoke. "We know, because we are those people." "What? How can this be?" Lillian asked astonished. "How did I not see it before? Jess you are the Northstin Wind aren't you?" Randy asked shaking his head in realization. "Most likely, my last name is Northstin. I am from Morganstin. I am going to marry Linder, who is the prophet. I have the magical ability to feel others feelings and I can change their feelings to whatever I want them to feel. I had never heard of the Northstin Wind before I heard it from you but I fit all the requirements." Jess admitted. "You're the Northstin Wind, and you're the Prophet! Holy smokes! No wonder there's dangers after you. Do you all have magic then?" Lillian exclaimed. "Yes, we all have magical abilities." Linder replied grinning. There came a knock on the door, everyone froze.

"Are you expecting anyone?" Marcus whispered. "No." Lillian answered her eyes growing wide in fear of who could be out there. The knock came again. "Go answer it but don't let anyone inside." Marcus instructed. Lillian nodded and left the kitchen. Everyone listened carefully while remaining in the kitchen, not wanting to be seen and trying to listen to see who was at the door. Lillian opened the door a crack and to her terror there stood a Black Dragon. "I am here for a routine home check, move aside." The man in the dark red cloak said strictly. "Can you come back later? My father isn't here right now." Lillian replied as calmly as she could. "So your home alone. That's not a problem at all. Move aside and let me in. This won't take long." he replied his tone loaded with malevolence.

He pushed Lillian aside and made his way into the house. "Close that door, and come here." He demanded. "We have to do something." Marcus whispered. Linder pointed to Randy and whispered, "Go out there and pretend like you're going to take advantage of Lillian and we will sneak around and stop him." Randy had an unsure look on his face, but could only image how terrified Lillian was. He nodded and strode out of the kitchen to face the Black Dragon. "Close the door girl and get over here! I don't have all day and you're going to make me day a whole lot better." The Black Dragon subjugated. Lillian slowly closed the door, truly hoping that the people in the other room were going to do something to help her. As soon as she got the door closed the Black Dragon grabbed her wrist and pulled her toward him. Just then Randy walked into the room.

"What do you think you're doing?" Randy spoke in a commanding tone. "What does it look like? I'm taking my benefits. She told me that she was alone. But this will still work, after me you can have her." The Black Dragon said after looking up and down Randy. "No, I was here first. I will take her and then you can but I prefer to do it alone. You can wait outside until I'm done." Randy stated and grabbed Lillian's wrist out of the Black Dragons.

"Outside! No I will wait right here! If you're not man enough to do it in front of me then you're not man enough to do it at all. That will be something to tell the others of the order. No, you do it now or lose your chance. I don't know why Wizard Soldum even let you army boys join our cause." The Black Dragon scoffed. "Fine, I will have her now and you can watch and then you can enjoy her yourself after." Randy replied angrily while jerking Lillian closer to him. "Don't worry, this won't hurt me..." Randy snickered towards Lillian pulling her body right against his, wrapping one arm around her waist trapping her next to him. "Trust me" he whispered into her ear and then smelled her neck. He moved his free hand onto her thigh and started pulling her skirt up her leg. "You better enjoy this girl because I'm not going to be as gentle as he is." The Black Dragon said leering at her while leaning his back against one of the walls. Suddenly the front door swung open and in came Linder sword drawn and at the same moment Marcus came out of the kitchen with his sword drawn, both directing the swords towards the Black Dragon.

It was over within seconds, the Black Dragon didn't even have time to react. One minute he was leaning against the wall the next his head was rolling across the floor, his body lay crumpled on the floor with a sword sticking out of his heart. Lillian screamed in horror while Randy turned her away and tried to block her from the site. She started crying and her body trembled. Randy led her out of the room and to where Erika and Jess waited. "Randy why don't you go take a bath while we calm her down. Then when you both are ready, you can go get supplies. We will take care of the body while you're gone." Jess offered as she reached out for Lillian.

"That would be good." Randy replied then set to his task. Erika started some water boiling on the still hot stove to make some calming tea for Lillian while Jess tried to calm Lillian's trembling body. Linder and Marcus moved the body and head of the deceased Black Dragon outside and buried it in the snow. When they came back in, Lillian had calmed and Randy should have been done with his bath but still hadn't come out yet.

"I wonder if he drowned." Jess teased. Linder washed his hands in the sink and then remembered something. "I didn't get him any clothes to wear; he might be done but doesn't want to come out here naked." Linder remarked then went to his packed and pulled out some fresh clothes. He took the clothes to give to Randy. Moments later he returned and asked which of the women knew how to sew up wounds, stating that when Randy was scrubbing his body his wound tore and started bleeding a lot and that it needed to be sewn to heal right. All the women replied that they knew how so Linder picked Erika to come with and help sew it. He didn't want Jess to come and he thought that Lillian wouldn't be calm enough to do it properly and Randy seemed to like Erika. He thought that Erika was the best choice.

Linder and Erika entered the bath room and during the time that passed, Jess made a list of supplies that they would need while her and Marcus tried to devise a plan for getting out of the city. Lillian sat at the kitchen table and listened to Jess and Marcus talk while drinking her cup of relaxing tea. Some time passed before Linder, Erika and then Randy returned to the kitchen. Linder and Erika looked the same but Randy was clean from head to foot. He had his damp dark brown shaggy hair combed down to lay flat against his head; he had brown facial hair growing into a small beard and a small mustache. He really needed a haircut and a shave but there wouldn't be the opportunity to do so any time soon. He wore some of Linder's extra clothes which consisted of a pair of tan pants, a long sleeved forest green button up shirt, and black suspenders. He wore his own boots that had been wiped cleaned.

"You look very handsome." Erika commented. "Yes you do." Lillian agreed. "Thank you." Randy replied. "Are you ready to go t the market now?" he asked Lillian. "Yes." "Here is the list of supplies that we will need. Don't draw attention to yourselves. If anything seems to be wrong return here and don't worry about the rest of the items." Marcus instructed and held the list out to Randy. "I understand." Randy replied taking the list. "Good" Marcus remarked. "Alright, shall we go now?" Randy asked Lillian reaching his hand out towards her. "Yes, first we need coats to wear. You can wear one of my father's coats." She replied then walked into another room.

Moments later she returned wearing a black frilly cloak draped on top of her dress that tied around her neck. "This is for you to use." She said and handed him a brown frock. "We can go now." Lillian answered taking Randy's once again outstretched hand while holding a wicker basket on the other arm. Randy led her towards the door. "Be safe." Linder told them before they walked out the door. Randy nodded then led Lillian outside, closing the door behind them.

"I guess I will go and get cleaned up next." Marcus said after Lillian and Randy had gone. "Okay, we will wait in the kitchen." Erika replied. Marcus nodded and retrieved clean clothes from his pack and headed into the bath room. Several hours pass while Randy and Lillian were gone. Marcus, Linder, Jess, and Erika all took separate baths and got all clean. Jess gave Erika some of her clothes to wear, since Erika had lost her pack earlier. Jess retied her long blonde hair into a single braid and tossed it over her shoulder. Erika brushed her shoulder length curly brown hair evenly and tucked it behind her ears. They wore cloaks to keep them warm and after they all repacked their belongings, as they anxiously awaited Randy and Lillian's return. Linder knew they couldn't go looking for them so all they could do was to wait. Randy and Lillian finally returned around lunch time. The wicker basket on Lillian's arm was full of items and Randy carried a large burlap bag full of different things and a wicker basket that looked the same as Lillian's.

"We brought lunch and here are the supplies, we were able to get everything that was on the list." Randy replied, placing everything onto the table. "We also saw my father and talked to him briefly. He wasn't able to talk to me in great detail because of the people around but he told me to be prepared for tonight. I am positive that means that we will be leaving tonight." Lillian acknowledged then placed her basket onto the table as well. "We will need to hear Judon's plan and compare it to ours to see if he has anything better that we could do. But for now let us go through the new supplies, and then eat lunch. Afterwards Lillian can do what she needs to, to get ready to leave." Linder stated.

The rest of the day went by slowly. They ate a lunch of chicken, rolls, raw vegetables and an apple pie all of which were bought from the market. They divided the supplies and Lillian got everything ready for her and her father. Judon returned home two hours before sunset, moments later the curfew bell rang. Looking out the window Linder could see at least four Black Dragons on the street, pacing up and down looking at each house in turn as they passed. Judon instantly asked why there was a large blood stain on his floor. They explained about killing the Black Dragon and putting the body in the snow outside of his house. Their dinner was the same as lunch and after eating Judon washed up, changed his clothes and then told Lillian to change her clothes into what he had brought home in a bag. "Father, these are men's clothes" she said while pulling the clothes out of the bag to look at them. "Yes they are. Go change into them girl and don't forget you are to wear your long johns underneath. It's cold out there and men's clothes are better for traveling. See even Jess and Erika wear men's clothing." Judon replied pointing to Jess and Erika, who were wearing men's pants and men's pull over shirts. Lillian paused for a moment to look at the women then left into a different room carrying the clothes. Afterwards Judon told everyone his plan for getting out of the city.

"The Black Dragon's change posts sometime after midnight, so I want to leave before then. My plan is simple. We will travel in the shadows heading southward in two groups, don't get caught, and keep traveling until we make it to Morganstin. The hardest parts will be getting out of town." "You know that Morganstin is around a three day walk don't you?" Jess asked. "Yes I do." Judon remarked casually. "We might be able to stop in Jensen City for a night if we have too. I have family there that we could stay with." Linder proposed. "I don't think we should stay with them, I don't want to bring any more trouble to them then we already have." Jess stated.

"There is a wayward pine tree that Jess and I stayed in for a night just before Jensen City, or in this case right after it that we could stay in if we had too." Erika offered. "That would be nice but I would really like to travel the whole time if we can until we get to Morganstin." Judon replied. "It takes around six hours to get to Jensen City, a few hours to get past it and then another day or so to get to Morganstin. I think that we should leave in a few hours and get as far away as we can tonight. We also should wear any extra clothing that we have so that we stay warm. I really need to rest before we leave so I am going to take a quick nap, and I need someone to wake me up in a few hours and then we can leave." Judon informed them. "I will wake you father. Go and rest." Lillian replied entered the room. Judon nodded then left the kitchen without another word. Everyone got everything ready to go while Judon took a nap.

Chapter Five- Going Separate Ways

The sun set and an eerie darkness settled over the city. Lillian lit one candle and placed it on the kitchen table to light the room as their shadows flickered on the wall behind them. Those who lost their packs or didn't have any to begin now had extra large burlap bags, which Randy and Lillian got from the market that they could use to put their stuff in. They tied a rope around the top making a loop that they could throw on their shoulders. All the supplies were divided equally. Everyone put on all their extra clothes and then they waited. Erika wore her golden brown wolf fur cloak with silver trimmings with a big fur hood attached to it which was her magical talisman which allowed her to use her powers to change the weather. It would keep her warm and allow her to use her powers anytime she desired if she need to do so. Jess wore her gold chain necklace with a small gold hollow heart hanging from the end of it around her neck, which was her magical talisman. She had never taken the necklace off since receiving it from Kedar.

Marcus wore his arm band that was made with a brown leather lining with hemp tightly woven through the center. The arm band will allow him to use his illusionist abilities, which he thought would be necessary for them to get out of the city. Linder kept the prophecy book in his pack always near him. Three hours later, Lillian woke her father. Judon didn't waste any time. Once in the kitchen with everyone else he repeated the plan. "Lillian you will go with Linder and Jess in the first group, the rest of you will come with me in the second group. Linder's group will leave and then we will wait for at least ten minutes then we will leave. If we don't see you before Morganstin, here is the address that we are headed too. Once you get there tell the woman that lives there that your father is part of the South Rebellion. She will know what you are talking about and let you in. Her name is Ellen. Stay there until we arrive." Judon informed Lillian and handed her a folded piece of parchment. She placed the piece of parchment into her pocket on her pants. Then she hugged her father.

"Be safe." He told her. "I will. See you soon." She replied. They released their embrace then he handed her a dagger. The dagger had wooden handle and a six inch blade. It sat securely in a sheath that fit it perfectly. "Take care of her, and be safe." Judon instructed to Linder. "We will." He replied. Linder and Jess shouldered their packs, while Lillian put the rope around her shoulder which was tied to a burlap sack that was full of supplies for herself. "Ladies, are you ready to go?" Linder asked Jess and Lillian. "I'm ready." Jess replied. "I have never done anything like this before. But I think I'm ready." Lillian answered nervously. "Then let's go. Once we go out there be as quiet as you can and watch me for instructions." Linder replied. The women nodded. He peeked out of the window and saw the same four Black Dragons pacing up and down the street. Each of the Black Dragons wore their dark red cloaks and had swords hung at their waists. "We're clear. Let's go." He said and went to the door and slowly opened it only wide enough for them to slip out into the cold dark night. Jess and Lillian followed. Marcus shut the door as soon as the others were out.

It was dark but the women were still able to see Linder's outline. Linder pointed southwards and the ladies followed. They quickly and quietly ran down the street. Linder pointed down to the ground and quickly dropped face first into the snow, holding perfectly still. Jess could hardly see him when he was lying like that. Jess and Lillian saw a Black Dragon heading their direction and did as Linder did. The snow on Lillian's face was so cold that she almost couldn't take having it pressed against her. She heard the sound of men running past them while she lay as still as she could. Someone nudged her; she turned her head and saw Jess and Linder getting up.

They all quickly stood up and continued running quietly down the street farther away from Judon's house. It took many cold hours of hiding and running to get to the edge of the town where to their horror were posted over twenty Black Dragons guarding the entrance and many of the houses around the entrance to the city which would have access out of the city. There were a few torches burning around the entrance so the Black Dragons could see anyone coming. They quickly backtracked and hid in a back yard of a house, with no sign of any person around.

"What now?" Lillian whispered. "I have an idea, but it's risky." Jess replied. "I trust you. Do what you have planned; we will follow your lead." Linder remarked. Jess lead them back a few streets to where there were only four Black Dragons guarding the streets. "Lillian, you stay here. Linder go across the street. Right after I get caught, give away your location and get caught, then Lillian you do the same. That's when I will use my power. I hope this works. If it doesn't work be prepared to fight and run." Jess informed Linder and Lillian. Linder shook his head, "You're crazy. Let's try it." He smiled, even though Jess wouldn't be able to see it in the dark. His voice gave away his acceptance. Jess crept farther down the street a few houses while Linder made his way across the street. Lillian stayed hiding in the back yard of someone's house.

Moments later the sound of commotion came from towards the direction that Jess had gone. "Gotcha! Thought you could sneak out of here did you? Well not hardly." a Black Dragon said while grabbing Jess's arm, as she pretended to flee. "There's another one." One of them shouted and ran and caught Linder. Lillian knew that it was her turn to run out and get caught. She was so nervous. What if Jess's plan didn't work? What if she had to fight? She had never fought with anyone before, especially where she would have to really hurt them or kill them in order to survive. She took a deep breath then walked out onto the street.

"There's one more." Another Black Dragon called and chased down Lillian who was caught within moments. All the Black Dragons gathered together with their prisoners, to figure out what to do with them, which is just what Jess had hoped for. Jess's wrists were being held behind her back by one of the Black Dragons. Desperately hoping her plan would work, she quickly pulled away from the Black Dragon that was holding her wrists and spoke these words and looked at each one in turn making eye contact with each one. "All of you Black Dragons believe my words! You have captured us and have been ordered by Karlsen Soldum, your master, to escort us directly to Morganstin without harming us. Now go!" All four Black Dragons blinked.

"We have orders to take you to Morganstin. Now move!" one of the Black Dragons demanded and gave Linder a push. The four Black Dragons led Linder, Jess and Lillian right to the main entrance of the city where the multitudes of Black Dragons were guarding. Jess could see the panic on Lillian's face as they drew near to so many Black Dragons. "Let us pass. We found these prisoners and have orders to take them to Morganstin." One of the Black Dragons said. "What orders? I haven't heard such orders." One large Black Dragon replied. He had Black Dragons tattooed on both sides of his face. This man seemed to be the one in charge; he had a bald head except for what looked to be another dragon tattooed on the top of his head. It was hard to tell what exactly was on his bald head in the flickering torch light. He held a ring of keys on his belt and had more weapons than any of other Black Dragon there.

"Soldum gave us the order. We have orders to take these prisoners to Morganstin unharmed." The Black Dragon replied. The leader looked up and down the four Black Dragons and their prisoners then called to the others. "Open the gate let them through." Some of the Black Dragons worked together and opened the gate to the city. "Move!" One of the four Black Dragons prodded Lillian, Jess and Linder forward through the group of Black Dragons that stood by the gate. As soon as they were past the gate Jess heard the leader speak in a hush. "Follow them. Something isn't right. Kill them if you have too." Jess didn't turn her head to look back to see how many Black Dragons where following them even though she really wanted to know.

The four Black Dragons pushed, poked, prodded and propelled them onward farther into the forest away from the city and into the dark looming trees with the ever darkening night sky. There were little stars shining this night, and the moon was covered by black clouds that filled the sky. Jess knew that she had to do something to get rid of these Black Dragons so they could get to Morganstin quickly and unharmed. An idea struck her. "Excuse me." She said then everyone turned to look at her. "Black Dragons believe me. You are all exhausted and cannot walk any farther; you must go to sleep right now." Jess declared keeping her voice firm while she pushed her power out towards them. The Black Dragons blinked then yawned then one of them suggested that they go to sleep, while starting to lie down on the ground. The others lay down on the ground right where they had been walking and all of the Black Dragons forgot about their prisoners and went right to sleep. Lillian looked completely shocked. Jess gestured to keep moving. They quickly and quietly left the four Black Dragons and continued to head towards Morganstin.

After a few moments of walking quickly, Linder suggested that they run for a while. Jess nodded in approval and they began running. Unsure of how long they had run Lillian's sore feet were telling her that she couldn't run anymore. Jess and Linder noticed Lillian slowing and they slowed with her to a fast walk. Linder heard the sound of someone running behind them. "We're being followed. It sounds like one or two people." He commented. "I hear them also." Jess acknowledged. "Is it Black Dragons?" Lillian asked somewhat scared that they had been found. "Most likely, we just need to continue on and if they catch up to us, Jess will have to use her powers or we will have to kill them. Let's just keep going for now." Linder replied.

They traveled briskly through the forest until the morning sun began to rise above the eastern mountain range. They passed the weathered wooden post which held wooden slats directing the different routes they could travel. All three slats had words carved into them stating the cities that lay ahead and behind. They followed the path that led towards Jensen City. "Can we stop for a rest now?" Lillian asked in a tired tone. Linder knew that Lillian and Jess really needed to stop to rest but with the Black Dragons following them he didn't want to stop until they absolutely had too. "Yes, but for just a few minutes. I haven't heard the Black Dragons for sometime but I believe they are still following us. Why don't we eat some breakfast, rest for a few minutes and then get moving again?" Linder suggested as he began to take his pack off. They moved off the trail into the untamed forest and found a spot to rest. They ate fruit, nuts, and rolls and drank from their water skins for breakfast. Resting for sometime letting their sore feet and legs have a break they remained silent, not wanting to draw attention to themselves just in case the Black Dragons should catch up to them.

It was a good thing they were being quiet because right as they were about to continue on, Jess whispered that she heard someone coming. Linder and Lillian nodded that they could hear them too. Linder gestured for them to lie down on the ground. Lillian and Jess lowered themselves onto their stomachs on the ground alongside Linder. They were a short distance from the path but if they were sitting or standing they would be spotted. Moments later two Black Dragons came running by, they didn't seem to be tired from running all night. They didn't seem to be tired at all. One of them slowed the other and pointed to the ground. With a thin layer of snow of the ground their footprints were easily visible with the rising sun shining on it. Both Black Dragons stopped and turned to face the direction the footprints led. Right to where Jess, Linder and Lillian were hiding. Jess looked at Linder and that's when it happened.

Marcus closed the door behind Linder then went right to the window and peeked out watching them leave until he could no longer see them. "Now we wait." He spoke into the dim candle lit room. "Now we wait." Judon repeated then blew out the candle. After some time of standing in the dark house the only sound audible was coming from their breathing. "Okay, let's go. Follow me." Judon instructed and slowly opened the door. Judon, Marcus, Randy and Erika slipped out of Judon's house and onto the dark street. There was only one Black Dragon on his street, who was headed the opposite direction that Judon headed. He wanted to get them off his street before the Black Dragon reached the end and turned around. He led them down the street until they saw a Black Dragon coming their direction so they quickly ducked into someone's back yard.

Judon led them through many backyards. They climbed over fences, dashed across streets, ran from one house to the next trying to not been seen and get out of the city. It took quite some time before they reached the road that led to the main gate out of the city. While hiding in the shadows of a building, Judon looked around the corner of the building and analyzed their situation and the sight he saw shocked him. Marcus held Judon back when he started to head onto the open street. "What are you doing?" Marcus demanded in a harsh whisper while keeping his grip on Judon's arm. "They have my daughter!" Judon replied trying to get away from Marcus.

Erika peeked around the corner and saw multitudes of Black Dragons standing around the gate and in front of them were four Black Dragons with Linder, Jess, and Lillian. Erika looked harder and tried to hear what the men were saying. "Let us pass. We found these prisoners and have orders to take them to Morganstin." One of the Black Dragons said. "What orders? I haven't heard such orders." One large Black Dragon replied. "Soldum gave us the order; we have orders to take these prisoners to Morganstin unharmed." The Black Dragon replied. The leader looked up and down the four Black Dragons and their prisoners then replied. "Open the gate let them through." "Move!" One of the four Black Dragons prodded Lillian, Jess and Linder forward through the group of Black Dragons that stood by the gate.

As soon as they were past the group of Black Dragons the leader spoke in a hush. "Follow them. Something isn't right. Kill them if you have too." Erika tried to figure out what had just happened. "Unharmed?" she whispered to herself. Then she quickly turned to face Judon, Marcus and Randy. Marcus was still holding Judon back while Randy stood a few paces behind them. "It's a trick." She stated in an excited whisper. Judon didn't listen and continued to try to get away from Marcus.

"Stop fighting! It's just a trick! They have tricked the Black Dragons to lead them out of the city. They do have some Black Dragons following them but I think they will be fine. It was just a trick. They will be alright, we need to move. I think they might have heard us." Erika stated. Judon stopped struggling and listened. Not far away they heard the sound of boots running towards them. They all started running away from the Black Dragons that were after them. Judon led them down two streets and then abruptly stopped and opened a house door and went inside. Randy, Marcus and Erika followed. As soon as they were all inside Judon closed the door quietly. "Get down." He instructed. It was near pitch dark in the house, as they all got down onto the floor. The only thing they could hear for a few minutes was the sound of their breathing. Then the sound of multiple people running down the street passed. Erika held her breath as the Black Dragons ran by. Randy started to rise when Judon pulled him back down, shaking his head in disapproval.

Randy got back down, just as another bunch of Black Dragons went running past. Each group of Black Dragons had many torches with them to light the way. They all turned to face the interior of the house when the sound of a squeaky door opening resonated towards them. From within the opened door flickering candle light spilled out onto part of the house. Everyone looked towards Judon to figure out what to do. He shook his head and pointed towards the floor. They all lay motionless in the shadows on the floor.

An elderly man walked out of the bedroom carrying a candle stick in his hand to light his way. He was wearing loose fitting trouser, and a long sleeved blouse. He didn't have anything covering his feet. He had a long white beard that covered his face and went down to his chest. His shoulders were hunched slightly. Raising the candlestick over his head with an old shaky hand he peered right at the strangers in his house. "With the looks of it, you're trying to hide from the Black Dragons. Am I right?" the elderly man asked. "Yes sir." Randy replied sitting up. "Military man? But not from here, correct?" the elderly man asked. "Yes sir." Randy replied. "What about the rest of you? Where are you from?" the elderly man asked, while he shakily held the candle. "I'm one of the cities blacksmiths." Judon answered. "I am from Delkija." Marcus replied. "I am from Morganstin." Erika stated. "What a collection I have found. All of you from different places yet all of you end up in my home in the middle of the night. Now I have a decision to make, I can either open that door and call for the Black Dragons to come and take you away or I can help you get out of the city. That is what you are trying to do right?" the elderly assumed.

"Yes sir that is correct." Randy answered straightly. "Well luckily for you, I'm opposed to the Black Dragons as much as you are, they've gone and ruined this town. It used to be a mostly peaceful place to live. There was no magic, and if there was it must have been only the good kind that helped people but none of this dark magic that has weaved its way into everyday life.

There certainly weren't Curfew Guards or Black Dragons prohibiting what you could and couldn't do and there wasn't anyone who took people away from their families with no good reason. We were content with things the way they were. So, I say if you can get away good for you. I will let you hide here until the coast is clear and I can offer one piece of advice for getting out of town but I do ask for something in return." The elderly man replied still holding the candlestick shakily above his head. "What is it?" Judon asked.

"If you are able to get away, one day when it will be possible come back for me. I hate living here, I know there are Black Dragons in other cities but I would like to at least get out of Hyrum. I can feel the darkness overtaking the city and I don't want anything to do with it. I need to live my last few years without oppression. So do we have a deal? I will tell you a way out of Hyrum that involves less Black Dragons then there are at the main gate and hide you here for a short time and when the time is right you will return for me." "Deal" Erika stated without hesitation.

"Smart lass." The elderly man replied. "Yes we have a deal. I don't know who of us will return but one day at least one of us will return for you and take you to a place without any Black Dragons." Marcus confided. "So how do we get out of the town?" Judon asked, getting to the point. "There is a house that has a broken fence in the backyard that leads into the forest outside of town. Depending on which way you're traveling, you may have to stay in the woods and go around the town to head south and to go north just head northwards and the path will connect to a small animal trail later on. The house is located at seven fifty five Jenks Street. But not only will you have to make it there without getting caught but the owner of the house is a spiteful man and will sell you out to the Black Dragons without a second thought.

Another thing, he owns dogs. Dogs that don't like strangers. If you wake them up they won't stop barking until Mr. Finkle tells them to stop. So don't wake them up. Well I guess that's all. You best be off soon so that you can have as much time as possible to get as far away as you can." The elderly man explained. "Thank you for letting us hide here, and for giving us such valuable information. We will return for you someday." Erika replied. "Good, the coast is clear. Go now and be safe." The elderly man stated. Everyone was standing now. Marcus opened the door a crack and peered out. "He's right. We can go now." He stated. "Wait we don't even know your name?" Erika asked turning around to face the elderly man.

The candle stick was flickering a soft glow while sitting on a small table, but the man wasn't in the room anywhere. "Where'd he go?" Erika asked as she peered around the dim lit room. "I don't know but we need to go now." Judon insisted then went to the front door. "He's right." Randy told Erika placing his hand onto her shoulder. Erika nodded then blew out the candle and followed Judon, Marcus, and Randy out of the house and onto the street. It took quite some time to sneak through the city, dodging Black Dragons on many occasions until they made to Jenks street. A couple houses away from the address that the elderly man told them Marcus whispered quietly to the others. "I have an idea for distracting the dogs." Stopping he pulled his pack off his shoulders he fished around in it for a minute and then retrieved two dried meat strips. They walked right to the dark house and headed towards the back yard.

Suddenly the barking began, Erika jumped in surprise as she heard the dogs coming closer and Marcus quickly broke the dried meat strips into pieces and tossed them towards oncoming dogs. The dogs stopped barking and began eating the meat strips. "Go!" Marcus sharply whispered. Judon, Erika, Randy and then Marcus quickly ran past the dogs and threw the opening the in the broken fence. They continued to run farther into the forest, Erika glanced back and saw that there was now a candle lit somewhere inside of the house.

They turned south and staying hidden in the forest skirted the town and went deeper into the forest. Many hours past without seeing any other humans and with the sun rising they decided to stop and have breakfast to gain the needed strength to continue. After eating miscellaneous foods from their pack and resting for a short time, they decided to find their way to the main trial. Shortly after sunrise they were following the main trail that lead to Jensen City and then to Morganstin. They passed a weathered wooden post which held wooden slats directing the different routes they could travel. All three slats had words carved into them stating the cities that lay ahead and behind. They followed the path that led towards Jensen City. Then they heard it, the sound of men in front of them.

"We should see who that is. Maybe its Linder and the others, but it could also be Black Dragons so to be safe we should do it sneakily and then reveal ourselves if it's our friends." Erika suggested. "I think that is a great idea. Let's go quietly. But be prepared to fight if needs be." Judon replied. They all made the weapons easily accessible then continued onwards. Within moments they could hear what the men ahead were saying and instantly knew that they were Black Dragons. Fear rose in the back of Erika's throat when she heard what they were talking about. They had found Jess, Lillian, and Linder's foot prints and were headed right toward them. Randy grabbed Erika's wrist and pulled her back while Judon and Marcus proceeded ahead. Marcus pulled his bow of his shoulder and retrieved an arrow from the quiver and knocked it in the bow.

Judon pulled a small ax from his belt and gripped the handle so hard his knuckles were turning white. Randy put a finger to his lips. Erika looked into his eyes and in that instant she could see that he cared for her and was trying to protect her. Staying back with Randy she watched Marcus and Judon stealthily shorten the distance between them and the Black Dragons ahead. Within moments they were out of sight and Erika's anxiety grew. She knew that she was safe with Randy but she feared for Jess. What if Marcus and Judon couldn't reach the Black Dragons before they reached Jess and the others? Her anxiety quickly rose when she heard a man scream in pain.

From their hiding spot, looking into Linder's blue eyes Jess whispered, "I love you" then that's when it happened. A man screamed in pain and everything after that seemed to happen instantaneously. Linder, Jess and Lillian all peered above the bushes to see what was happening. An arrow hit one of the Black Dragons, Marcus appeared on the trail running towards them with his bow loaded and knocked. He released the second arrow right into the second Black Dragon's heart.

Judon ran up next to Marcus yielding a blood soaked ax in his right hand. Linder jumped out of their hiding spot before Jess could stop him, pulling his dagger off his belt as he went. He ran past Marcus and Judon flinging his dagger towards an oncoming Black Dragon. The dagger hit the Black Dragon's arm, cutting a small gash through his clothes and into his skin then fell onto the ground. Linder ran head long into the Black Dragon. He pulled the Black Dragons dagger away from him and they both fell to the ground. The Black Dragon struggled to get Linder off him as Linder tried to cut the Black Dragon with the dagger he had confiscated.

The Black Dragon was much bigger than Linder and after only a few seconds had Linder thrown off. Furiously he attacked Linder, seeking his revenge. "Linder move!" Marcus yelled. Linder jumped into the foliage away from the Black Dragon, landing on his stomach knocking the wind out of him. Marcus shot two arrows at the Black Dragon before the man fell down dead. Linder rolled onto his back trying to catch his breath. Jess was standing and watched the whole thing happen.

"Stay here" she instructed Lillian then ran to help Linder. Marcus walked around all the dead Black Dragons and retrieved his arrows back, wiping each one on the dead bodies and placing them back into his quiver. Judon put his ax onto his belt and went to Lillian. "Come girl. We're safe now." He told Lillian reaching his hand down towards her. She took it and he pulled her up to her feet. They embraced in a hug. Jess ran to Linder and knelt down beside him. "Are you okay?" "Yeah, I just got the wind knocked out of me and a few bruises. I'll be fine." Linder replied sitting up. "Good" Jess stood up and helped Linder to his feet. She gave him a hug once they were both standing. He winced in pain. "Sorry, I'll be gentle." she loosened her hug and then let go completely. Judon, Lillian, and Marcus were watching them. "Let's go get Erika and Randy and continue on." Judon suggested. "I will go retrieve them, no sense in all of us going back." Marcus offered. "Alright" Judon answered then Marcus left. Judon, Lillian, Jess and Linder all waited while Marcus retrieved Randy and Erika.

Erika saw Marcus coming towards them alone and her heart seemed to stop. "Where is Judon? Did you find Jess, Linder, and Lillian? Are you hurt?" "I am fine. Judon is with the others. Everyone is fine. I came to show you the way to where they are waiting." Erika released a long breath. "Oh good." Marcus led them to the others and soon they were all together traveling towards Jensen City. It was around supper time when they came upon Jensen City. They were going to go around Jensen City staying hidden in the forest but the closer they drew the worse the city looked. Many of the buildings were burnt down, some still had smoke rising from the blackened ashes that remained. The air was thick with smoke causing it hard to breathe. The snow laden ground was black with soot.

"I have to go in town. I need to know if Loni and her boys are alive, they are the only family I have left." Linder told the others as they looked at the city sprawled before them. "It's not safe. We should stay in the forest. We can't risk going into town." Judon stated in his gruff voice. "I am going into town. The rest of you can keep going and I will meet you in Morganstin once I am done." Linder declared. "I am going with you." Jess remarked gripping his hand in hers. "If you go in there with all your gear on, you will be spotted and then captured or killed. If you insist on going, hide your gear in the forest and then retrieve it after you done. The rest of us will continue on and you two can meet us in Morganstin later." Marcus remarked then scratched his black beard.

"Very well, here is the address that we will meet at in Morganstin." Judon said and handed Linder a piece of folded parchment. "I can find the address easily; I am from there so I know the town well." Jess commented. "Good. Until we meet again, be safe." Judon remarked and turned to leave. "Go with them. I will see you when we get home." Jess told Erika. "Alright, see you later, and be careful." Erika responded. Judon, Lillian, Randy, Marcus and Erika then left Jess and Linder standing alone.

Hand in hand Jess and Linder walked closer towards the city. The smell of burnt wood, amongst other nauseating smells hung in the smoke filled air. Linder found a fallen hallow tree to hide their packs and swords. They both still carried daggers on their belts because Linder didn't want them to be completely unarmed. He covered their gear with snow and brush until it was well hidden and then they made their way into the city. He didn't waste any time going straight to his house. They passed many houses that were burnt beyond repair; most were burnt to the ground. But the peculiar thing was that only some of the houses were burnt while others seemed untouched right next to them. Coming up the street Linder's house was on they could see there were many houses burnt down. Before they reached it they could see the destruction. Linder's house was burnt to rumble, only one large wooden beam still partially stood. It leaned against the large pile of rubble. Panic and despair rose in Jess. "Loni! Nolin! Laken! Is anyone here?" Linder yelled. "Loni!" Linder frantically reached towards the rubble, attempting to dig them out but found it still hot causing him to burn his hand. He pulled his hand back and cried out in pain.

Chapter Six- Lottie

"They're not here." A small voice said from behind them. Linder and Jess turned to see a young girl standing behind them. She wore a long soot stained blue dress, her long brown hair was in a tangled ash filled mess. Her face was almost completely black with ash except streaks running down from her eyes that looked as if she had been crying. "What?" Linder asked. "The lady and her little boys left." The girl replied. "When?" Linder asked. "Right after the bad men started the fires. I saw her ran out of the house with her boys and run away. They went that way." The girl stated pointing down the street. "Thank you. Can you tell me what the bad men looked like?" Jess asked. "Yes. They had red cloaks and had dragons on their faces. They were scary. They burned my house too and my family is deaded now." The little girl replied. "How do you know they are dead? Didn't they escape? How did you get out?" Jess asked. "I was going home when the bad men went to my house. I saw them but they were scary so I didn't want them to see me so I hideded by the house next to mine. Some of them went to the back of my house while some were at the front. Two bad men threw fire on sticks into my house and wouldn't let my family get out. They blocked the back and front door. My family screamed for a long time. The fire got bigger and then my house fell down and the screaming stopped.

The bad men left and went to another house. I ran to my house to get my family but the fire was too big and hot so I couldn't get close. When the fire went away everything was still too hot to touch. I called for my mom and dad and little brother for a long time but no one answered. They were deaded. The fire made them deaded. After that I cried for a long time until I saw the bad men coming back so I ran away. I ran and ran and ran until I was too tired then laid down in the snow and went to sleep. I woke up when someone screamed.

The bad men were across the street, they were throwing fire on sticks into someone's house. A lady ran out of the house with two little boys and ran that way. The bad men didn't see her because it was getting dark but I saw her. I hideded back there until the bad men went away and then went back to sleep until I heard you yelling." The girl answered. "What is your name?" Linder asked her, kneeling down to face her. "Sharlottie Agnes Smith, my dad calls me Sass because of my initials, whatever those are, but my mom calls me Lottie. I like Lottie better." "Well Lottie, would you like to come with us? We have to go and find my sister, the lady you saw run away. She is a nice lady, do you want to come with us and help us find her? You will be safe with us." Linder asked her kneeling down to be at her level, taking her hands into his. "Really, I can come with you? I would love that." Lottie replied excitedly. "We would love it if you would come with us." Jess replied. "Yes I want to." Lottie said and wrapped her arms around Linder's neck. Linder picked her up off the ground with her arms gripped around his neck.

"Let's go check at Loni's old house and then we will check at the shop." Linder told Jess. Jess nodded and then followed Linder's lead. It took fifteen minutes of walking fast through the rubble of the city to get to the street where Loni's house should have been. They past many burnt buildings, there were men, women and children calling and crying for their loved ones. Linder stopped walking at the beginning of the road when he saw that Loni's house no longer stood. An instant passed and then he turned around and headed a different direction. He was heading towards Loni's husbands shop. He still carried Lottie in his arms as they made their way through the city. Linder released a long breath when they rounded a corner and saw that the shop was still standing.

"If Loni isn't in there, then I don't know where else to look for her. If she isn't in there then I fear we will just have to leave and go to Morganstin without her." Linder told Jess. Linder set Lottie down then tried to open the door but it was locked from the inside. He tried again but wasn't able to open the door. Lottie took Jess's outstretched hand. He tried to peer in the windows but there was too much soot built up on them to see inside well. He knocked on the windows, but no one answered. "I have an idea." He said then began spelling Loni's name with a question mark at the end in the soot on the windows. He wrote it backwards so that if anyone was inside they would be able to read it. He finished and waited. He didn't have to wait long until he saw a finger spelling something in return. Three letters was all it took to lift his spirit. Y.E.S.

He took his hand and smeared all the writing and went to the door. Turning the handle the door opened. He opened it wide enough for Lottie, Jess and himself to go inside then he closed and locked it once more. It was dark inside the shop but light enough to see the shadowy outline of a woman nearby. "Linder is that you?" she whispered. "Yes sis, it's me." "Who is that behind you?" "Its Jess and a new friend named Lottie. Loni, where are the boys?" Linder asked noticing that Loni was alone. "They are both asleep back there in the corner. We have had quiet an ordeal these past few days so I am going to let them sleep as long as they can." Loni replied. "What has been going on with the Black Dragons?" Jess interjected. "Sit down and I will tell you what I know." Loni replied. They all went to the back of the shop and sat down on the floor close to Loni's sons, Laken and Nolin, who were still sleeping. "It started a few weeks after you left. An army of Black Dragons showed up one night and that's when the devastation started. They said it was their duty from the king to prepare the city for the new order that was starting and only those who supported the Black Dragons were allowed to live.

The first few days there were only a few executions, most of the people were hung for treason against the king. The Black Dragons said that they were uncooperative and were plotting against the king. Days following more people were hung, different excuses were given but the people knew that none of them were true and began to fear the Black Dragons more than they did before. More and more people were being executed and there were also a lot of disappearances happening during the nights, mostly woman. They were even killing children.

The merchants at the markets were dwindling quickly, everyone was either too scared to go out and sell the merchandise or they were dead. Food became scarce except for the Black Dragons who took all the food that they wanted from wherever they could find it. They posted and enforced many new rules for the city to follow, most of which gave them rights to do whatever they want to anyone they want, including rape and murder. This continuously went on until a few days ago then that is when they started burning down the buildings. My boys and I stayed hidden as much as possible, I only went out when we needed food and I tried not to draw attention to myself. I knew it was only a matter of time until they spotted me. No one was safe; some people tried to leave the city but were killed on the spot. One day at the market, one of them stopped me and asked where I was headed. I told him I lived in the house next to the Inn. He followed me around the market telling me all the things he was going to do to me and that there was nothing I could do about it because it was the law. When I was done shopping I waited until his back was turned then snuck behind one of the carts and joined a crowd of people walking away from the market. Luckily he didn't see me and I was able to get back to my boys safely. When they started burning down everything they were picking certain house and buildings to burn down first but then they went around the city burning down whatever buildings they wanted. They trapped the people in the buildings and listened to them scream as the flames grew.

Then when they started burning down houses on my street I knew we couldn't stay there any longer, I was packing a bag full of clothes and food and was planning on leaving when they weren't around and go to my old house but they came before I was ready. Luckily it was a dark night when they came because as soon as they threw the torch in the house I grabbed both boys and ran out of the house and kept running in the dark. I never looked back. I ran to my old house but it had already been burned down so we can here, I don't know where I would have gone if this was gone. We can't stay here though. It's only a matter of time until they have the entire city destroyed." "We will find a way to get all of you out of the city." Jess replied. "Really?" Lottie asked. "Yes. With everything we have been through, getting out of the city shouldn't be too difficult." "You promise we will be safe?" Lottie asked. "Yes. I promise." Jess answered. "As do I. All of you will be safe." Linder acknowledged.

"Is that Lottie Smith?" Loni asked hopefully. "Yes" Lottie replied meekly. "I thought you had died with your family. You are one brave girl to still be alive." Loni said to Lottie. "Linder how did you find her?" Loni asked. "Actually she found us and told us that see saw you run away with the boys. We couldn't just leave her alone. She is coming with us; you and your boys are coming with us also. We are on our way to Morganstin. There is someone there that can help us stay safe." Linder replied. "Who?" Loni asked as glanced at her sleeping boys and then back to Linder. "We have an address on a piece of parchment where we are supposed to meet the others where the lady lives that can help keep us safe." "Also I live in Morganstin so you can stay at my house if you want to." Jess noted. "Good, but how are we going to get out of the city safely? There are Black Dragons all over the city." Loni stated. "I didn't see any Black Dragons as we made our way here. Maybe they are still sleeping so now would be the best time to leave or we will have to wait until tonight. I think now would be best though." Linder informed everyone.

"Let's go now. We will have to carry both boys, neither one of them have shoes." Loni acknowledged. "That's fine. Lottie, can you run?" Linder inquired. "Yes, I am a good runner." She remarked proudly. "Good because we are going to have to run for a long time. Even if one of us gets hurt you have to keep running with the others okay. Can you do that?" Linder asked Lottie while kneeling in front of her. "Yes I think so." Lottie replied then wiped her face with the back of her hand. "Good girl." "Linder, what about our weapons and gear, there on the other side of the city, we are going to need to get them. It's not safe for all of us to go back but one person can't carry all the stuff. What are we going to do?" Jess asked. "You will lead Loni and the children towards Morganstin while I go back and get what I can carry. I will have to leave some of it behind but we are going to need the food that is in our packs and some of our weapons."

"No, you can't leave me. I don't want to be away from you. I'm afraid of losing you." Jess inclined. "I'll be safe and will meet up with you as soon as I can. I promise. You know the way to Morganstin and I need you to keep them safe and they won't be safe if we all go back for the supplies, so it has to just be me." Linder replied then pulled Jess close to him. "Trust me, this is the only way. I won't be gone long. I finally have you in my life so I won't take any chance of losing you. I know you can do this and I will be with you as soon as I can. It will be alright. I love you Jess." Then he placed his lips on hers and kissed her. She returned the kiss then softly said "I love you Linder." He kissed her once more then released the embrace. Jess had a terrible feeling about Linder leaving but she knew he had to go. "Loni and Lottie, I need both of you to follow Jess and do what she tells you. I am leaving now. I will see you soon. Be safe." He stated and then he went to the door, opened it slowly and slipped out onto the street. "Good bye brother." Loni said but was too late for Linder to hear.

"Well…I guess we leave now." Jess stated. "I will carry Laken because he is bigger and you can carry Nolin." Loni suggested. "That sounds good." Jess replied. "Boys, it's time to wake up. We need to go for a run before we can have breakfast though okay." Loni told her boys as she slightly nudged them to wake them up. "Mo meal" Laken said as he sat up and yawned. "No oatmeal today. We will have something different. But right now we have to go run and when we are done running then we can have breakfast. I will carry you and my friend Jess will carry Nolin alright." Loni said softly to the sleepy boys. "Mommy" Nolin said and reached his arms up to Loni. She picked him up and gave him a hug. "Jess is going to carry you. Mommy will be right next to you." She said then handed Nolin to Jess and then picked up Laken. "Alright, Lottie are you ready?" Jess inquired. "Yeah I think so." "Okay, let's go." Jess stated then headed for the door. Lottie and Loni followed.

Quickly and as quietly as they could they made their way through the rubble filled streets, passing burnt house after burnt house. Corpses lay strew on what use to be yards, people curled into balls trying to stay warm and sleep near the rubble, while others dug through the ashes of what remained of their homes. Still others in soot covered clothes sobbed for their lost loved ones. There was no sign of any Black Dragons around as they ran towards the surrounding forest. No one seemed to notice them as they passed. Jess and Loni who were slowed by carrying the little boys were still able to run at the same pace as Lottie. To Jess's surprise Lottie was really a good runner. A short time later they heard a loud bell ring. The sound rang through the air, followed by men shouting. Jess's heart pounded so hard in her chest with worry for Linder. "We have to go faster." Jess stated. With that Lottie and Loni started running as fast as they could alongside Jess.

Minutes later they were out of the city and into the forest. They didn't slow at first because Jess wanted to get them farther away before they stopped. Jess found a spot hidden well in the trees and bushes where she told Loni and Lottie that they could stop and rest for a time. Breathing hard, heart pounding and sweat pouring off her face even with the cold winter air Jess set Nolin down on the ground, took off her cloak, moved Nolin on it and sat down on the ground to rest. Placing her elbows on her knees and her head in her hands, she tried to catch her breath but she was too worried about Linder to calm her breathing down. Lottie sat down beside her. Loni set Laken down next to Nolin then looked back towards the city for a long moment then turned to Jess.

"Linder will be alright. He is very resourceful and he is a smart man. There isn't anything to worry about, he will be fine." Loni said to Jess trying to not only comfort Jess but herself as well. She believed everything she said but she too was worried. She then sat down next to Nolin and Laken. "Mo meal now?" Nolin asked. Jess raised her head to look at the little boy. "No sweetie, we have to wait until uncle Linder comes back and then we can eat." Loni replied. Jess looked at everyone in turn and realized that now was not a time to break down and that she couldn't worry about something she couldn't control. Linder would be fine. He would be back with her soon. He promised. She told herself. "We can't stay here for very long. We can rest for a few minutes and then we need to keep moving." Jess stated in a determined tone and then looked back towards the city.

Chapter Seven- The Black Order Attacks

Linder kissed Jess good bye and headed out for the supplies. He hated leaving Loni, Lottie, Laken and Nolin, but he especially hated leaving Jess. He knew that Jess could lead them to Morganstin without him, but desperately wished he could be with her now, but he knew that they needed the supplies that they had left in the forest on the other side of the city. The quickest way to get to their supplies would be going right through the main part of the city. It wouldn't be the safest way but definitely the quickest. He hadn't seen any Black Dragons yet and was hoping that he wouldn't. Knowing his way around the city he ran past street after street. As he drew near the center of the city he could see a mass of people gathered together, he wanted to avoid any chance of running into Black Dragons so he quickly turned onto a street away and kept running past the group of people.

There were many people and he ended up running past some that were at the edge of the group. As he passed he thought he heard someone yelling at him but he kept running. Seconds later a loud bell rang and people were shouting "He went that way." A fearful stomach clenching feeling came over him as he realized that the people were yelling about him. After that came the sound of people running after him and men yelling orders at him, all of which consisted of words such as "The Black Dragons order you stop!" "Cease in the name of the Black Order" "Halt for the Black Dragons and accept your consequences."

Linder ignored the shouting and continued to run. The smoke was thicker in the air in this part of the city which made it hard to run. He began coughing as he ran, knowing he couldn't stop running he tried to hold his breath as much as he could to minimize the intake of the bad air. He was able to get many streets away before they caught him. Large men with Black Dragons tattooed on the faces, and blood red cloaks waving behind them seized his shoulders and threw him to the ground. "You shouldn't have run, now you're going to suffer the consequences." One of the Black Dragons implied with a big grin on his face, whom was one of the men that were holding him to the ground.

There were two Black Dragons holding him down while the last stood over him looking down at him. Linder tried to escape their grip but was unsuccessful. "We have ourselves one from the rebellion here men. We love rebels." The Black Dragon that stood over him leered. Then without any warning the Black Dragon kicked Linder in the ribs. Recoiling back in pain as much as his captives would allow Linder tried not to show how much it hurt and tried not to make any sound. He knew that is what they wanted. They wanted to see him in pain. The Black Dragon kicked him again. This time a moan escaped his throat. He was sure he had a broken rib or two now. He would not let them see how much pain he was in. "Stand him up." The Black Dragon ordered. The other two Black Dragon hoisted Linder to his feet. As soon as he was standing, with the support of the two Black Dragons that had him pinned to the ground the Black Dragon that had kicked him, punched him right in the stomach. Linder doubled over in searing pain and lack of breath. "Welcome to the new order." One of the Black Dragons said then they pushed him out of their grip and he stumbled to catch his balance.

He fell onto the ground on his back. At that point all three Black Dragons started punching, kicking and beating him all over his body. He tried to defend himself, and was able to punch one of the Black Dragons in the face breaking his nose but the pain of the continuous beating was almost too much to handle. The Black Dragons were much bigger and stronger than he was. His ribs hurt, his stomach hurt, he couldn't intake enough air to refill his lungs, and one of his eyes was beaten so bad he couldn't open it anymore. His head spun as blood trickled down his face. He couldn't think right. Everything was going black. All he wanted was to make it stop. Make the pain go away. Please just make the pain go away. He thought to himself as the three Black Dragons continued to beat him. I can't stop them, I am going to die now, he thought to himself. I want to die. He closed his good eye and embraced the darkness that was overpowering him.

Just then a vision appeared in his mind. The most perfect vision he could ever imagine. It was Jess. He saw the first time he met Jess and the realization it was the woman from his dreams, he saw the first time he saw her hair unbraided after she bathed in the waterfall, also the awful moment when Jess was struck with an arrow in her back and thinking she was going to die, the moment when Kedar saved her with magic, the moment he proposed to her at Kedars castle in the flower garden when she was recovering then a flash from his earlier visions of Jess standing at an alter dressed in a white wedding gown with flowers in her hair holding his hand as they become man and wife, and then a new vision of Jess flashed in his mind, she was standing in a forest with bright green pines trees surrounding her, it was summertime and the sun shone brightly through the pines. She looked so happy. She was holding a small child in her arms while he stood behind her with his arms around her. She turned her head towards him and whispered, "I love you Linder." Then the words he told her earlier that day rang in his head over and over. "Trust me, this is the only way. I won't be gone long. I finally have you in my life so I won't take any chance of losing you. I will be with you as soon as I can. I love you Jess." And the words "I promise" echoed in his head.

No! I can't die! I promised Jess I would return to her. I can't die, she needs me. She loves me and if I die then she won't have the strength to defeat the Black Dragons and free everyone that was taken captive by the Black Dragons and rid the world of the black magic that plagued that world. He wanted her to live her life freely, and be happy. She loves him and if he died she wouldn't be happy. I have to live for Jess. He told himself. With those thoughts running through his head he realized that his head was no longer spinning, his ribs ached but no longer felt broken; he tried to take a full breath and realized that it was no longer hard to breathe. He slowly opened both eyes, which felt itchy and he was surprised to be able to open them but what shocked him the most was what he saw. Or what he didn't see. He saw that he was alone. All the Black Dragons were gone, they must have thought that they had killed him and left his corpse to rot.

He wasn't sure how long he had been lying on the ground unconscious. His body was bruised, sore and ached. He also had blood covering many parts of his skin. He took a deep breath, stood up, spit out blood from his mouth then with absolute resolve he began running again. With Jess on his mind, and knowing that he would have been dead now if it wasn't for her, he continued to run. He couldn't run as fast as he had before because of his sore body but he pushed himself as fast as he could. He changed course several times trying to avoid as many people as possible. He made it out of the city without being noticed and into the forest to where he and Jess had hidden their gear and weapons. He sunk to his knees next to the fallen log where their gear was hidden, in relief and exhaustion. He was thankful that he had made it this far alive.

He dug out the packs, swords, bows and quivers full of arrows from inside the fallen snow covered log. Knowing he couldn't carry everything he replaced the bows and quivers back into the fallen log then moved the swords off to the side so he could hook them onto his weapons belt after he would go through the packs. He opened his pack and checked the contents, removing all his extra clothes and his bedroll, and then he went through Jess's pack. He moved all the food and an extra blanket from her pack into his. He looked through everything in Jess's pack to make sure he wasn't forgetting anything important. Then he put Jess's pack back into the fallen log along with their bows and covered it with dirt and snow so that it was unseen.

He stood up, his legs not wanting to work anymore. They were stiff, bruised, blood covered, and stinging from the pain and cold; they did work though and held him up. He flung the pack onto his back and situated it on his shoulders comfortably. Then he unbuckled his weapons belt and placed one sword in its sheath on one side of his belt and the other in its sheath on the other side of his belt. After buckling his belt back up, he headed southwards towards Morganstin. He wanted to get as far away from Jensen City as he could and return to Jess.

He tried to run but with his legs hurting, his stomach clenching and his ribs starting to ache again he could only manage a fast paced walk. Many miles later and hours past with the light in the sky fading fast, he decided that he was going to have stop for the night and camp where he was. He thought about how worried Jess and Loni were going to be because he wasn't back with them yet. Then he thought about how hungry the children must be. They didn't have any food with them; he had all the food in his pack. Hopefully Jess found them some nuts to eat or met up with Marcus and the others, who had food in their packs. Linder thought to himself. He knew there were only a couple of hours left to travel until he would be at Morganstin but with his hurting body and failing sun light he didn't want to risk traveling in the dark. Propping himself against a tree, he took off his pack and placed it on the ground next to the tree then he sat on the ground with his back against the tree. Knowing he needed to eat, even though he felt bad about it he reached inside his pack and pulled out an apple, a roll and a piece of dried meat. After eating he put a blanket over his legs, wrapped his cloak around himself, closed his eyes, leaned his head back against the tree and thought about Jess until he went to sleep.

"Alright, let's get going." Jess insisted. Loni nodded in agreement then moved her boys off Jess's cloak. Jess picked up her cloak and retied it around her neck then picked up Nolin. Loni picked up Laken. "Lottie are you ready to run some more?" Jess asked looking down into Lottie's soot covered face. "Yeah" she replied in her soft little girl's voice. "Good girl. Let's go then." Jess lead the way farther away from Jensen City, hoping that Linder would return with her soon and that she could find Judon and the others because they had food that they could share with the children. They traveled a few hours, alternating between walking and running with no sign of Judon and the others or Linder. Jess kept on eye out for anything that they could eat as they traveled but with no prevail. The little boys, Nolin and Laken were starting to cry because they were so hungry and little Lottie's stomach growled numerous times but she never once said anything about her hunger. After another hour of traveling, Jess decided to let them stop and rest. Her legs were tired and her arms were getting sore from carrying Nolin. She stopped them right on the trail and let everyone sit down and rest their legs.

"My tummy hurts" Nolin cried. "I know sweetie, once Linder gets here we can eat something." Loni replied softly then looked towards Jess. Jess looked back towards the way they had just come. She stood up and knowing it wasn't wise, shouted Linder's name as loud as she could, hoping that he was close enough to hear her. No reply came. Please come back to me. She whispered to herself. She sat back down next to Lottie. "He will come back, he promised." Lottie said and put her hand on Jess's. Jess smiled. "Jess!" shouted a male's voice calling her. "Jess!" the voice shouted again. Jess jumped to her feet. "Over here" she shouted back and looked around for the voice that had called her. "Stay there, I'm coming to you." The voice shouted. "Okay" she replied.

She heard someone running towards her. A minute later Marcus appeared out of the trees. "Oh I am sure glad to see you." She said as he emerged from the trees. She was happy it was him but also disappointed that it wasn't Linder. "Is anyone hurt? Where's Linder? Where's your gear? Who are these people?" Marcus asked in a rush. "We're not hurt. These kids are starving though. Linder went to get our gear that we hid before going into the city and he hasn't returned yet. This is Linder's sister and her two boys and this is Lottie, she is coming with us. Her whole family was killed by the Black Dragons. Can you share your food with us please?" Jess asked Marcus in reply to his question.

"Yeah sure, take what you need." He replied and took off his pack and handed it to Jess. She reached inside and took out a bag full of food then handed it to Loni. She took the bag of food, then gave each child a piece of a roll, and broke a carrot and divided amongst them. Jess cut an apple into pieces using her dagger and gave the pieces to the children. Loni gave Nolin and Lottie some nuts and dried meat to eat. Laken was too little to eat nuts but was given some dried meat to eat. "You need to eat also." Jess told Loni. "I know I just don't want to take all his food away from you." She replied. "Don't worry about it. You eat as much as you want; I think you need it more than I do." Marcus remarked. "Thank you." Loni replied than ate some food.

"Where are the others?" Jess asked in between eating bites of dried meat. "They are about thirty minutes ahead now. We were traveling at a fast pace until Randy's leg started bleeding and hurting him really bad to where he could barely walk. We all slowed to his pace. Erika is trying to help him as much as she can but I don't know if he will even be able to make it to Morganstin without the leg giving out. Erika thinks that it got infected and that's why it's hurting him so much now. But there's nothing else we can do until we get to Morganstin to help him. That's when we heard the sound of little children crying. I decided that I would come and see if it was someone who could use help. The rest of them continued on while I came back to see who it was. I was just about to turn around and catch up with them since I didn't hear any more crying when I heard you yell." "Well thank you for coming to help. We appreciate it." Loni said as she sat on the ground holding a roll in her hands. "You're welcome." Marcus replied then turned to Jess.

"We can't stay here, we only have a few more hours left of sunlight, and I think if we go now we might be able to make it there before it gets to dark. Are you ready to go?" he asked as he repacked the remaining food into his pack and then placed the pack back onto his shoulders. "I am, but can you take a turn carrying one of the little boys. They don't have shoes and are getting heavy to carry." "No problem. Which one is the heaviest?" Marcus asked. "Laken is." Loni acknowledged. "I'll carry him." Marcus stated then Loni stood then handed Laken to him. She then picked up Nolin in her arms. Jess reached her hand down to Lottie. The little girl gripped Jess's hand and was pulled to her feet.

Jess bent down to be at Lottie's height then softly said "You have been so good, and are a great runner but now we are going to have to walk farther. I know you're tired, but do you think you can keep going?" Jess asked while looking into Lottie's brown eyes. "Yeah I can but when is Linder coming back?" "I don't know Lottie. I hope he returns soon, but I don't know. He promised he would be with us soon and I believe he will keep his promises. He will be fine." Jess replied strongly. "I hope the bad men don't get him." Lottie said. "Me too." Was all that Jess could say, and then patted Lottie's hand. She didn't want to show Lottie how scared and worried about Linder she really was. "Alright let's get going." Marcus instructed.

Everyone cooperated and soon they were traveling once more. The sunlight faded into night as they traveled. They continued on in the dark until they made it to Morganstin with Jess leading the way. As soon as they reached the cities borders Jess breathed a sigh of relief when the city looked the same as it did when she left. There were a few Black Dragons patrolling around the streets but hardly any compared Hyrum City. Jess led the way through the city to her house. When she arrived she turned the door knob and pushed open the door. She knew that no one would be there but the absence of her grandma and brother was still a surprise. Then she remembered where her grandma was. Linder had told her about a vision that he had shortly after they met. He saw her grandma being taken away and her little brother hiding underneath his bed with a note that Jess had written to him to tell him to hide then go to the neighbor's house. His vision hadn't happened at the time, which gave Jess the chance to write a warning note to her grandma and brother before the Black Dragons came. The Black Dragons had taken her grandma away and her little brother was hopefully at a neighbor's house right now.

After her, Marcus, Loni, Lottie and the two boys were all inside the small house Jess closed and locked the door. She wished she couldn't see the inside of her house but the light of the moon shinning in through the curtains she could see that the furniture wasn't where it should have been. Not wanting to draw attention to her house she chose not to light a candle. "This is my house; we should be safe here for tonight. The Black Dragons have been here. They took my grandma away and tipped over the furniture. She felt around the living room and picked up furniture while Marcus shared what food he had left from his pack with everyone as they sat down on the up turned chairs.

Jess walked through her entire house, which only took a few minutes but saw that every piece of furniture had been tipped over except Zander's bed. Every drawer emptied, and every content of the cabinets were now of the floor. The Black Dragons must have been looking for something. But what? What would we have that the Black Dragons would want? She thought to herself but couldn't think of any answer. She stood looking into her bedroom. "It looks like they were after something." Marcus said from behind her. Jess didn't hear him come up behind her so when he spoke she jumped from being startled. He apologized then went on. "What do you think they were looking for?" "I don't know. What is strange to me is that the only furniture that isn't tipped over is my brother's bed. The one he hid under. I don't understand that. I just hope that he is alright." Jess said. Marcus placed his dark hand onto her shoulder. "There's nothing we can do right now. Come on; let's help Loni with those kids. They will need to rest." "You're right." Jess answered then turned around and went back into the living room with Marcus.

There she saw Loni sitting in her grandma's rocking chair holding both boys on her lap. She was rocking them to sleep while singing sweet lullabies. She had them both covered up with a blanket that Marcus had given her from his pack. "Lottie, you can wear some of my brother's clean clothes if you would like. I can help you change, and then you can sleep on my bed for tonight." Jess suggested. "Okay." Lottie answered then walked to Jess's outstretched hand. Jess took Lottie to her bedroom, helped her change out of her dirty dress and into some boy trousers, a long button up shirt and then a brown jacket on top. She gave Lottie a clean pair of Zander's knitted socks to wear. The clothes were a bit too big for Lottie, even though her brother and Lottie seemed to be around the same age. While Lottie put on the socks Jess turned her bed upright and then tucked Lottie into her bed with blankets that were tossed onto the ground. "I will be in the living room if you need me okay. Good night little Lottie. Sleep well." Jess said softly. Lottie reached up and wrapped her arms around Jess's neck. "Good night. I love you." She said then released Jess's neck, lay down and closed her eyes. "I love you too." Jess whispered then left the room.

"Loni, you can sleep on Zander's bed with your boys, and Marcus you can sleep on my grandma's bed." Jess informed them. "Thank you. Can someone help me carry the boys in there?" Loni asked. "Sure." Jess replied then took the sleeping Nolin from Loni's arms and carried him into her bedroom. Loni followed carrying Laken who wasn't quite asleep yet. Jess laid Nolin down on the bed. "Jess, I wanted to thank you for everything you have done for us. I really appreciate it and I know that your journey with Linder has just begun and that there is much more to come but for everything so far, thank you. You saved us." Loni whispered in a gentle tone. Jess's throat was chocked up and all she could say was "Your welcome." Then she turned and left the room. Marcus was still in the living room waiting. He turned to look at her as she entered.

"I can't sleep yet." He stated. "Me either. I keep having this feeling that something is wrong. I can't stop thinking about everything. Like where is Linder? Is he alright? Did something terrible happen to him? When will he be here? Where are Judon and the others? Is Randy okay? Where are we supposed to meet at? Judon and Linder have the address that we are supposed to meet at so how we are going to find them. How is Erika handling all this and what is going to happen to Loni and her boys and little Lottie?" Jess explained in a troubled tone. "Here eat this." Marcus said and tossed her an apple. "Everything will work out. We will just see what tomorrow brings and take it in stride. But for now you need to eat and then rest. I will be up for a while and keep a watch for anything unusual. When I get tired I'll sleep out here." He told her. "Okay." She said then brought the apple closer to her mouth.

Suddenly the apple disappeared. Marcus held up his hand with the apple still in his hand. He acted like he was going to toss it to her again but instead of an apple coming her way it was an orange that flew towards her. She tried to catch it but it disappeared before it reached her. "That's a great illusion. I really thought the fruit was real." She replied smiling. "It made you smile now didn't it?" Marcus stated. "Yes" Jess replied. "Good, now here is the real apple." He said then tossed the real apple to her. "Thanks." She responded after she caught it. "You're welcome." Marcus replied. Jess took the apple with her into her grandma's room and not bothering to take her boots off she laid on her back on the bed, starring at the darkness above her.

Chapter Eight-Morganstin

Jess awoke with a start to the sound of someone knocking on her front door. She hadn't realized that she had gone to sleep. It was early dawn; there was a soft morning glow that seeped in through the curtains. Jess jumped to her feet and ran to the door, with fear and hope in her heart. Marcus was standing next to the door and turned to look at her as she came up behind him. Someone on the other side of the door knocked again. Marcus had his hand on the hilt of his dagger. Jess motioned for him to back up. He backed up a few step with his hand ready to draw the dagger if needed. Jess unlocked the door and opened it a small sliver. To her surprise Judon and Lillian were outside her door. "Jess?" Judon asked in curious tone. "Judon? Come on in. Where are Erika and Randy?" she asked as Judon and Lillian entered her house. "Erika took Randy to her house since it was closer. She said that her mother could help heal Randy's leg. I gave Erika the piece of parchment with the address we are going to meet at. Then we came straight here. How did you get here before us?" Judon asked as he looked around the room and noticed Marcus as he closed the door. "This is my house. We traveled into the night and I led them here, to stay the night." Jess replied.

"This is 1498 Nesry Road right?" Judon asked with his brow furrowing. "Yes, but that is my address." Jess answered. "That is the address we are supposed to meet at. Do you know Ellen Whitaker?" "Yeah that's my grandma." "Really? Is she here?" Judon asked hopefully. "No. She was taken by the Black Dragons" Jess answered dolefully. "Oh I'm sorry. She was the one who was going to help us. She was your grandma….That means you are…." Judon began to say then his eyes grew wide. "I am what?" Jess asked confused. "You really don't know do you?" Judon asked. "What?" Jess asked unsure at what he was trying to say. "Have you ever heard the lullaby Come Little Leaves?" he asked. "Yes, my grandma would sing that song to me when I was younger and then taught me the words when I got older. What about it?" Jess replied. "Wow, I can't believe this. All this time, you've been right here and alive and safe and now…oh man." Judon said stroking his beard while looking at Jess in admiration. "What are you talking about?" Jess asked exasperated.

"Where's Linder?" Lillian asked from behind her dad. "I don't know. He had to go back through Jensen City to get our gear and weapons that we hid before entering the city and he hasn't returned yet." Jess replied to Lillian's question. "Linder… Jess…Linder….Jess…" Judon whispered to himself as he began pacing the small area. "What about us?" Jess asked, raising her tone. "Answer this question. Can you make people believe whatever you want them to believe?" Judon asked. Jess was taken off guard by his question and unsure whether or not to answer the question but decided to tell him the truth. "Yes." She replied. "Yes, Northstin, Come Little Leaves, the Black Dragons, that's it!" he replied with each word emphasized. "Jess you are royalty." He stopped pacing and excitedly answered. "Yeah right, I'm not royalty. I was born here and lived here my whole life. There's no way I'm royalty." "It seems to me that you are. With what I know from reading old books about myths, prophecies and foreign cities and what Randy has told me. It sounds like you are part of the royal family of Northstin's that created Morganstin a long time ago. You are the Northstin Wind from the prophecy from Tasintall which just happens to also be the lullaby Come Little Leaves, and Linder is the prophet isn't he?" Judon inquired with excitement. Jess just stood there dumbfounded looking at Judon, trying to wrap her head around everything he just said.

She knew that she was the Northstin Wind and Linder the prophet from the prophecy that Randy had told her about, but being royalty that was too much. She wasn't royalty but everything that Judon had said sounded right. She would have to figure everything out with Linder, once he returned. "Yes, he is." She answered after a moment of pause. "That's wonderful then. That means you have the capability to defeat the Black Dragons." Judon explained. "Well actually…" Jess started to reply when Marcus interjected.

"Jess, Linder, Erika and I are all on a mission right now to destroy the Black Dragons and rid the world of the black magic. This stop in Morganstin is just temporary. We have to stick to our mission or we will fail." "Yeah that's right." Jess responded. Just then Loni showed up in the living room. "Who's this?" Judon asked. "I am Loni. I'm Linder's sister. Jess helped me and my little boys escape from Jensen City. Who are you?" "This is Judon, and his daughter Lillian." Jess replied as she introduced everyone. Just then someone knocked on Jess's front door. "Jess, it's me. Let me in."

Jess recognized the voice immediately and opened the door for Erika to come in. "Why does this parchment have your address on it? I took Randy to my mother, man was she glad to see me but I told her that I had to make sure you made it back safely but really I was going to go to whatever address was on this parchment to see if you and the others made if there but when I read what address it said I was surprised that it was your address, then I came right here. What is going on?" Erika asked in a rush.

"A simple hi, how you doing, I'm glad you made it here alive, would be nice." Jess replied with a smile. "Hi. How are you doing? I'm glad you made it here alive. Now what is going on?" Erika insisted. "Well I'm royalty. My family owns a kingdom somewhere far away, my grandma was taken by the Black Dragons, and I have no idea if my brother is safe at a neighbor's house or taken away by the Black Dragons. Linder hasn't returned yet and I have a terrible feeling that he is hurt. We also rescued Loni, Laken and Nolin plus met and saved a little girl named Lottie whose entire family was burned to death in their home, and to top it all off we still have to go into the forbidden forest, find the Circle of Power Platform, get our magic powers bestowed into us and become wizards, then we have to find where the Black Dragons are keeping all the people that they have stolen and free them plus destroy the black magic and not to mention restore the forest, and Linder and I are going to get married sometime.

Also Linder and I are part of some prophecy involving Randy's army that will help rid the world of the black magic, and I have no idea how to do any of that so to sum it up…. I've been better." Jess explained. Erika gave Jess a hug then quoted something that Jess had told her at the very beginning of their journey. "Desire the difficult times because with them you will learn, grow and become a better you." Jess smiled. "That's what my grandma always said. You remembered. Thank you." "What are best friends for? So now what?" Erika asked. Jess looked around the room at all the faces looking at her. Erika, Marcus, Judon, Lillian, Loni, and Lottie, who had quietly entered the living room and was standing in the shadows near the hallway, all awaited for her answer. Jess closed her eyes, took a deep breath then opened her eyes and replied in a determined tone.

"This is the plan. Judon, Lillian, Loni, her boys and Lottie will stay here. You can take care of each other while I am gone. This will be your home for now. Stay inside unless you absolutely have to go out. You should have everything you will need here. Erika will tell her mother about all of you and she can help get you food and anything else you might need. Stay here until I return. Erika go tell your mother about them and also once Randy is healed enough he will stay here too. Marcus I want you to go with her to make sure she stays safe. Both of you meet me at the path we took into the forbidden forest, where we found the talismans. Erika, you know the spot right? I am going to look for Linder. Once I find him we will meet you there, then we will all go together to find the Circle of Power Platform." "But…" Judon started to say. "No. That is the plan. That is what we are going to do. If you don't like it too bad, that's final." Jess dictated.

Erika told Marcus to follow her and then they left without any questions. Erika knew that once Jess got determined like this there was no way of changing her mind. She was going to do and expected everyone else to do exactly what she said to do or they were going to get hurt if they didn't. Once she punched a boy in the face who kept poking her with a stick when they were little girls. She told him to stop and he didn't so she punched him in the face so hard it broke his nose. Also when they were in Hyrum and were looking for Jusdan or Judon at the City Jobs Office when after finding out that Jess didn't have the money it took for the worker to tell her where Judon worked the worker eyed her entire body and then suggested that she could pay him in other ways with her body. Jess did not like to be treated like that and instantly pulled out a dagger and held it against the man's throat, until he obliged to her needs.

The set in stone determined look that was on Jess's face made it clear she wasn't going to budge on her decision. "That will be fine. We can stay here and help take care of each other until you return." Lillian replied. "Your right, we will be safer here than in Hyrum." Judon answered. "Or Jensen City. Thank you Jess, we will do as you say." Loni interjected. "Can I come with you?" Lottie asked coming closer to Jess. "Not this time. You are going to stay here; I will be back soon okay. You will be safe here." Jess kindly answered then gave Lottie a hug. "Good bye." She said then went to the front door, looking one last time at the people that remained in her house she said goodbye then left.

Linder awoke with his eyes hurting, ribs, stomach, legs, arms, and back aching and sore. Along with a pounding in his head that felt he was being hit in the head with a hammer. When he stood up he realized that he was having a hard time breathing as well. Like his lungs weren't getting enough oxygen. It was early dawn, he wasn't sure what had awoken him but he knew that he needed to get to Jess as soon as he could. He put his pack onto his shoulders, tightened his weapons belt then set off towards Morganstin. He tried to run but the pain was almost unbearable and brought him to his knees.

He stood back up, and determined to continue he walked as fast as he could. Each step he took shot more pain through his body which worsened the more he went. He rubbed his hands across his eyes many times as if trying to wipe away the pain but the pain continued. His vision slowly went blurry and darkened the farther he traveled. He felt like he was getting beat again. He took off his pack and leaned against a tree to catch his breath and tried to control the excruciating pain. He was unsure if he could go any farther and with his head spinning he thought he heard someone calling his name. Not sure if the sound was real he didn't reply. The sound came again, someone was calling his name. He recognized the voice. "Jess?" he asked meekly.

"Linder" Jess called again as she ran through the forest toward him. She had been running for the past thirty minutes looking for him. That's when she saw someone who looked kind of like Linder ahead of her leaning against a tree. He seemed to be hurt. She stopped running and called his name. He didn't answer. Maybe he didn't hear me. She thought to herself then called his name again louder this time. He replied with her name very meekly. Jess ran to him. As soon as she got close she gasped. "Oh Linder, what happened?" she quickly asked as she approached him as she saw how bad his body looked. "Jess is that really you?" he asked as he started to slump to the ground. Jess helped him to the ground. She couldn't believe that he was still alive. It looked like he had been beaten to death but somehow he was still alive. "Yes Linder it's me."

"I promised I would return, I tried, I really tried. I love you Jess." He quietly said. "I love you too." Jess replied, holding his hand as he lay on the ground struggling to breathe. "I'm sorry." He whispered. "For what?" Jess asked. "Dying." He slowly said then took the hand that Jess was holding and using the intertwined hands he wiped his eyes. "Linder, you're not going to die." Jess replied tears forming in her eyes as she looked into his eyes. She noticed that they were no longer blue but didn't say anything. "The Black Dragons got to me, I'm sorry. I… promised." Linder quietly replied then closed his eyes. His breathing slowed more. "No, you can't die! I need you. I love you! Stay with me, please don't go." Jess cried as desperation filled her body.

Just then a loud cawing sound caught her attention. She looked up. There sat an oversized crow on a branch that flew down and landed on the ground next to Jess. She didn't move. The crow started drawing something in the dirt with its beak. Once done, Jess saw a picture of what looked exactly like the magical talisman that she wore all the time. It was the heart shaped necklace that gave her the power to make anyone believe what she wanted them to believe. She used her free hand to grab the necklace around her neck. She looked between the picture in the dirt and the crow. "I can't. I can't use my power on him." She said to the crow. It cawed over and over and over again. Jess looked at Linder, who was slowly dying and then at the cawing crow.

Jess had promised herself to never use her power on Linder but she couldn't think of anything else she could do for him. She leaned in close to his ear, "Linder" she whispered. He moved his head slightly. The crow stopped cawing. "Linder, you need to believe that you will live. You have to live. I love you." She whispered to him then kissed him on the lips while sending a flow of her magic into him. She moved back and sat on the ground next to him, holding his hand once more praying that her magic would work and save him.

Suddenly his body convulsed, his eyes opened wide and the brown sunburst in the center of his eyes grew wider as if taking over his entire eyes. Jess never let go of his hand. He didn't look at her, he seemed to not actually be looking at anything, his eyes were glazed over as the brown sunburst took over his eyes. That hand that Jess was holding became very cold. She felt his trembling head with her free hand, which felt ice cold as well. "Linder come back to me." she pleaded.

Instantly his body stopped convulsing, he lay motionless; his temperature started getting warmer, his skin was warm to touch, his wide glazed eyes stared at nothing. Jess watched as the brown sunburst withdrew from his blue eyes. It looked as if the brown sunbursts were being sucked into his black pupils. When the brown sunbursts were all but gone, only a small brown ring around his pupils with small brown streaks coming off it remained. Linder blinked and gasped. He turned his head towards Jess. His eyes were focused on her. They were his original light blue except for the small brown sunbursts that remained in the center. "You saved me." He stated with the special smile that Jess loved seeing on him.

She released a long sigh in relief. Then smiled and replied. "Now we're even." "That's right, now we are even. Can you help me get up now?" Linder remarked as he let go of her hand and tried to sit up. "Are you sure that's a good idea?" Jess asked, concerned about him. "Jess look at me. I am all healed. I feel great and it's all because of you. I no longer have any broken ribs, my bruises are gone, my head no longer hurts, I can breathe regularly so my lungs must be healed, my eyes….well actually my eyes still itch a little but at least I can see and with that I can see the most wonderful person in the world. You. Jess I am really alright. I haven't felt this good in a long time. Can you just help me get up now so I can give you a hug and kiss?" he asked as he reached his hand out to her. Jess stood up and grabbed his outstretched hand. She pulled him to his feet. He tipped a little and then got his balance.

Jess was prepared to catch him if he fell. "I'm good." He told her then pulled her close to him and wrapped one arm around her waist and put his other hand on the back of her head then pulled her in to kiss her. His lips touched hers and she felt the warmth of his body against her own. She kissed him in return. The kiss was soft and gentle and had a sensual feeling about it but then at the same time it brought on more feelings of desire. Linder tightened his grip around her and then kissed her harder. She embraced the kiss, enjoying the feel of his lips to hers. The way he held her made her feel safe and also desirable. She then thought about the magic she had used on him and pulled away from him.

"What's wrong?" he asked. She looked up and down his body and noticed that he was right. Every red, blue, black and purple bruise's that covered his body were gone. She was glad she had healed him but hated having to use her magic power on him. "I used my magic on you. I promised myself I would never do that, but I had to, to save your life. I'm sorry but I need to stop the flow of the magic on you. I don't know how this will affect you. I hope this doesn't hurt you. I'm really sorry." She explained then ended the magic flow. Jess saw the faint flicker of the magic power as it left Linder's body. She watched Linder for any change and thought she was prepared for anything. Nothing happened. Linder just stood there and smiled. Jess didn't know what to expect but was confused when nothing changed.

Linder shrugged and then replied. "I already believed that you could save me, even before you used your power. The magic just healed me faster, but your love is what kept me alive. Come here." Jess went to him. He put his arms around her and pulled her in close to his body once more. "I love you Jess and I…" Linder began to say but Jess cut off his words by kissing him. She wrapped her arms around his neck and they enjoyed each other's embrace while kissing for many minutes. Jess once again pulled away but this time it was slowly and untroubled while keeping a hold of his hand. "I am so glad that you're alright. You really had me worried. I don't want to live without you. I love you." There was a short pause then she continued. "But I think we should go now. Erika and Marcus are waiting for us by the forbidden forest. We still have a lot of responsibilities we need to take care of and little time to do it." Jess stated. "That's one reason why I love you. You have such a strong determination. You know what needs to be done and will do it. Thank you Jess, I am here to stay and will never leave you again. I don't want to live without you either. Well let's go and become wizards." Linder responded while holding on to Jess's hand and giving her that special smile that she loved.

Jess picked up the pack from the ground, Linder took it and put it on his shoulders, then gave Jess her sword. After Jess situated the sword onto her belt Linder took her hand back in his. "Lead the way" he insisted. They walked together quickly through the forest. When they reached the spot where Marcus and Erika should have been, no one was insight. Jess looked around, the snow was almost completely melted, not like before when the snow had been knee deep when they first found the talisman's in the forest. There was no sign of anyone around. The sun had risen and the town's people would be awake now. Jess didn't want to risk being seen so after a quick evaluation of her surroundings she led Linder into the forest.

She followed what she thought was the same route that she had taken previously and came to the spot where the trail bent and lead deeper into the forest out of sight from the street. Jess stopped and looked toward the big pine tree a short distance away where Jess and Erika had found the red and silver drawstring bag which contained Linder's prophecy book and Erika's magical fur cloak. There sitting on the ground waiting patiently were Erika and Marcus. They were both looking at Jess and Linder. "It's about time." Marcus said cooly as Jess and Linder joined them. "We had some business to take care of first." Jess stated promptly. "What happened to your eyes?" Erika asked Linder. "They just itch. I don't know it must be something in the air." Linder remarked. "Linder, I didn't tell you earlier but your eyes have changed." Jess admitted. "Changed? What do you mean changed?" "I mean, they are no longer all blue. You have a brown sunburst shape around your pupils and then your original blue on the outside. When I found you it was worse and when you were dying the brown took over your entire eyes. But when I was healing you the brown sunbursts seemed to get sucked into your pupils but then stopped where it is now and you seemed fine other than saying that it itched so I didn't tell you. I didn't want you to worry about it. I was just glad that you were alive." Jess admitted.

"You were dying!" Erika stated in astonishment. "You don't look like you were dying." Marcus observed. "Jess used her magic on me to make me believe that I had to live. The magic healed my body but her love kept me alive. That was actually the second time I almost died. The first time was when the Black Dragons attacked me. The beat me so bad and left me for dead. I am surprised that I'm not dead already. It was thoughts of Jess that kept me alive and gave me the strength to go on. The pain was dramatically lessened when I thought of her but the farther I traveled and the more I used my muscles the worse I got. If Jess hadn't found me at the time she did I would have died. If my eyes are stuck like this forever, then so be it. I would rather be alive and have itchy changed eyes and be with Jess than to be dead and Jess be alone." "Wow, that's incredible that you're still alive. Sorry for giving you a hard time." Marcus apologized. "It's alright. I know it sounds hard to believe. But it's the truth." Linder answered back.

"Everyone's alright so let's get going. The sooner we find the Circle of Power Platform the sooner we can start on the harder parts of our mission." Jess stated. "Jess is right, we need to get moving." Erika agreed. "Okay. Which way do you think we should go?" Jess asked to no one in particular, looking around at her surroundings. Erika burst out laughing and shook her head at Jess. Jess laughed as well. "What's so funny?" Marcus asked confused by the sudden change in mood. "It's Jess. She is always ready to go and do but doesn't think about the hows of it. She just charges in without thinking things through sometimes." Erika replied smiling. "Hey I keep things interesting." Jess replied lightheartedly. "That's true." Erika remarked smiling.

"I think we should head that way. We need to go deeper into the forest so why not start there." Linder interjected. "Okay." Jess replied. The others agreed. Linder held Jess's hand and led the way with Erika and Marcus following close by. They went deeper into the forest. "Why is this forest forbidden?" Marcus asked as he stepped over a large tree branch that had fallen on the ground. "The forest is said to be a dangerous place where there are beasts and unspeakable creatures that live there. It's said that no one has ever entered the forest, or if they have they have never returned.

Everyone that I know always avoided the forest. They were too scared to go in or near it. Except for one person…Jess." Erika answered pausing to emphasize the name. Jess just shrugged. "Well we have encountered many terrible creatures already so if this forest is anything like the Kahidon Mountains then we should be prepared for what comes our way." Marcus replied then scratched his small black beard that was growing on his dark face. "I think your right but we need to stay alert and prepared for any attacks." Linder stated as they headed in the direction he suggested. They traveled for almost an hour without any sign on life. There were no birds chirping, no critters rustling through the brush, there was no wind blowing through the trees, there was no sound in the forest besides the sound of their breathing and the snapping of twigs with every step they took.

"There is something wrong here." Jess stated as she looked around the forest nervously. Her attitude had completely changed from the light hearted joking to very weary of her surroundings the farther they went into the mysterious forest. Erika jumped in surprise from her voice. No one had said anything for some time and the sound of Jess voice broke the silence. "Your right, this forest isn't natural. It feels like we are the only things alive here and I have the feeling that we are being watched." Marcus replied as his eyes darted all around his surroundings. No one replied. Tall dark pine trees loomed over them with a light dusting of snow. Spindly dark shadows clustered near trees and seemed to be alive and watching their every movement. The ominous silence crept around them once more. They traveled farther and farther into the forest with the silence encasing them. All of a sudden a large black shadow was cast over them, blocking out the sunlight momentarily and then was gone. "What was that?" Erika asked apprehensively as they all stopped and peered around. There was nothing to be seen. "It must have been a bird." Marcus replied, gazing at the trees. Erika didn't believe it was a bird but nodded in agreement anyways. They started walking again.

The black shadow flew by once more, followed by a high pitched bone chilling screech. Every stopped and looked around for the source. Linder and Marcus drew their swords and stood closer to Jess and Erika to protect them. Once more they didn't see anything out of the ordinary at first and then they saw it. The dark shadow flew by again. "There!" Jess pointed to the sky as the dark shadow fly past them. Erika gasped; Jess tried to take a step back to distance herself but stumbled into Linder. He caught her and helped her back up. "What is that?" Marcus asked in fright as his grip tightened on the hilt of his sword. "I don't know but run!" Linder replied as he watched the nightmarish creature turn in the air and start to heading towards them. The creature was something worse than anything Jess had ever imagined. Its furry body was pitch black and longer than a grown man was tall, its dark brown wings were almost double wide the length of its body, stretching at least eleven feet wide. It looked like it could have been a gigantic bat except one thing. Its face almost looked human. It had a round fleshy face with pitch black eyes with no pupils, its lower jaw held equally spaced serrated fangs and it had large pointed bat ears.

They all ran away from on the oncoming creature. It was hard to run fast because of the dense forest around them. They jumped over brush, fallen trees, and boulders as they weaved their way through the forest as they tried to get away from the creature. The creature dipped, ducked, turned, weaved and zipped its way through the forest with ease. Linder saw that there was not going to be any way of out running the creature so he decided to do the next best thing. "Everyone get down!" he shouted. Jess looked behind her and saw the creature closing the distance and realized what Linder had planned.

She stopped running and dropped to the ground along with Erika. Linder stood his ground. Marcus did the same as Linder. Swords drawn the two men waited the last few seconds until the creature was upon them. It dove through the trees to attack the men. Linder swung his sword high as the creature dove at them with its fangs bared. His blade sliced at the creature, slashing one of its huge wings. It screeched and flew higher into the sky as blood dripped from its injured wing. It circled above the tree tops as it screeched over and over and over again. "Let's get out of here!" Marcus shouted while keeping an eye on the circling creature. Jess and Erika got up from the ground and they all ran away.

They hadn't run very far until they all tumbled into a large pit that had been dug into the ground. It had been covered with brush, branches, small trees and even a layer of snow. No one had noticed it until they were falling into it. Everyone tumbled onto each other as they hit the bottom of the pit. After they untangled themselves from each other they stood and looked around. Luckily no one was hurt from the weapons that they carried. The pit was at least ten feet deep and had a few small rotting animals inside of it along with all the brush they had fallen through. The pit was clearly man made. "How do we get out here?" Erika asked. Marcus looked around and then replied. "Linder and I will hoist out you and Jess and then I will hoist Linder out then you all can pull mc out. I am the heaviest so I will go last." Marcus said. Linder intertwined his fingers together leaving a spot for Erika foot to be placed and Marcus did the same. Erika placed one of her feet on Linder's hands and the other on Marcus's. The men hoisted her upwards. She gripped the edge of the pit and pulled herself out of the pit. Next it was Jess's turn. Soon she was standing outside of the pit alongside Erika. Moments later Linder pulled himself out, leaving Marcus alone in the pit. Linder reached his arm down into the pit, Jess did the same. Marcus grabbed their outstretched arms and together they pulled him out of the pit with some strain.

Once everyone was out they looked around to see if there was any immediate danger. The cost was clear so they continued traveling farther into the forest. Their feeling of safety was short lived as moments later another high pitched screeched was heard from above them. Frantically they all searched the trees with their eyes, searching for the monstrous creature that the sound originated from. Suddenly the creature appeared out of nowhere and came diving towards them with its serrated fangs bared. Marcus drew his sword and slashed at the creature. The creature was to quick and avoided Marcus's slashes. Marcus slashed at the creature again as it attacked them again. His blade was true, and slashed right down the middle of the gigantic creature. It toppled to the ground splattering blood as it fell. Marcus examined the fallen creature with his sword tightly in his hand and prepared to stab it if it was still alive. No movement came from it.

Blood poured out of his stomach and soaked the ground. The creature was truly something straight from the depths of darkness. "What is that?" Jess asked in revulsion. There came a gut wrenching stench that exuded from the corpse. "I have no idea. I have never seen anything like that beside the one we saw earlier. Hopefully that's the only one around here. Let's get out of here, just in case there are more though." Linder responded, then took Jess's hand and led her away from the creature. Marcus and Erika followed. "I was hungry but not anymore. I think I might lose what I do have in my stomach." Erika said as they walked away from the gruesome creature. She covered her mouth and nose with her hand, trying to block the awful smell from reaching her. She looked as if she would hurl at any moment.

For several minutes they could still smell the horrific smell that came from the dead creature. Then something even worse happened. They heard the sound of numerous high pitch screeching animals near them. They looked back to where they had just come from and saw at least a couple dozen of those terrible creatures flying in circles above where the dead one lay and some were diving down through the trees toward where it lay with their fangs bared.

"Run." Linder stated loud enough for everyone to hear but also trying to be quiet so that they wouldn't draw the attention of the terrible creatures toward them. Marcus led the way as they ran. What seemed to be many miles later and no creatures in sight they stopped to take a rest. "I am so hungry. I need to eat something." Jess said as she tried to slow her pounding heart. "As I am. Let's eat something really quick and then we need to keep moving. I am hoping that we can find the Circle of Power Platform before nightfall." Linder replied, catching his breath. "How are we going to know if we're going the right way? We don't have any idea of where the Circle of Power Platform is. What if it's in the opposite direction from what we're traveling? And what if we don't find it by nightfall? I don't want to stay here for the night. That would be suicide." Erika stated anxiously.

Marcus touched Erika's arm to calm her down and then replied. "I think that we are going the right way. Why else would there be so many creatures. I think they are guarding it. Also if we don't find it within the next few hours we will just have to turn back and get out of the forest before nightfall and try again tomorrow." Erika seemed to relax slightly. "Okay." She replied and nodded. Everyone sat on the damp ground and ate dried meats, some fruit, and small section of cheese and shared a hard loaf of bread together. They each drank water from the water skins they carried. After a short time they continued traveling with the sun shining through the trees against their backs they made their way deeper and deeper into the forbidden forest. Erika was getting concerned with the late hour approaching when they finally saw something besides trees in the distance ahead. It looked to be a several giant stones in a circle together with an opening in the middle.

Once they drew nearer they saw that inside the circle of stones was a stone altar held up by six stone pillars. The stone altar stood three feet off the ground and had symbols carved into it on the top along with many symbols on the stone pillars that held it up. Neither Marcus nor Erika recognized any of the symbols. Linder recognized one symbol that he had seen in his prophecy book the first read through it. "This symbol represents magic or power. One of the old prophets mentioned it in a prophecy he wrote about. I guess that prophecy hasn't come true yet because it's still in the prophecy book." He said as he pointed out which symbol was familiar to him. The symbol was a straight line which then turned into a small spiral ending back onto the straight line.

"This must be the Circle of Power Platform." Erika stated as she admired her surroundings. "Wow, we made it." Jess said looking up at the huge stones that encircled them. "Kedar said that we place our talismans on the stone then we will become wizards." Marcus explained. "Is that all?" Jess asked. "That's all I remember him telling us about it." Erika conferred. "Very well, everyone place your talisman on the stone and we will see what happens." Linder instructed. Jess took of the gold chain necklace with a small gold hollow heart hanging from the end of it, which was her talisman. It gave her the ability to recognize feelings that are being experienced by another but along with recognizing someone's true feelings it gave her the ability to change their feelings and make them believe and feel whatever she wanted them to believe. She placed it onto the stone altar, and instantly it began to change color. It went from gold to a pulsing white light that felt alive.

Marcus untied his arm band that was made of a brown leather lining with hemp tightly woven through the center. It gave him the power of illusion. He could make almost anything out of thin air and it would appear and look and feel real. The illusion could only sustain itself while Marcus concentrated on it. If he stopped concentrating the illusion it would disappear. He had been able to make some illusions look and feel real and last for several minutes without his full concentration. Even in the shape of people. He placed his arm band onto the stone then the white light that pulsed around Jess's necklace grew to encompass Marcus's arm band.

Erika took off her golden brown wolf fur cloak with silver trimmings with a big fur hood attached to it and placed it onto the stone altar alongside the others. It too was engulfed in the white light. Erika's cloak gave her the ability to control the elements, wind, earth, water, fire. She could make trees grow bigger, make leaves fall, change the weather from hot to cold, make wind, make it rain, move clouds around in the sky. She had also conjured a beautiful fruit tree and flower garden at Kedar's castle. Linder was the last to place his talisman on the stone. He placed the book of prophecy on the stone and it was instantly covered by the white light. Suddenly the white light grew bigger and brighter, everyone had to shield their eyes from the bright light. It poured off the alter and completely filled the space in-between the giant stones that formed a circle around them, trapping them inside then shot upwards. The light went through the sky until it touched the clouds and then very quickly shot back down into the talismans. With their eyes shielded from the intense light they didn't see what happened next until it was too late. The white light shot out from each the talismans and hit them all right in the chest, knocking them all to the ground. The light vanished and everyone stood up.

Chapter Nine-Mahonri Dumas

Jess looked around; everything seemed to be the way it was before the light appeared. She look at herself, she didn't feel any different besides a sore back from the fall. Their talismans were still sitting on the stone right where they had placed them. "What just happened?" Erika asked. Before anyone could answer they heard a crow cawing, they all looked around and saw an oversized black crow slowly drifting downwards towards them. Marcus drew his sword. Jess studied the bird for a long moment. "That won't be necessary." She told Marcus and pointed to his sword. "I think this is the crow that helped us earlier." "Jess are you sure?" Linder asked, keeping a vigilant eye on the lowering bird while his right hand tightly gripped the handle of his dagger. Jess watched the crow land on the middle of the stone in between all of their talismans. "Yeah I…" But before Jess could finish answering something started to happen to the crow.

The bright white light covered it and it began to grow. It grew bigger and began to change its shape. It went from looking like an oversized crow to a crouched man wearing a black furry cloak. The white light dissipated and the man stretched his body upwards and stood to his full height. Linder pulled Jess back away from the platform. Marcus held his sword erect and ready.

The man looked at everyone in front of him in turn then did something no one expected. He hopped off the altar and went to his knees and bowed his head. "Thank you great wizards for freeing me, I have waited many centuries for all of you and now you have finally come. My name is Mahonri Dumas. You can call me Dumas. I am here to help you in defeating the Black Plague." The man said then lifted his head. The man looked to be in his late thirties with long shoulder length straight black hair and dark brown eyes. He was very fit, and wore a long black furry cloak with a black hood attached to it. He wore old torn black trousers and a holy tan shirt underneath it. He had no shoes on and his entire body had dirt smears on it, as if he had just rolled in the dirt.

"Did you just say your name is Mahonri Dumas?" Erika asked with confusion in her voice. "Yes." The man replied smoothly then stood. "Wait a second. Your saying that you are Mahonri Dumas, the prophet from centuries ago that wrote the prophecy about us? The prophecy that is still written in that book that says…" Linder began to say but was cut off by Dumas quoting the prophecy that was about all of them.

"When north and south meet the prophet, the spark will be lit. The guardian will show them the way. The illusionist will show himself in his truest form. With talismans in hand their journey shall begin, once bestowed with power the platform awaits. Place the talismans on the stone and with this comes their fate. Wizards shall they become, a marriage shall await, free the stolen and misjudged ones, destroy the blackness too, restore the forest to its real form then life will be anew. But beware if all doesn't precede then destruction and darkness will feed. The darkness waits and will attack if all the wizards fail to act."

"So who is who? I am so excited that my prophecy is finally taking place. It's about time. I was starting to think that I would remain a crow forever." Dumas replied much like a child would when waiting for a birthday to come and it seemed like it was taking forever. "Who figured out what the part means about when north and south meet? Also who is the prophet, oh and the illusionist? I am so eager get to know all of you." Dumas asked with a giddy smile on his face.

"Oh, I just remembered that when Kedar was telling us about Dumas he said that after he wrote down his last vision he used a powerful shape shifting spell and turned himself into a crow and flew away so that the black wizards couldn't kill him. Why didn't I remember that earlier?" Jess stated shaking her head.

"You. You were the crow that helped us earlier wasn't it?" Jess asked. "Yes, of course and to me it seems like you could use all the help you can get. Weren't you taught about the black magic creatures when you all were younger? You all acted like it was your first time dealing with black magic. I had to help you or you all would have been dead by now. Well maybe not Jess. But the rest of you would be. I had a feeling to follow you at first and then I realized that you might be the wizards from the prophecy. So I did what I could to help, knowing that if you were then I would be freed and the prophecy would be taking place and that means that soon the Black Plague would finally be defeated." Dumas replied nonchalantly. He rubbed his hands together. "So am I going to get any answers to my questions or I am just going to have to guess, who is who?" he continued without giving anyone else a chance to speak.

Jess thought that Dumas acted more like an energetic child than a grown man. Marcus spoke up first. He still held his sword in his hand but had it pointed downward to the ground. "I am Marcus. I am the illusionist." "Perfect, show me something." Dumas instructed. Marcus reached for his arm band but stopped when Dumas said that he wouldn't need it anymore. Marcus raised his hand and instantly there was an arm band around his wrist that looked identical to the one that sat on the stone altar. Marcus was surprised that he didn't need the real talisman to do magic. Dumas drew closer and looked at Marcus's arm and shouted in excitement. "Brilliant! Can you make people?" Marcus slowly waved his hand across the air. His arm band disappeared and there in front of him stood... himself. The copy of himself had his right hand raised the same as Marcus's. "Fantastic!" Dumas stated while waving his hand through the copy of Marcus. Which wavered slightly as he did so, then the copy of Marcus shortly vanished.

"Keep working on that one and you will have it mastered soon. Then you can make it move and feel solid and then the real fun will begin." Dumas encouraged with a big smile on his face. "I can create solid small items, like this." Marcus said and acted like he was throwing something at Dumas but had nothing in his hand. Dumas put his hand out and caught a shiny red apple. He turned it in hands studying it closely. Suddenly it changed into an orange. Dumas's eyes grew wide. "That is remarkable. I have never met anyone with quiet the ability that you have. When I was younger I met an illusionist but he never created anything quiet so life like to the touch, like this is. And to be able to change it while someone is holding it. That is just remarkable." Dumas exclaimed. "Thank you." Marcus replied. "You are going to create much mayhem when the time is right." Marcus was unsure what Dumas meant by his last statement but didn't have a chance to say anything before Dumas turned his attention to the others.

"So, let me see. I am guessing that you are the prophet. Am I right?" he asked Linder. "Yes" Linder answered. "Now tell me, did you have any visions or prophecy's before you became a prophet or just after?" "I have had visions my whole life." Linder replied as he watched the man. "Have any of your visions come to life? Oh they have. I see." Dumas said, answering his own question and glancing at Jess, who was holding onto Linder's arm. "The marriage from the prophecy is about you two isn't it? I hope I didn't miss it. Have you two already had the wedding? Wait, no you haven't. You had to become wizards first and you have to…..oh never mind that's not important. So what's your name young prophet?" "Linder" "Any last name?" "None to mention." "Very well, Linder my young prophet friend I would love to hear about some of your visions at a different time. We haven't much time left before….Ahh….Oh lovely lady, what is your name? Dumas said changing his attention towards Jess. "I'm Jess."

"Jess? What a peculiar name." "My name is actually Jessalyn Northstin." "What? Did you say Northstin, as in the Northstin army from Tasintall? Wow wee…why didn't you tell me sooner. Where is your army now? How many forces do you have? Have they found the book yet? Does the Northstin Wind have control over the armies and lands yet and who is it? I have read many prophecies about the Northstin Wind and the prophet defeating the black plague along with the four wizards which are all of you. This day just keeps getting better and better." Dumas stated excitedly. "Listen, I don't have any armies, I just recently found out about Tasintall and the Northstin Wind. I don't know who the Northstin Wind or the prophet is sorry." Jess told him but in fact she did know who the Northstin Wind and the prophet were, it was her and Linder but she didn't feel like explaining that to Dumas.

"Oh I see but there still is a city named Tasintall that is ruled by the Northstin family right?" he asked hopefully. "Yeah of course." She lied. "Oh good, because that plays a big part in defeating the Black Plague that riddles the world and for defeating those who use black magic for the black plagues purposes. So what powers do you have?" Dumas continued on. "I have the power of empathy including making others believe what I want them to believe." "That is wonderful can you show me." Jess nodded then raised her hand towards him pushing her power towards him. "I want you to believe that you have forgotten everything you have heard in the past few minutes." Dumas blinked and had a strange expression on his face as if he didn't know where he was.

He looked down at himself and then looked at everyone who was watching him. "Who are you? How did you break the spell on me? Where am I?" Dumas asked in confusion. Jess stopped her power and the magic left Dumas. He blinked once more then looked at Jess. "That was amazing. What did you do? I really couldn't remember anything from the past few minutes. I was so confused. I thought I knew what had happened but then had no recollection of it. You will be very useful against the black wizards." He insisted. "I hope so." Jess imparted. "Now last but definitely not least." Dumas said as he turned to face Erika.

"My name is Erika South. I have the elemental powers."
"North and South, that's you two. It's your last names. Meet the prophet, and the illusionist, Linder and Marcus. Wow this is so exciting. Wait who is the guardian? No, that's not important right now. Defeating the black plague is priority number one." Dumas rambled on seemingly to himself. He looked at Erika then turned his attention back to her.

"Sorry, I would be grateful if you would be willing to show me something with your powers?" he asked her. Erika looked around at her surroundings then raised her hand up straight palm up above her head. The normal tingly feeling that she got when she used her power ran through her fingers and shot upwards. Instantly it began raining. "Really? Rain? Couldn't you have made it hot and sunny instead of cold rain?" Jess asked as the rain seeped into her clothes. Erika smiled then closed her raised hand into a fist and the rain stopped. She lowered her hand then waved it in the air as if shooing a bug away. A gust of warm wind blew past them then faded away. "Excellent." Dumas shouted in excitement. Everyone was still damp from the rain but not cold anymore.

"This is so great. Now we can go to Tasintall and get the army then we can defeat the Black Plague and its instigators. So which way is it to Tasintall? Things look so different from when I was a crow. I'm unsure of directions now." Dumas stated, looking around at the forest. "We have to go to Morganstin first. I have to check on my brother and we have some friends that need taken care of before we can go to Tasintall. And besides one of our friends is a Sergeant in the Northstin Army. He is healing from an injury in Morganstin. When he is healed he can show us the way to Tasintall. We can stay at my house until we are ready to go." Jess noted.

"If your friend isn't healed soon we will have to leave him because there is no time to waste. If Karlsen Soldum is still in charge of the Black Plague then he or his minions will have noticed the magical rays that shot through this forest and will be coming for us. You say you have a place for us to stay? Is it safe?" Dumas asked, now aware of his surroundings. "I think so." Jess replied. "Good, which way?" Dumas asked, his curiosity gone from his voice now replaced with caution. "We have many hours of traveling that direction before we will be out of the forest." Marcus answered and pointed to the way they had come. "What about our talismans?" Erika asked. "Take them if you want to keep them but they're not necessary anymore, except for the Prophecy book. We will need that." Dumas replied without looking at them. His eyes scanned the forest as if he was searching for something.

Jess watched the peculiar man, who was so much different from what she had imagined him being from what Kedar told her about him. "I have an idea for getting out of here faster and it's a much safer way to travel. By the way, how did you get past all the creatures and spells that guard this place? And where are they now?" Dumas asked. "We injured one creature and killed another. The one we killed served as a distraction to keep the others busy while we ran away. For spells we haven't noticed any." Linder replied as he packed the book of Prophecy back into his pack. "That's odd. There should have been spells to keep anyone away." Dumas commented. "Kedar couldn't find it when he searched and told us that we might be able to find it easier because we had the talismans. I think he was right. It was like we were drawn to it." Erika remarked.

"Either way, we made it; we are now wizards and now have to find a way out. It's going to be dark soon. We only have an hour, maybe two before it will be too dark to see." Marcus stated. "Together you all have the answer." Dumas stated. "What? How?" Erika inquired as she re-tied her golden brown wolf fur cloak around her neck. Linder placed Jess's necklace over her neck while Marcus tied his arm band securely to his arm. "Use your powers of course." Dumas concluded as if it was obvious. Erika, Jess, Linder and Marcus all looked at each other confused. "Oh I have so much to teach all of you. Okay, everyone grab hands in a circle and think about the griffins that helped you earlier and send some of your powers outwards. That's about it. The magic will transcend distances and because griffins are magical creatures they will feel the need for their help through the magic and since you are familiar with them and have earned each other's respect they will come and help. Then they can fly us out of here. It's easy." Dumas explained as if explaining the simplest things to a child.

Jess shrugged then took Linder's hand then outstretched her other hand. Marcus placed his hand in hers then took Erika's hand while she linked her other hand with Dumas who then grabbed Linder's other hand. "Alright, everyone think of the griffins and send some of your power outwards." Dumas instructed. They all did what they were told and suddenly a white spark that resembled a lightning strike, struck out from the middle of their circle and shot into the sky, above the treetops and zoomed out of sight. Dumas let go of the other's hands. "That's it. Now we just wait." He said then sat down on the ground next to the stone platform and closed his eyes.

Moments later they all heard several sounds emitting from the forest. It sounded like different creatures fighting. A high shrill twitter and a bone chilling screech along with the sound of wings beating hard in the air are the sounds that Jess couldn't distinctively pinpoint. The sounds made everyone nervous, except for Dumas who sat calmly on the ground with his eyes closed. "What was that?" Erika asked as she gripped the hilt of her sword that was placed on her belt and pulled the sword free. Jess, Marcus and Linder all had swords in their hands also. The noises drew closer and everyone kept their eyes to the sky preparing themselves to fight, except Dumas.

Just then they saw something through the tree tops that surprised them. There were the three griffins that they had met earlier. They were fighting the giant bat like creatures in mid air. Many black bat creatures bared their fangs and dived at the griffins. The griffins were much bigger than their opponents and using their sharp beak bit and tore the fleshy heads off the bat like creatures that attacked them.

Once the heads were bit off the griffins dropped it and the body and heads fell to the ground as they tumbled through the tree tops and landed on the ground. Some of the bodies were strew in the tree branches that had gotten stuck when falling. Soon the many terrible bat creatures that attacked the griffins were gone and only one remained. The largest griffin killed it quickly. When the threat was gone all three griffins landed on ground and pushed their way through the trees until they reached the outside of the Circle of Power Platform stone circle. They all bowed their heads and waited for the people to respond. Dumas opened his eyes then stood as if this was normal. He walked through the stone circle and knelt in front of the griffins, bowed his head then rose. The griffins rose to their full height. The largest griffin twittered then shifted its eyes between Dumas and the Circle of Power Platform. "I am sorry. I will do what I can. You have my word. " Dumas said to the griffin and patted its large furry leg. Jess could have swore that she saw the largest griffin glance at her directly but wasn't sure because it turned its gaze away to quickly. "Put away your weapons. We need to show them respect remember. We did ask for their help so we don't need our weapons out." Jess instructed as she put away sword. The others followed her instruction.

Jess stepped out of the Circle of Power Platform and bowed in front of the griffins. She was joined by Linder, Marcus and Erika who all bowed in respect. All the griffins bowed in return then lowered themselves to the ground. The second largest griffin twittered and tilted its head to the side. "They're inviting you to ride them." Dumas stated putting his arm out in invitation. Erika was first to climb on one of the griffins. Marcus climbed onto the same as Erika. Jess and Linder climbed onto another one together then Dumas climbed onto the last one all by himself. "Tell them which direction to go." Dumas said as he tightened his grip on the griffin as it rose to stand its full height. "Can you take us to Morganstin? It is several miles that direction." Jess asked as she pointed to the direction they had traveled from. The griffin she was sitting on had its eagle head turned to watch her. The other griffins twittered and nodded.

Suddenly they all flapped their giant dark brown eagle wings and they rose into the sky. Linder wrapped his arms around Jess's waist as she gripped onto her griffin's soft tan lion's body. Tree limbs whipped past them as they rose above the trees until they were in the open air.

Jess looked down at the forbidden forest and saw that most of the forest was black because of the thick trees and from that height she could see creatures that looked like Therion's prowling around in the forest, as well as many large bat like creatures hanging upside down from tree limbs. Amongst the black magic creatures there were also the ordinarily dangerous forest animals such as bears, coyotes, wolfs, and mountain lions. Jess felt Linder poking her shoulder. She turned her head to him. He was pointing down at a spot in the forest. Jess looked at where he was pointing and her stomach clinched. Below them in a group of at least twenty were many figures weaving their way through the trees, all of them were wearing blood red cloaks. None of them seemed to notice the griffins above them. But what disturbed her that most was that the Black Dragons were dragging struggling people behind them. Why would they be taking people into the forbidden forest, especially with all those terrible creatures there? Jess thought to herself. That's easy because they are evil. She answered her own question silently.

The griffins flew past and continued on towards Morganstin. It didn't take long for them to reach the edge of the forest. The griffins landed in the forest near the spot where Jess and Erika had found the talismans at the start. Everyone dismounted and thanked the griffins. The two smaller griffins flapped their wings and rose into the sky. The largest griffin looked at Jess for a long moment then flapped its wings and joined the others. Together all three griffins flew out of sight once more. The sun was in its last few moments of daylight as they made their way down the city streets as they headed to Jess's house.

Chapter Ten-More Surprises

When they walked into Jess's house they were surprised to see Randy sitting on Jess's grandmothers chair with his healing leg propped onto a kitchen chair sitting in the living room. He had a look of relief on his face as they entered. Erika's father was there also. He was a big brawny man. He was bald but had a light brown goatee and brown eyes. It looked as if he had just emptied a bag full of food onto the table where Lottie, Laken and Nolin sat with wide eyes looking at the assortment on the table. He held the empty bag in his hand. Erika saw him then gave him a hug and asked him why he was there. "Your mother sent me here with some food and some supplies along with something or should I say someone that might be important to you." Erika's father replied and glanced at Randy. Erika didn't miss the look and looked towards Randy. Erika's father cleared his throat. Randy reached his hand out to Erika. She looked back at her father then at the others, which included Loni, Judon, Lillian, Marcus, Dumas, and Linder and Jess who were holding hands. They were all standing near the walls out of the way. The little house was full of people.

Erika turned back to Randy and took his outstretched hand. "Erika, this isn't how I had planned to do this but due to my injured leg it will have to be so. I haven't known you for very long but you have struck my heart and inspired me to be the best I can. I feel a need to protect you and the desire to always be around you. I know that you are a caring, compassionate and loving person who will do all she can save to a person's life. You have saved mine. You have shown me more compassion than I have ever seen. Despite the fact that we don't know each other very well I feel compelled to open my heart to you. I have discussed my feelings about you to your parents and asked them for their permission to marry you. Unfortunately your father told me that he would not allow you to marry me." Randy stated. Erika cut him off. "Dad!" she exclaimed, her face flushed.

"But he said that he would allow me to court you for some time and if I still feel the same after getting to know you better than to ask you instead of him." Randy finished with a big smile. "So will you, Erika South will you join me in a courtship and hopefully in time want to marry me?" Randy asked while looking into her big brown eyes. Without hesitating she replied. "Yes." Randy pulled her towards her and gave her a hug and whispered in her ear. "Will you kiss me? Your father told me he would break my good leg if I kissed you first." Erika smiled then gave him a kiss on the lips. "Oh, don't do that in front of me." Erika's father stated and turned his head away smiling. Jess laughed, "She's not your little girl anymore." She said to Erika's father. "Yeah and I see you've got one of your own now. What is this world coming too?" he replied shaking his head teasingly. "Well enough of this mushy stuff, I need to go before the Curfew Guards or Black Order or whoever they are now get out there. I don't want to leave your mother alone for very long. Come by the house tomorrow and let us know what you have planned. Your mother says that you all are on some kind of mission and we want to stay informed. Well good night and no funny business." He told Erika then said goodnight to everyone else. "Goodnight Mr. South." Jess commented and then he left.

"Well that was exciting, now where is that good smell coming from?" Dumas asked as he walked to the table. "We didn't think you all would be back so soon. Did you do what you needed to do?" Loni asked. "Yes we did one part but there are still many things we must do." Linder replied. "How about right now we eat and then we can discuss the rest of our plans. That does smell delicious." Jess offered. "I agree." Dumas replied as he peered over all the contents on the table. "Who is this?" Judon asked as he eyed the man from bottom to top. "This is Mahonri Dumas; he's a wi....our friend." Jess replied stopping herself from calling him a wizard. "He is going to help us defeat the Black Dragons. He has skills that will be very helpful." She continued. "Good. The sooner the Black Dragons are destroyed the better." Judon answered.

"Okay, let's eat." Jess said. Loni and Linder helped sort through and serve the food. There weren't enough plates in her house for everyone so some people had their food in bowls. Erika's father brought many individual meat pies, which were loaded with meat, potatoes, and vegetables. There were rolls, biscuits, loafs of different types of bread including Jess and Erika's favorite honey raisin bread. There was also salted pork wrapped in cloth that could be cooked later on. Included with the breads were three jars of homemade jam. Raspberry, apple and peach were the flavors of the jam. There were raw apples, carrots and potatoes also a large brick of cheese, a bag of oats and a bag of dried beans. Loni put herself in charge of the food and moved all the extra food off the table and divided out the remaining amongst everyone. Before a single person could eat Loni suggested that they say grace. Some of the people in the house seemed a bit awkward about this suggestion but said nothing and joined the circle around the table. Randy had to stay sitting in the chair in the living room for his leg to heal so Erika said she would hold his hand in prayer. Linder offered to say the prayer.

"We come together this night in prayer to thank thee for this food that has been given to us by the kindness of the South family and for the shelter we have from Jess and also for the companionship that we bring each other whether in love or friendship and we ask thee for protection from the evil that is trying to control the world and the guidance to know what is right from wrong as we go our separate ways and try to do what is right. Amen." After that everyone ate and enjoyed the food until their stomachs could hold no more. Erika retrieved Randy's food for him and brought it to him and she ate right next to him. After everyone was done eating, it was time for the children to go to bed. Jess tucked Lottie into what used to be her own bed and wished her a good night. Loni put her two boys into the other bed in the room, which belonged to Zander, Jess's brother. All the adults congregated in the living room to discuss what had happened during the day and what tomorrow had in store for them. Then everyone found a spot in the house to go to bed.

Jess awoke lying on the kitchen floor wrapped in Linder's arms. She was still tired but knew she couldn't sleep anymore. She opened her eyes and saw Erika cleaning and re-bandaging Randy's wound. The only problem with that was to get to his wound he had to take his pants off. He had a blanket tossed across his lap but his bare legs told Jess he wasn't wearing any long underwear. Jess thought about saying something but she could tell his face was red enough from embarrassment. She closed her eyes and just lay in Linder's arm relaxing. She wasn't sure how long it had been until she opened her eyes once more and saw that Randy had his pants back on and Erika was leaning over to kiss him. His face glowed when she kissed him. He truly had deep feelings for Erika. Jess slowly moved her way out of Linder's arm's and got up. She looked around her little house. There were people everywhere. Erika and Randy were in the living room along with a sleeping and loudly snoring Dumas who slept on the floor. Marcus who looked very uncomfortable asleep on a kitchen chair that had been moved into the living room, Linder was asleep in the kitchen. There was no sign of Judon and Lillian. Jess presumed they were asleep in her grandmother's bedroom and Loni was in her room with her sons and Lottie.

Erika and Randy noticed Jess and quietly said good morning. Jess replied and asked them if they were ready for breakfast. They both said yes and luckily for her Loni and the others had cleaned up and organized her house after being ransacked from the Black Dragons. Jess found the ingredients she wanted and began to make breakfast. After sometime she had a fire going in the little stove and the batter was ready. She made pancakes for everyone as they all awoke and trickled into the kitchen. The one jar of syrup that her family possessed had been broken by the Black Dragons so Jess put the jar of raspberry jam available to top the pancakes with. Just after Jess had finished her third pancake there came a knock on the door. Jess went to answer it, making her way through the others. She opened the door and to her surprise it was her neighbor, Mrs. Morris.

Mrs. Morris was a kind old woman with a slight hunch. Mrs. Morris lived at the end of her street, about five houses away. She had many children of her own but all of them but one were grown into adults now. Her youngest was a few years younger than herself. She was the person Jess had told Zander to go to until she returned. Jess knew that she wouldn't stay in her hometown for very long so she hadn't gone to get her brother from the neighbor woman because she would be leaving shortly and wanted Zander to stay safe. She knew if she even went to visit Zander he would want to come with her or even follow her so she couldn't risk it. Mrs. Morris had tears in her eyes as she began to speak. "Jessalyn, it's about your brother. Two nights ago he told me that there was someone in your house. I told him that no one was here. I didn't see any light coming from the windows and didn't see any sign of anyone here. Well last night he told me again that someone was here and he was determined that it was you and that you had come to bring him home. I told him that we would come and check this morning but he didn't want to wait.

He ran outside after curfew. I called for him but unfortunately the Black Dragons were out and saw him. Jess they took him. I saw it happen from my front porch and I told them that he belonged to me. They told me that he now belonged to the Black Order and that he would become a valuable asset for them. He fought with them until they hit his head and he stopped moving. There was nothing I could do. I was up all night long, as soon as the sun came up and hurried over here to see if you really were here. I am so sorry Jess. I was responsible for him and now he is gone. I'm sorry. " Mrs. Morris said as tears streamed down her face.

Jess's mind went into hyper drive. What? What was she talking about? Zander is safe. Zander is at her house right now playing with her cat. No. Zander couldn't be taken away. The Black Dragons couldn't get him. He got her letter; he went to Mrs. Morris's. He was safe. This can't be true. Zander is fine. She thought to herself. Linder came up behind Jess and asked what was going on. Mrs. Morris explained what had happened. Linder's face went white and pushed his way out of the house. "Which direction is your house?" He frantically asked the old woman. She pointed towards her house. Linder ran down the street past a few houses and then stopped and looked towards Jess's house. His heart sunk. There he saw a familiar window with a single candle sitting in it. In his vision it was dark and the flame from the candle was clearly visible. But the window was very recognizable.

"No!" he shouted in frustration and sadness. He walked back to where Jess and Mrs. Morris waited. "I am sorry." Mrs. Morris said as she touched Jess's arm. Then she left and started to walk back to her house. Jess felt a small tingle where Mrs. Morris had touched her arm but thought little of it. Linder took Jess's arm and led her away from her house, the opposite direction of Mrs. Morris. "Jess, you know how I had a vision while at Kedar's castle and wrote it down in the prophecy book but I told you I didn't know who or what it was about. I fear I know the answer now." "No! Not Zander!" she pleaded. "Yes, I think he is part of the prophecy." "What is the prophecy exactly?" "Well it came in flashes and phrases. The phrases went in this order.

They searched for the light but got caught in the darkness, ages unknown in time, they are willing and they are not, friend or foe nobody knows, if saved it will not succeed if forgotten it will end.

Jess I saw a young boy looking at that window with a candle lit in it. Your neighbor said that Zander saw the candle and went searching for you, then got caught in the darkness by the Black Dragons. I feel that the boy from my vision was Zander. There are others also. I don't know what it all means but Jess I'm sorry." Linder admitted and put his arms around her embracing her.

She tried not to cry but the tears ran down her cheek and onto Linder's shoulder anyway. He held her tight trying to comfort her. A tear ran down his face and landed on her hair. He had brought her so much pain.

After several minutes they walked back to Jess's house. Linder felt guilty that he had given her bad news about her family once more. Well Mrs. Morris had given her the bad news but he had just made it worse. The moment Jess and Linder entered the house all the adults knew something was wrong. "What did Mrs. Morris want?" Erika asked. "Zander has been taken by the Black Dragons." Linder answered gripping Jess's hand. "What? When? I thought he was safe with her. What happened?" Erika asked shocked by the news. "Last night. He saw the candle we had burning and came to see if I was here but the Black Dragons caught him and took him away." Jess replied, as she tried to hold back the tears.

"We will get him back Jess. I know we will." Erika stated and gave her best friend a hug. "Thanks." Jess replied. "This doesn't change our plans though; it just makes them more imperative." Marcus responded. "You're right. Now I have even more reasons defeat the Black Dragons." Jess commented seriously. "Good. The plan is still set for tonight then." He stated matter of fact like. "Yes it is." Linder replied. Then they all started preparing for what they were going to do next. Erika's father had brought extra food but with so many mouths to feed. Jess and Erika decided that all the extra food would stay at the house with Loni, Laken, Nolin, Lottie, Judon, and Lillian while the rest of them traveled to Tasintall.

Erika would have preferred if Randy stayed at Jess's house so that he would have longer time for his leg to heal. The injury on his leg he had received from fighting with a Therion. The Therion slashed his leg with its claws cutting a large gash onto his leg. It had gotten infected and made him almost immobile. With Linder, Jess and Erika's help he was able to make it to Morganstin. There Erika's mother cleaned, disinfected, sewn, medicated and bandaged it. She also gave him herbs to eat that would help speed the healing process and reduce the pain. The best medicine for it would be rest, but unfortunately Randy was the only one who knew the way to Tasintall, his home town, which is where their next destination was.

The plan was simple, they would go to Tasintall, Randy would present Jess and Linder in front of the royal family as the Northstin Wind and the Prophet, Jess would convince the royal family that she had to take control of the Northstin Army, then they would capture, torture and even kill the Black Dragons including the leader of the evil group, a dark wizard named Karlsen Soldum, once they retrieved the information about the people they stole. Then they would find and free everyone who had been stolen from their homes and families, like Jess's brother and grandmother, Linder's brother in law, some of Marcus's family and many more and then return to Morganstin and then they all would use their magic restore the forbidden forest to its true form. After all that is done then Jess and Linder would get married with all their families joined together. Jess realized that it wasn't such a simple plan after all but it's the best one that they could come up with.

"Jess are you ready?" Linder asked placing his hand on her shoulder. "Yeah" She replied. Linder had his traveling pack situated on his shoulders, his weapons belt held his sword and a dagger that had a six inch blade on it which was fastened around his waist and he had his dirty brown boots on that were fastened tight. Jess couldn't help but admire how handsome he was with his brown hair and blue eyes and the look of love she saw in his eyes every time she looked at him. She took his outstretched hand. Judon had given Dumas an outfit of his own to wear, and was now wearing it as he leaned against the wall by the front door. Erika's father had given Dumas a pair of his old boots to wear. Randy stood leaning on his cane that Erika's father had quickly made for him. Erika stood next to him with her travelling pack on her shoulders, that her father had brought her, and her weapons belt strapped to her waist as she held on to Randy's free hand. Jess couldn't help but notice the big grin that was on Erika's face. She had never seen Erika so happy.

Marcus had everything of his stuffed into his pack which he had flung onto one shoulder with his weapons also readily available on his belt. He also had a bow and quiver flung over his shoulder. Jess looked around at the people she was leaving behind at her house Loni, Laken, Nolin, Lottie, Lillian, and Judon, who all sat and stood together in her little home. This was going to be their home for awhile. She took a deep breath and then let Linder lead her outside. Marcus, Dumas, Erika and Randy followed. They all traveled to Erika's house where Erika told her parents what they had planned and took food from her house for everyone. She said goodbye to her parents and then they left Morganstin.

The first few days of traveling went by quickly. They traveled at a brisk walk most of the day and then slept by a low burning fire during the night. Everyone took turns keeping watch during the night, just in case there were any Black Dragons or black creatures looming in the woods. Jess typically felt comfortable in the woods but she had never traveled this direction and these woods were unfamiliar to her, and not knowing what type of creatures could be lurking there it made her nervous. They decided not to travel through any cities unless to resupply, it would be safer that way. Dumas talked almost nonstop for days. He was very helpful though in teaching all of them how to strengthen their powers and improve their abilities. He knew so much about all their powers, even though his power was prophecy he was able to teach them all skills and tricks to use with the powers to make them stronger. He emphasized that their powers were going to have to be perfect if they were to use them against Soldum.

Linder was fascinated by the visions of prophecies that Dumas had seen. The visions that had come true and also the ones that were still written in the prophecy book that hadn't come true yet. Dumas was born with the gift of prophecy just like Linder. They spent many hours discussing all possible ways to interpret the prophecies they had seen and what outcomes they could create from them. Dumas also taught Marcus ways to create illusions that looked, felt and lasted longer than any he had created before.

Marcus was able to create an illusion of any person he had ever seen before that could move a short distance and almost feel real. He was currently working on making his illusion people feel real and move much farther without his full concentration. Dumas taught Erika how to control her powers with ease. She was able to start fires and extinguish them with a snap. She conjured wind storms that were confined to a small section of trees. She made it rain on a whim, made the temperature raise and fall to her liking, and she grew bushes with full grown fruit on them, that they piled into their packs. Dumas tried to teach Jess how to control her power but she just couldn't concentrate well enough and she didn't like making her friends believe and do what she wanted.

Dumas explained that if she couldn't use her powers on her friends than she wouldn't be able to use her powers on the Black Dragons and anyone else who opposed them. Jess tried to control the others emotions and make them believe simple things such as they believed their boots were untied, that the temperature was different, that the food they were eating was either delicious or disgusting but her heart wasn't in each action. Jess was just too worried about her brother, and grandma and the impossible tasks that lay ahead. "It's alright Jess, you can try again later." Linder said as he placed his hand on her shoulder trying to comfort her. "Dumas is right. If I can't use my magic on my friends, then I won't be able to use it on Soldum and the Black Dragons. This should be easy for me. But I just can't do it. I am so worried about Zander and my grandma that it's affecting my ability to use my magic. But I can't stop worrying about them. I don't know what to do. It's going to take us weeks to reach Tasintall, then we don't know if our plan is going to work, and how are we suppose to find and especially rescue all the people that have been taken by the Black Dragons. It sounds like an impossible task. I don't know what to do. I feel so helpless." Jess replied.

Linder took Jess in his arms and hugged her. "You are never helpless. You are the most determined woman I have ever met. I know everything will work out. I am here and I will help you any way I can. I would give my life for you Jess. I love you." Linder softly replied to her. Jess was silent for a long moment. "I love you too." She replied. Linder held her in his arms for a long time before she pulled out of the embrace. There were tear streaks running down her face. Linder took his hand and wiped the tears away. "Why don't we go and eat dinner now and then we can go to bed. I think that some food and rest will do you good." Linder offered. Jess nodded in agreement. Linder started a fire while Jess retrieved food from Linder's pack. Erika and Randy had gone to get water from a stream nearby. Dumas and Marcus were a short distance away practicing creating illusions.

The crackling of the fire drew the attention of Dumas and Marcus who decided to join Linder and Jess. Marcus, Linder, and Erika were the only ones with packs so they each shared with the others. Not long after Randy and Erika joined them and they all enjoyed dinner together. Linder offered Jess his blanket for the night. She accepted and shortly after eating dinner she went to sleep. Sometime later she felt Linder's arms around her and felt comforted. Erika awoke Jess sometime in the night for her turn for the nightly watch. Jess got up and pulled her cloak tight around her body. "It's been a peaceful night." Erika said to Jess. "Jess are you alright?" she asked looking at her friend in the dim fire light. "Yeah, I'm just worried about my family." Jess answered rubbing the sleep from her eyes. "Are you sure? There seems to be something else wrong. You're not acting like yourself." Erika remarked. "Yeah I'm fine, really." Jess answered bluntly. "Alright, I will see you in the morning then. Good night Jess." Erika said then lay down next to Randy. "Yeah good night." Jess replied faintly and starred off into the dark forest.

Jess had the last watch of the night and before she realized the time the sun was rising and the others were waking up. "Good morning Jess. I hope you slept well and had an uneventful watch." Linder said as he put his arms around her from behind her. "Yeah it was fine." Jess remarked as she starred into the fire, barely noticing Linder. He kissed her on the cheek. "What did you say?" she blinked and her eyes focused on Linder. "I just asked how you slept and how your watch went." Linder replied surprised by her reaction. "Oh, sorry I must have been daydreaming. I slept great and my watch was very boring. Nothing happened, I just sat and listened to all of you snore and boy some of you can really snore loud." Jess smiled and then kissed Linder. "Yeah I know you should hear yourself." Linder teased. Jess shrugged and smiled. "Well you all can't be as awesome as I am." She replied teasingly. "You seem in a lot better mood than you were in yesterday." Erika said as she sat by Jess. "I guess so." Jess shrugged then scratched her arm. "So, how much farther until we reach Tasintall?" Jess asked Randy as he sat down next to Erika. "We still have at least three more weeks. We travel a lot faster than my army did but it will still take some time. If we could get horses somehow that would speed things up but I don't know how we could afford that." Randy replied. "We can't and we can't risk going near any town." Marcus remarked. "If only we could use the Time Tricksters." Dumas said then sighed.

"What are Time Tricksters?" Erika asked with curiosity. "Long ago, there used to be a spell that a group of wizards would perform together and it would in a sense stop time for them. They would say the spell before a journey then travel for days and when they got to their destination say the last part of spell and in most cases only a few hours had past, a single day at most. They had stopped time while they kept moving. That's why it's called Time Tricksters because the wizards who used it were tricking time. But unfortunately all those who knew the spell are long dead and the spells that were written down have been missing for hundreds of years. It would have been so nice to use that spell right about now." Dumas explained. Jess scratched her arm again.

The bug bite on her arm that was making her arm itch so much was really starting to annoy her recently. "I used to know the beginning of the spell but I never learned the last. I hardly used the spell and when I did it required at least four wizards so there was always someone else who recited the last part. I do admit I was fascinated by the world in a slow motion state. People seemed to be frozen, tree limbs stiffened to one side as it swayed in the wind. Birds stuck in mid flight in the sky. It did have a very odd sensation though, like it was all a frozen dream with no sound or movement. It was wonderful." Dumas stated as he reminisced the memory then bit into an apple as he sat on a log near the fire. Jess starred into the burning fire as she scratched at her ever present itch on her arm.

"Seconds, minutes, hours and days pass me by. Time creates all, time destroys all, time never ends but with time I change my course and subsequently change time itself." Jess whispered.

"What? That's it! That's the ending of the spell. Jess how do you know that?" Dumas asked excitedly. Jess looked at Dumas and put her hand to her head as if she had a headache. Shaking her head she replied. "What? What spell? What are you talking about?" "The time tricksters spell. You just recited the portion we were missing. With that we can trick time and make it to Tasintall within a few days instead of weeks." Dumas explained. Jess shook her head and scratched her arm. "I don't know what you are talking about." She answered honestly with a confused look on her face. "Jess you were sitting right here when he told us about it." Linder explained while we looked at her. Jess itched her arm again. "No, I had my turn keeping watch and then everyone else woke up. Linder kissed me, Erika teased me about feeling better than yesterday but I felt fine yesterday and today. Why is everyone looking at me like that?" Jess asked as she saw that everyone was looking at her strangely. Jess shook her right arm, trying to shake away the constant itch.

"Jess, what is wrong with your arm?" Dumas asked in a serious tone. "Nothing, just some bug bites on my arm keep itching." Jess replied. "What type of bug bites? Can I see them?" Dumas asked as he stood and reached down for Jess arm. "Why? They are just spider bites. They will go away soon if I can stop itching them." "Please show me." Dumas insisted. Jess rose to her feet. Linder stood up next to her. Jess untied her cloak and handed it to Linder then rolled up her sleeve. Erika gasped at the sight. "That is no bug bite!" Marcus stated as he could clearly see what was on Jess's arm from across the fire. "No! You can't be! Jess, what is going on?" Erika demanded as she stared at Jess's arm. "You betrayed us." Randy said with disgust as he pulled Erika closer to him. The sight was so shocking to everyone around her but it was the most shocking and disturbing thing Jess had ever seen and it was on herself. Jess almost fell over in horror when she saw what it was that had been making her arm itch. Linder caught her and helped her to her feet.

"Jess, why?" Linder whispered. "I didn't! I don't know how that got there! My arm just started itching after we left Morganstin. I looked at my arm at first and there were just a few red swollen bumps on my arm that looked like spider bites. I just tried to ignore the itching and didn't look at it any time after that. How could this have happened? I am not a Black Dragon!" she exclaimed as she looked at the black dragon tattoo that was permeated to her right arm. The black dragon looked as if it were clinging itself to skin. It's sharp front talons looked to be dug into Jess's wrist while its long black jaggedly body weaved its way up to her elbow where its spiked tail wrapped around her elbow and ran up to the middle of her upper arm. The dragon's wings were spread outward wrapping around to the underside of her arm which ended in pointed ends. The dragon's mouth was open with numerous fangs bared and ready to strike. What bothered Jess more than anything were the black soulless eyes on the dragon that seemed to suck her mind into them and the two small red blood stains that were tattooed onto her skin right under the dragon's fangs as if the blood had dropped off the fangs and onto her skin where they sat in a puddle.

Everyone started shouting at once but Jess zoned them out and just starred at the monster that had invaded her arm. Unaware of anything that was going on around her she tried to figure out how it got on her arm. She moved her arm back and forth studying the awful creature on it. I am not a Black Dragon! She thought to herself. How could this happen? She scrambled through all of her memories of everything that had happened since leaving Morganstin. What had happened? Nothing. Nothing had happened that would have caused this. Maybe it happened before we left Morganstin? She thought to herself. But what? What or who could have done this to me?" Who? That's it. Someone had done this to her! But who? It couldn't have been any Erika, or Linder. Neither Marcus nor Randy. Dumas. Dumas could have done it. He has magic and he was a black crow. He could be a black dragon. Jess didn't want to believe it but who else could it be. She hasn't been around anyone else. Jess looked up from the dragon and stared at Dumas who was watching her. She didn't want to believe it. Looking right into his eyes without speaking she searched for something to tell her that he was responsible. He starred right back into her eyes, in the corner of her eyes she could see everyone else yelling and arguing with each other.

"Jess, come back to us." Dumas said. But his lips didn't move. She heard his voice in her head. "Jess, come back! You do not want to go there! You are not a Black Dragon! Fight it Jess! You are not a Black Dragon!" he shouted in her head while she stared at his eyes. Jess scratched at the black dragon on her arm and then put one hand to her head. Her head hurt, her arm itched, her eyes hurt, and she felt extremely nauseas. She blinked and when she opened her eyes she was sitting on the log next to Linder. Dumas stood in front of her grabbing her wrist to pull her to her feet. Everyone else was still in the same spot they had been at before Jess showed them what was on her arm. Dumas looked surprised and looked at Jess with confusion on his face. He pulled her to her feet. Jess looked around at everyone, they were all watching. Dumas moved Jess's cloak over her shoulder, slid her sleeve up only a tiny bit. Jess could see the black tip of the dragons head on the exposed part of her skin. It wasn't a dream it really was there. She thought to herself. Dumas glanced at Jess's eyes and winked then slid the sleeve back over the dragon to cover it before anyone else could see it.

"Well you were right. Spider bites." Dumas lied. "I will help you find leaves you can crush up to put on those bites to reduce the swelling and itching. Let's eat breakfast and then find those quickly before we have to travel on." he suggested. "Okay."Jess agreed. "What about her not remembering the talk about the time tricksters and then quoting the last part of the spell?" Linder asked with worry in his voice. "I don't think she is getting enough sleep and so she wasn't fully awake when we talked about that. She will be fine. She just needs more rest, don't we all though. After we eat, I will help her get rid of those spider bites and then we can be on our way." Dumas clarified. "I just remember hearing someone say that poem about time and I thought it fit well with what we were talking about. Sorry I don't remember all the words, I probably messed it up. I am tired. Dumas is right." Jess stated trying to verify what Dumas said. "Okay." Linder acknowledged.

Everyone ate a breakfast of oatmeal and bread. Afterwards while everyone else packed up the gear, Dumas led Jess away from the makeshift camp. Linder had offered to come along to help but Dumas declined and said that his help wouldn't be needed. Once they were far enough from the others so that no one would be able to hear them Dumas spoke. "I had a vision of you." He said. "I know. I was there." Jess replied. "That must be what Linder has told me about. How he can share visions with you. It is really incredible."

"This is not incredible." Jess remarked as she rolled up her sleeve, exposing the black dragon on her arm. "No it's not. I just meant that sharing visions is incredible. This is a serious problem." He said gesturing towards her arm. "Have you figured out who gave this to you and no it wasn't me." Dumas confirmed. Jess shook her head. "Did anyone touch any of your exposed skin and shortly after you felt a tingle or pain? Dumas asked. "No not that I can remember." She replied as she tried to recall any such incident.

"Wait. Mrs. Morris! Mrs. Morris touched my arm after she told me that my little brother had been taken by the Black Dragons. My arm tingled afterwards and then shortly after that it started itching. I looked and I had few red swollen bumps on my arm. Within a few days the bumps had spread the length of my arm from my wrist to my elbow. After that I tried to ignore it. The itching was driving me crazy though. I didn't dare look at it, I knew it was getting worse but until your vision I didn't know what it looked like and then when you hid it from the others I realized that your vision was true. Dumas how could this happen to me? How could Mrs. Morris put a black dragon on me and why would she do such a thing? I trusted her." Jess ranted. "I don't know why anyone would bestow such a terrible thing on someone unless they were in a desperate state themselves." Dumas stated.

"What do you mean?" Jess asked. "I mean, say this Mrs. Morris didn't really have choice. Let's say the Black Dragons threatened to take her life unless she helped them. In that case she would do anything they tell her to do instead of dying. Or maybe the black dragons took one of her family members and told her that they would return her family member to her if she helped them. That of course would be a lie from the Black Dragons but she would still do anything to get her family member back. Even hurt innocent people.

I used to see that kind of thing a lot when Soldum was first putting together his group of black wizards and dark magic. He would trick innocent people into doing terrible things that would only benefit himself." Dumas explained. "But how is this possible and how can I get rid of it?" Jess asked. "Anything is possible with magic, even terrible things. As to how to get rid of it, I'm not sure. Sorry I have only witnessed this once and it destroyed him before he figured out how to get rid of it."

"Destroyed him!" Jess shouted. Dumas shushed her. "Yes and it has already began to destroy you." He said and pushed Jess's sleeve up to view all the black dragon on her arm. "The talons have dug into your skin and began to spread the poison through your body." "Poison!" "Yes the poison of the Black Dragons. You couldn't remember the discussion about the Time Tricksters and some then days you act like you're not even there. Your mind is going somewhere else. Do you know how many days we have been traveling?" "Yes. It's been nine days." "No, it's been twelve. There have been three days where you were not you. Your body was there but your mind was not. That's why Erika commented about you being in a better mood or feeling better because the day before you were not the strong willed wizard that I have seen you as, you retained some sense of your surroundings but mostly you were just zoned out. Can you try to remember those days? Like when we tried to control your powers." Jess struggled to remember.

"I remember trying to use my powers but there was something there in my mind that was stopping me. I tried several times but could never reach my powers after those first few times I just stopped trying and haven't used my powers since." Jess admitted. "Try to use them right now." Dumas instructed. Jess concentrated as hard as she could. Suddenly she was flung backwards and landed on her back. Dumas walked over to where she landed and helped her up to her feet. "There is a black dragon in my mind blocking me. It looks just like the one on my arm. It was like I was inside my mind and there was an actual black dragon guarding a chest which held my powers. I tried to reach it but the dragon flipped its tail at me and then I went flying backwards. That hurt." Jess said as she looked at the black dragon on her arm in disgust. "I was afraid of that. You will not be able to use your power until you get rid of this dragon. I am sorry I don't know how to get rid of it. I do know that the drops of blood are the number of people that you will kill that are close to you."

"What? You're saying that I am going to kill two people that are close to me. No. I won't." Jess defended. "Jess you won't have a choice, unless you can somehow tame the beast and rid yourself of it before that happens or die first. My advice is to not show anyone, even Linder. Don't tell him anything about this. For now you need to fight the dragon until we can figure out a way to get rid of it. Fight it with all your might. If you feel like you are not in control fight it. Always stay alert. Ask questions to make sure you haven't missed anything. The dragon also holds its own knowledge like the last part of the time trickster spell. If you are able to learn anything from it that would be great but also be careful because this dragon is going to try to completely destroy you, mentally and eventually physically. If you don't fight it you will lose yourself and either become a Black Dragon wizard or the dragon inside you will…" he trailed off while looking into Jess's bewildered eyes. "Or what?" she asked. "It will tear your body apart into piece from the inside out as the dragon tries to escape your body, which would kill you in the process." He answered regretfully. "Is that what happened to the person that you knew?" Jess asked despairingly.

"Yes. The dragon that took over his body was one very similar to the one that has you. He wasn't a very strong wizard. He was a very good man though but his powers and willingness to fight weren't strong enough and one day the dragon inside him wanted out and ripped its way through him. Once the dragon escaped it grew rapidly into its true giant size. Luckily we were able to kill it soon after it was out of him but it shredded him to pieces. He was an innocent man but one day someone in a blood red cloak with a black dragon on his face came through town and he got mixed up with him. The man in the red cloak bragged about how much power he had and drew my friend near.

The Black Dragon looked at my friend and told him he was destined for greatness then grasped him arm then left. Shortly after that my friend began itching his arm a lot like you have. He itched his arm nonstop it seemed like and it changed from red bumps to black bumps and then one day the dragon was there and that is when his real problems began, until he died. I was curious about you because you were acting just like my friend did. I knew it wasn't a bug bite because it is still too cold for many bugs to be out yet and curiosity got the better of me and I asked to see your arm. I am glad that I did. Now we must find a way to rid you of it. I will not stand by and watch another friend of mine be destroyed because of the black dragons." Dumas stated.

"Linder could really help in finding a cure." Jess suggested. "Yes he could but his worry about you would hinder his thinking and ability to focus on our present goal. He is a better help to us if he does not have to worry about you." Dumas replied. "You're right." Jess agreed. She hated keeping secrets from Linder but Dumas was right, Linder would focus all of his energy into finding her a cure and that wasn't best for the mission. "We better get back or all of them will start worrying. Don't tell anyone about this. Hopefully Linder won't have a vision about this and we will figure something out. Remember to fight it." Dumas instructed. "I will." Jess replied. Dumas started to walk away, Jess grabbed his shoulders. "Wait! What if I can't find a way to get rid of the black dragon? I will be changed or shredded into pieces. I don't want either or those to happen so I need you to make me a promise. You need to promise to kill me before any of those happen if it comes to that. Please promise me that you will do that for me. Kill me if we can't find a way to cure me." Jess pleaded. Dumas look right into Jess's blue eyes which were desperate for an answer. "I will not let it come to that." He replied. "But if it does. Will you?" Jess asked with her gaze never leaving the Dumas's. "Yes I will." He replied straightly. "Good. Thank you." She replied with a sigh of relief then let go of his shoulders. They walked back together towards the others in silence.

Chapter Eleven- Traveling through Time

Once Linder saw Jess and Dumas returning he rushed to Jess's side. "Are you alright?" he asked. The concern in his voice and on his face was clearly visible. "Yeah, never better. We took care of the bug bites. I'm surprised that no one else had them. I will be fine now." Jess responded calmly. "As long as she doesn't itch them anymore she will be fine." Dumas chimed in. "Yeah, see no problem." Jess smiled and took Linder's hand in hers. He smiled back. "Good." "Alright, everything is good so let's get traveling. We still have a long way to go." Marcus commented. "What if we try that Time Trickster spell?" Erika suggested as she held Randy's hand who was wearing Erika's pack that him and Erika were sharing. "I guess that depends on if Jess can remember every single word from the poem that she told us earlier." Dumas stated as he glanced at her. "I will try." Jess remarked.

"What if she doesn't remember every single word?" Linder asked. "Then we will be stuck in a time trap. We can trick time to travel the distance within days but would never be able to reset it to normal. We would never be in the real world's time again. I don't know if that's such a great idea unless Jess can really remember every word." Dumas admitted as he scratched his facial hair trying to act nonchalantly. "Jess do you remember every word?" Erika asked hopefully. "Let me think." She said then glanced towards her right arm. She put her left hand to her head and rubbed the left temple on her head. "When I say the words everyone listen so that I'm not the only one to know it. I have a terrible memory so it would be nice if you all knew it too. Let's see it goes like this.

"Seconds, minutes, hours and days pass me by. Time creates all, time destroys all, time never ends but with time I change my course and subsequently change time itself."

Jess quoted then scratched her right arm. "Jess don't scratch it." Dumas instructed as he watched her closely. Jess clinched her right fist and winced then shook her head in pain. Dumas knew what was going on inside her head but didn't say anything. Jess was fighting the black dragon to keep control over her own mind.

"Well you have convinced me. Let's go ahead and try it."
Dumas responded. "Okay, what do we do?" Jess asked as she rubbed
her left temple once more. Dumas looked around at everyone. "Well
I have never tried it with someone who doesn't have any magic, so I
don't know how this is going to work." He answered while looking
at Randy. "Randy keep a hold of Erika's hand at all times, no matter
what. Erika, you will need to share your magic with Randy. I don't
know what will happen if you don't. He might die. Hold his hand
and push your power into him like you do when you use your power
to change the elements. Don't use the fire element though, that
would kill him and never let go of his hand while we are traveling
through time." Dumas instructed. Erika grasped Randy's hand
tightly.

"Couldn't we trade on and off for each person to share their
magic with him?" Jess asked as she stood near Linder. "No. If we
were all to take turns sharing our magic with him there would be a
moment in between switching people that would leave him without
magic and that could kill him. No. Only one person can share their
magic with him and it has to stay constant throughout our trip. Erika
is the best person for that job." Dumas explained. "I would love to."
Erika replied and smiled at Randy. "Good. Now everyone join in a
circle and hold hands and I will say the spell that will trick time and
let us travel through it. When I am saying the spell all of you will
need to push your powers outward to the middle of our circle. It
requires the magic of at least four wizards to work. Once I am
finished speaking the spell we will know instantly if it worked or
not. If it worked then we can let go of each other, except Randy and
Erika, and travel to Tasintall. Oh yeah, some people have
experienced nausea and get dizzy when traveling through the Time
Trickster spell. I never have but I thought you might like to know
that it could happen. Okay everyone ready?" Dumas asked and
outstretched his hand.

Jess looked around at the others. "I'm ready." She said. "As
am I." Linder replied. "Me too." Erika stated. "I'm ready." Randy
acknowledged. Everyone looked at Marcus. "I'm ready too." He
remarked. Everyone joined hands. "Here we go." Dumas said then
closed his eyes and began the spell.

"As time will come it will also go. Time shall reap which it has sown. Time comes slowly and time goes fast. The time we take will help us at last. This time is where we are and this time is where we've been. Time will be lost and then be found again. Let this time give me distance and this distance and time are now mine." He said respectfully then opened his eyes. "Let go of each other." He instructed. Everyone let go of each other's hands except Erika and Randy. The world instantly slowed to a stop. There was no sound and it felt just like a dream. The world around them had seemed to stop. Nothing moved except them. Dumas took a step away from the group. There was a quick blur of motion and he was gone.

"Well come on." Dumas said. "Where are you?" Erika asked looking around for him but he was nowhere to be seen. "Take a step and you'll see." Dumas replied. Erika and Randy both took a step forward with their hands clasp together. There was a quick blur of motion and then they were gone. "That was awesome!" Erika announced excitedly. "We must have traveled at least fifty steps with just that one." Randy replied in an astonished tone. "Isn't it remarkable?" Dumas asked as he stood nearby Erika and Randy. Before they could answer three quick blurs appeared and then focused into Marcus, Jess and Linder. "Good we are all here. That first step is the hardest. We will know soon if anyone is going to get sick from the motion of traveling through time or not. Let's continue on and try to stay together." Dumas implored. Everyone take several steps forward. With each step the world around them became a blur of colors and objects.

Whenever they stopped the world was completely still and silent. Everything looked to be unmoving and unreal. The motion of traveling through time was both exhilarating and terrifying. Jess was afraid that she was going to step into tree or a boulder. Within the first hour of traveling they had got many miles through the forest. They stopped when they saw a small village ahead. Standing in the unmoving world they gazed upon the village in astonishment.

There were cattle, sheep, and horses grazing in the fields nearby, people with carts in the center of the village and children playing with each other while dogs ran by their feet near the small buildings in the village. All of which looked to be frozen in movement. One child was stuck in mid air while jumping over another's child's back. "Are they going to be alright?" Linder asked. "Yes. To them the time is normal. The child will land on his feet just fine. The cattle will continue grazing and the people will continue their lives as normal. The time appears slower for us when we stop moving. But in real time only a second has past. We need to go around the town because if we were to go through and touch anything it would be as if a stampede hit it. We would destroy anything we touched; even people so it's best to just avoid that." Dumas explained then lead them around the village which disappeared after a few steps.

They traveled for many hours with the world blurring past them before they decided to stop to rest and eat. "I'm not even tired." Jess acknowledged in awe. "That's good because I didn't want to mention it earlier but we can't sleep until we are out of the spell. If we go to sleep the connection will be broken and we will be stuck here. The only magic that will work here is the spell that stops the time trickster spell. No other magic will work. None of your powers will work here. So we have to keep going until we reach our destination. I think we can stop and eat some food though. At least that part doesn't change, I'm hungry." Dumas informed them then pushed his shoulder length black hair behind his ears. All of a sudden Jess screamed and fell to one knee.

"Jess! What's wrong? Are you hurt?" Linder frantically asked as he bent down to help her. Jess was gripping her right arm tightly with her left. "Jess are you alright?" Erika asked as she pulled Randy with her to get closer to Jess. Inside her the dragon was pushing its way deeper into her mind causing her to lose focus on what was really happening. Her mind was being taken over. The dragon that invaded her mind did not want her to have control and was sending pain through her body. She screamed as it forced her consciousness away. She could hear Linder speaking but couldn't concentrate on the words. Erika and Randy drew near her while the others watched. She was losing her consciousness. Why is everyone above me? She thought to herself. She tried as hard as she could to concentrate. I'm on one knee. I have to stand up. They can't know what is going on. I will fight this. She thought to herself, noticing that she was gripping her arm where the dragon was. I will fight this. She told herself then released her arm and with a clenched fist to control the pain that shot through her body she focused her mind on Linder's worried face.

She stood and the pain subsided and she was able to take control of her thoughts. With her right hand clinched into a fist she released her left hand from her right arm and rose to her feet. Assuming that the others were going to ask how she was doing she forced a smile, and hoping it looked genuine as she said. "I'm fine. My arm is just itching really bad right now and I know I can't itch it or it will make it worse. It's just driving me crazy. I'm fine though. Let's just eat and then keep going and get my mind of my arm." "I think that's a good idea. Jess says that she is fine and I believe her so let's keep moving." Dumas remarked.

"Jess are you really alright?" Linder asked her softly. "Yes I am." She replied with a smile and unclenched her fist and took Linder's hand into hers. Linder was unsure whether Jess was really alright or not but took her hand into his nonetheless. Erika kept an eye on Jess. Since she had known Jess for many years she usually could tell when something was wrong with her even if Jess said that there wasn't. This time Erika couldn't tell if Jess was alright or not. She was worried about her. Linder looked at Jess studiously then agreed to plan.

Everyone ate a quick snack of apples, biscuits, and dried meat without any more questions about Jess. Randy looked around at his unmoving surroundings and estimated that if they were walking at a normal pace it would take them a week and a few days left until they would reach Tasintall. "We have traveled almost half way there already. At this rate we will be there by tomorrow afternoon. You are all going to love Tasintall. It's an amazing city." He declared as he held onto Erika's soft hand.

"I just hope that the royal family will help us." Erika remarked. "I was sent to find you so I'm sure they will help." Randy replied. "Are you sure? You did lose your princess and let her get killed." Jess stated. "Jess!" Erika yelled. "Well? It's true. If he returns and tells the royal family what happened to their princess, how happy do you think that are actually going to be? Do you think that they will trust us? We are from the place where the princess got killed. I'm just saying that we should be prepared with a different plan if that happens." Jess commented. Her words came out sounding worse than she had planned them to. Erika thought Jess was being rude about it. "You're right. I can see your point but I think that they will still help us. They have been searching for you and Linder for a long time and even though the princess is now dead, we have faith that you two will be able to save our country from the black plague. One death compared to thousands is hardly anything to what could happen without you. I think that the royal family will see it that way also." Randy indicated. "Let's hope so." Jess inclined.

No more words were spoken except Marcus indicating that they should get moving after they had finished eating. Many hours passed with the blur of motion passing them while the blurred sky turned from light blue to pink, orange and eventually dark blue then black. The night had come at last. Jess thought it would be difficult to see in the dark but she could see just fine and with Linder holding her hand she felt safe in the constant movement. No one could keep up a conversation because of the distance between everyone that happened every time someone took a step.

The morning light came in streaks through time as they continued to travel onwards. Randy and Erika lead the way because Randy was the only one who knew the way. They stopped together and yelled for the others to stop so that Randy could get his bearings and estimate how much longer it would be until they would reach Tasintall. The moment they stopped the world seemed to be motionless. Nothing moved and nothing made sound. The trees were inert. The clouds stationery and the birds were stuck in mid flight in air. It was like living in an unmoving dream. "If we were walking normally we would be to Tasintall in around three hours." Randy stated as he looked around at the familiar woods surrounding his hometown. "We will need to get out of this spell in around five time trickster steps or what would be around two hours in real time. We will need to be fully acclimatized back to normal before we enter Tasintall. That requires walking in real time for the last hour remaining before we get there." Dumas insisted. Everyone acknowledge and took five more time passing motion blurring steps then regrouped.

"Alright, although it doesn't feel like it, it's been a long journey so once we are out of the spell you may be hit with fatigue, exhaustion, or temporary sickness. Those are normal reactions that happen so don't be concerned if any of those happen to you. Everyone gather in a circle and join hands and Jess will end the spell and put us back into the real time." Dumas instructed then extended out his hands. Jess grabbed Dumas's hand while holding onto Linder's with her other. Linder grasped Marcus. Marcus grasped Erika. Erika was holding tight to Randy's hand then Randy grasped Dumas's other extended hand to complete the circle.

Jess looked at everyone in turn then spoke then words to end the time trickster spell. *"Seconds, minutes, hours and days pass me by. Time creates all, time destroys all, time never ends but with time I change my course and subsequently change time itself."* Once she finished speaking the last word of the spell the unmoving world around them began to move once more and a wave of sound rushed into their ears.

Tree branches rustled and swayed in the light breeze, leaves rustled on the ground, birds fly speedily by above the tree tops. The scattering of small animals were heard in the forest around them. They were back in the real time of the world. Jess's head spun as she took in all her surroundings. She swayed slightly on her feet as she tried to keep her balance. The dragon inside her tried to take control of her mind, causing her to stumble. Linder caught her arm and helped her to her feet, then held on to her waist to keep her stable. Jess's sight went fuzzy, while pain pulsed through the dragon tattoo on her arm where Linder was holding. She was able to tell Linder that she needed to sit down before her mind went blank.

When Jess awoke the sun was setting on the west side of the sky. She lay on the ground with Linder sitting next to her. He had his knees bent and his head resting on his arms which were folded on top of his knees. His eyes were closed. Jess noticed a tear running down his cheek. She moved her eyes around and saw that they were alone. She tried to sit up, which drew Linder's attention to her. He helped her to a sitting position against a tree. "Jess please tell me the truth. Are you alright?" he asked, concern strong in his voice. Jess felt weak, and tired and extremely hungry. She looked at her arm where the dragon tattoo was imprinted on. Her cloak lay under her and her sleeve was still covering her arm when she replied. "No Linder I'm not." "I know about the black dragon. When you fainted at first I thought it was just from the time trickster spell but then you started mumbling words very quietly. You wouldn't respond to anyone as we all tried to wake you. You kept repeating the words, black dragon and stupid arm. I went to roll up your sleeve but Dumas stopped me.

He explained what was happening to you. I didn't believe it until I rolled up your sleeve and saw it there. Jess, I just don't understand why you didn't tell me about it. I know you would never become a Black Dragon so I would know that it wasn't from your own actions. Dumas explained the vision that he shared with you and what would happen if the others found out." Linder said. Jess began to ask a question but Linder cut her off. "No, the others don't know about it. Shortly after we realized that you weren't waking up and wouldn't respond to any of us Dumas sent Erika, Randy and Marcus ahead to Tasintall to get help. He told them that he would help me get you comfortable and stay here with me to take care of you just in case you woke up. Once the others were gone I saw the Black Dragon on your arm. You have been fighting with the dragon inside you for many hours. I felt so helpless. I could do nothing to help you. I could only watch you as you silently fought the dragon inside you as it tried to take control over your mind. You had me so scared. I didn't know what to do besides wait and hope that you would return to me. Dumas and I performed a spell that would allow me to speak to you in your mind. I told you to fight it and come back to me. You didn't respond. That was over an hour ago. But now you have awakened, so I'm assuming that you have the black dragon under control for now." Linder asked hopefully as he watched her.

She looked into his blue eyes with the brown sunbursts in the center and replied. "I did want to tell you but in Dumas's vision you didn't understand and that scared me. So Dumas told me not to tell anyone, including you. I was afraid you would leave me and I didn't want to lose you so I didn't tell you." "Jess I would never leave you. You're my dream come true. I just want to be with you. I would do anything for you. I love you Jess." "I love you too." Jess replied then reached out and hugged Linder. After their embrace Jess asked, "You said that Dumas was staying with you to help take care of me. Where is he then?" "He went to find more water. Our water skin was empty and the others took the only other water available." Linder replied. "Oh okay." "Jess are you sure you're alright now?" he inquired as he watched her. "Yeah, I'm just tired, and really hungry." Jess replied emphasizing the last word. Linder laughed. "Erika said that when you wake up the first thing you would say is that you are hungry. She sure knows you well." Linder commented. Jess laughed. "Yes she does."

"We have some food left in our pack. I'll get you some." Linder offered then rose to his feet. He walked a few steps to where his pack lay on the ground and retrieved it and carried it to where Jess sat. He sat back down next to her and retrieved a meat pie wrapped in cloth out of his pack and handed it to her. "It's the last one." He told her and handed her a fork from his pack. "We can share it." Jess offered. "You need it more than I do. I will eat bread and fruits." Linder insisted. "I'm so glad you're conscious now. That must have been quiet a battle going on in your mind. You were out for many hours but I told Linder that you were tough and were going to subdue the dragon and here you are. Did someone say something about food?" Dumas asked as he came strolling to where Jess and Linder sat. He was carrying Linder's water skin in his hand that was glistening with water drops on the sides. Dumas looked as if he had either fallen in the water source or had tried to take a bath but with his old torn dirty clothes it didn't help make him look much cleaner.

"Did you fall in or decide to bathe while you were gone?" Jess asked as she saw water drip of his long black hair that he had tucked behind his ears. His facial hair looked much cleaner than she had ever seen it and his dark brown eyes stood out on his dirt free face. "I figured if I'm going to meet royalty then I should at least be clean, even if my clothes aren't and I'm not the only one around here that could use a bath." Dumas stated smiling then handed Linder the water skin. "So how you are feeling?" he continued. "I'm tired and hungry." Jess answered. "Good. Nothing else?" Dumas asked as he joined the others on the ground. "Nope." "Tired and hungry, that sounds like me. We can eat and fix the hunger part but you won't be able to rest until we get to Tasintall though. That won't take very long. I expect that Randy will send some people to help us and they will arrive within the next hour or two. I think if you are feeling up to it that we should eat and then start walking towards Tasintall until we reach our help." Dumas offered. "Okay." Jess agreed on the plan then took a bite of the cold meat pie.

Linder took out a variety of fruits, nuts and breads for him and Dumas. After they finished eating Linder repacked what remained into his pack, stood and situated it onto his shoulders. He reached his hand down for Jess. She grabbed it and was pulled to her feet. She wavered slightly but balanced herself before she fell. "I'm alright. Really." She stated to Linder and Dumas's concerned faces. She raised both arms high and twirled in a circle, like a dancer would do. "See. I'm fine." Dumas and Linder nodded and then Dumas led the way towards Tasintall.

It was a little over an hour when they heard the hooves of many horses galloping towards them. Linder placed his hand on his sword handle. Once the horsemen came into view Linder released his hand. Randy had sent a troop from his army to help them. There were about twenty men on horseback all dressed the same. They all wore bright red military shirts that had two rows of buttons running down the front it, black pants, and dark green cloaks that had different symbols embossed on them. Some men had stars embossed on their cloaks along with the other symbols that Jess didn't recognize. The man with the most stars on his cloak stopped his horse a few feet away from Jess, Linder and Dumas. He was wearing a two cornered hat with a white feather sticking out of one side. He had dark brown hair that was neatly cut to match all the rest of the men on horses.

"What are your names?" he asked firmly. "I am Linder, this is Jess and this is Dumas." Linder replied gesturing to each in turn with their names. The man on the horse spoke to another man on a horse right next to him. "Tell the men that we have found them. I will assess the situation and instruct the men accordingly shortly." "Yes sir." The second man replied then turned his horse around and began shouting to the other men on horses that had stopped in a line following the first. He shouted that Jess, Linder and Dumas had been found and to hold their positions. The man with the feather in his hat dismounted and bowed.

"I am General Jackson. I am at your service. We were told that one of you is the Northstin Wind and that all of you were in desperate need of help. My men and I are here to help you in any way possible." The man stated. "Thank you." Dumas replied. "We did need help earlier but now were okay. We could use a ride to Tasintall though." Jess answered. "Yes ma'am." General Jackson replied with a smile then reached his hand out to her. She looked at him studying his features and secretly using her powers on him to determine what his true feelings were. He was a handsome man with a rounded chin, dark brown hair, brown eyes and a small dimple on the right side of his face when he smiled. He had a red birthmark on the left side of his face that was noticeable under a brown beard that grew on top of it. He looked to be in his late twenties.

Jess determined that his feelings were simply kindness with a hint of curiosity. She reached her hand out. General Jackson took her hand and kissed the top of it. Jess's face flushed red. Then she felt something in her mind pulling her attention away from the world. Jess tried to keep her balance but she could feel herself falling backwards before she could do anything about it. General Jackson gripped her arm tightly and caught her before she fell all the way. Linder also caught Jess from behind. Linder instructed the general that they should lower her to the ground. Jess watched both men's faces as she was lowered to the ground. Once down they released her they moved back to give her some space. Dumas and the other soldiers watched from the side. Jess clinched her right hand into a fist, closing her eyes at the same time. She had to fight the dragon inside her. She would not let it take control of her. Without saying a word within a minute later she opened her eyes quickly, unclenched her fist and stood on her own then spoke.

"Well, what are we waiting for? Can we get a ride to Tasintall or not?" she said in a neutral tone trying not to show the pain that was pulsing through her. "Of course. But are you sure that your fit to ride?" General Jackson asked as he rose to his full height. He was a few inches taller than Jess. "Yes. I just got dizzy. I will be fine. I think that we should get to Tasintall to inform our companions that everyone is alright. They must be very worried about us." Jess explained. "Sergeant Randy Porter was particularly worried about you because he said that you are the Northstin Wind. Is that correct?" The general asked. Jess wanted to disagree but instead nodded to the general. Chatter ran through the group of soldiers on horses as Jess admitted to being the Northstin Wind. "Wonderful. If the prophecies and rumors are true about what you can do then you will be greatly important for our people." The general stated.

"Well I haven't heard the rumors but I will try my best to do what I can to help." Jess confessed. "So if you're the Northstin Wind that would make you the Prophet and you the wizard that Sergeant Randy Porter told us about." The general stated to Linder and Dumas. They both agreed. Chatter ran through the soldiers once more filled with even more excitement. General Jackson looked to the officer with the second most stars on his cloak that was sitting atop of a black horse nearby. "Major Peterson take ten of the men with you and ride back to Tasintall. Five of you go to the palace and inform the royal family that the Northstin Wind, the Prophet and a Wizard will be coming to the palace soon. The rest of you go and find Sergeant Randy Porter, his new wife and their black friend and take them to the palace to wait. I'm sure the royal family will want to congratulate him for finding these important people." General Jackson ordered.

"Yes sir." Major Peterson replied then followed the orders given to him and soon half of the men on horses were heading back through the forest from the way they had come. The remaining men waited patiently for their instructions. "We don't have any extra horses so all of you will have to ride with one of my men. I hope that is alright." General Jackson stated. Linder looked at Jess reassuring her that it would be fine. "That will be fine." Dumas answered first. "Good. The lady can ride with me, and you men can ride with my best riders, Sergeant Green, and Lieutenant Daniels." General Jackson instructed. The two officers whose names had been spoken moved their horses out of formation and drew near. General Jackson mounted onto his horses and reached his hand down to help Jess mount onto the brown stallion. Dumas and Linder mounted the horses behind the officers who were already mounted there. "Alright men, we're headed back to the palace." The general announced in a loud voice so that all could hear. There was a conjoined "Yes sir." That came from the officers. Then they uniformly turned their horses around and started trotting towards Tasintall with General Jackson in the lead.

Jess felt awkward holding the waist of the general during the ride to Tasintall but had no choice but to hold on. The ride took half an hour until they reached Tasintall. The first thing Jess saw as they drew near the city was the immense palace that sat atop a hill with two roads leading up to it from either side of the city that sat below. It had many spires, two towers, and multiple windows that glowed from the candlelight that emanated from inside them. The palace look like it could hold all of the people from Morganstin in it with room to spare. Jess thought to herself. There were flags waving in the dimming light on top of the palace. Jess couldn't make out what most of the symbols on them were but saw that one matched the one that was embossed on the soldier's uniforms.

The night was coming quickly as the soldiers trotted their horses in a line through the many streets of Tasintall. It was getting hard to see so Jess kept her eyes on the glowing palace that sat on the hill that drew ever nearer. It took almost as much time to get through the city to the palace as it did to get to the city of Tasintall from where the soldiers had found them in the forest. The soldiers rode right up to the front steps of the palace where they stopped. Dumas, Linder, Jess and General Jackson and four other soldiers all dismounted. The general handed the reins of his horse to another soldier then dismissed them all. General Jackson and the four soldiers led the way up the staircase and in the massive front doors to the palace.

Chapter Twelve- A Night in the Palace

The interior of the palace was breath taking. The floor was white marble that ran through all the hallways and doorways that Jess could see. Towering above her was a large spiral marble staircase that lead to unseen rooms above. There were flowers in glass vases sitting atop marble stands that encircled the room. Jess wondered how the flowers could be alive in such cold weather. A grand fire place sat in the far wall stocked with logs for a fire but not a blaze yet. Above the fire place hung in the center of the wall was a large painting. The painting was of the city of Tasintall with the surrounding forest painted around it. The painting was done so well it looked as if you were looking at it from a window from the palace. Jess had never seen a painting so nice as this one. There were many candle holders mounted on the walls with lit candles to illuminate the room. There were many exquisite chairs sitting in a half circle near the fire place.

Before Jess could admire the room any longer a servant woman came rushing down the hallway and into the entrance room. "The king and queen have sent me to tell you that they have retired for the evening and request your presences at breakfast. They said that you are welcome to all of the services of the palace and I am to show you to your rooms for the night when you are ready. Is there anything you need before that?" she asked. "We want food, a real bath with soap, clean clothes and a soft bed to sleep in." Dumas stated. Jess was a little shocked by his forwardness to the servant woman but then also not surprised because Dumas was odd that way and she was secretly glad it was him that had spoken up first. If she had to answer than she would have told the servant no and just let her show her where she could sleep. "Very well, in what order did you want those sir?" the servant asked without any thought or hesitation to the demands. "The order I listed them." Dumas replied. "Yes sir. The dining hall is this way. Please follow me." she stated then retrieved one of the many candles from the walls and began walking away.

The seven people followed the servant down a hallway, up a narrow stone stair case, which was used as the servant's stairway then down another hallway and finally into a grandeur dining hall. There to Jess's surprise sitting at an extremely long wooden table sat Erika, Randy and Marcus all of whom had plates full of food sitting in front of them with platters of various foods that lined the table also. "Somehow I'm not surprised that this is where you would come first. Forget resting or bathing you came right to where the food is." Erika teased as she rose from her seat. Randy stood also as Erika got up and walked to Jess. "Well you know me, I'm always hungry." Jess replied with a smile. Erika gave Jess a hug. "I'm so glad that you're alright. You really had us worried." Erika stated. "I've been in worse situations than that one." Jess remarked. Erika shook her head. "You really are crazy you know that." "Yeah I know, and that's why we're best friends." Jess retorted.

"By the way, what are you wearing?" Jess asked as she looked at Erika's clothing. "I've been told it's the latest fashion in women's clothing here. I do prefer trousers and a blouse but they said that it was unacceptable to be wearing men's clothing in the mansion. They told me that I should dress like a woman so this is what they had for me to wear. It's a bit to extravagant for my taste but I do like it." Erika replied as she looked down at the red and black top that had a slightly squared neckline and narrow lace frills at the bodice and elbow length cuffed sleeves. The floor length skirt she wore was cream colored with red and black roses embossed on it. "Erika you look beautiful." Randy stated. Erika smiled towards him. "Well I can't decide whether I should be jealous or you should be. I can still move around without my clothes inhibiting my movements." Jess teased.

"Yeah but I kept my boots." Erika replied with a mischievous smile then lifted the skirt up so that Jess could see her dirty mud covered boots under the pristine skirt. Jess and Erika laughed so hard their stomach's started to hurt. The men in the room and the servant woman waited patiently for Jess and Erika to stop laughing. "Please sit. I will retrieve more plates and goblets so that you also may enjoy the palace's food and wine." The servant insisted. The general's men sat down as the general went to pull out of chair for Jess. Linder stepped in his way and grabbed the chair first. "I will do it." He insisted. The general nodded and sat himself down on a chair at the table that could hold at least twenty people. Jess sat down on the chair Linder held for her then he sat down next to her. Erika sat back down on her chair next to Randy. Jess then noticed that Randy was dressed in a clean military uniform that matched the soldiers that also sat at the table, except without the cloak. Marcus was wearing a brown pair of trousers, a cream colored shirt with a navy blue waistcoat. "You all look great." Jess commented to her friends. "Thank you." Randy and Marcus replied proudly.

Just then the servant came into the dining room carrying a stack of plates and seven goblets on a platter while another woman servant carried a pitcher of wine. The first servant set down the dishes in front of each person and then the second servant filled each goblet full of wine. "Can I have some water to drink?"Jess asked one of the servants. "Yes ma'am. I will retrieve some for you." She replied and bowed then left the room. The first servant told everyone that she would return once they were finished eating to accommodate their other wishes then she left the dining hall.

Everyone helped themselves to the many platters of food that were placed before them. Jess had just filled her plate with roasted chicken, mashed potatoes with gravy; pork roast with carrots and onions, rolls topped with creamy butter, and there was some type of white meat in a creamy white sauce that Jess later found out were doves and many varieties of fruits and nuts that she loaded onto her plate. She was enjoying the potatoes when the servant returned with a pitcher full of water. Jess thanked the servant who also brought an extra goblet and filled it full of water for Jess. The servant then placed the pitcher on the table and left the room. Most of the food was still warm and Jess and her friends relished the delightful taste and abundance of their meal.

Once their stomachs were stuffed to the point where they couldn't eat any more the two servants returned along with three more and began cleaning off the table. The first servant woman led all seven guests out of the dining hall and up a stair case. "Here are the bed chambers, the men sleep in the rooms on the left and the women on the right. You may pick whichever room pleases you. Each has a fire place that can be lit if desired and in each room is a cord to pull when you desire our services. The bath hall is located down the stairs, and is the fourth door on the right. The bath is ready for you whenever you are. There are servants there that can help you wash, and help with your clothes. Is there anything else I can do to serve you?" the servant woman asked properly.

"Do you have any books to read?" Dumas asked. "Yes sir, we have a library right here in the palace. What is the topic of choice that you desire?" the servant replied. "Prophecies." Dumas replied without hesitation. The woman's features blanch and she shifted her feet then she regained her composure. "I will retrieve a book about prophecies from the library and bring it to you for your enjoyment." "Good, I will take this room. You can put the book in there. First I'm going to take a bath and I would like a fire going when I return." Dumas instructed. "Yes sir. Right away sir." The servant replied then turned her attention to the others. "Is there anything else I can do for you?" "I'm good. Thank you though." Jess replied. "No but thank you." Linder stated. "My men and I are grateful for your service but do not require anything else this evening. Thank you." General Jackson told the servant woman then kissed her hand. "Very well good night." She replied than headed back down the stairs and out of sight.

The rest of the night was the most awkward moments of Jess's life yet. She knew that she was expected to take a bath and she wanted to be clean but the array of women and men in the bath room was unnerving. She asked if the men really had to be there and the servants politely answered that it was the duty they were assigned to, so that had to stay. Jess started to take off her clothes but one of the women servants told her that they were supposed to do that and if Jess didn't let them do then they would be punished. Jess sighed then nodded reluctantly. They all helped her undress. Most of the servants got scared and nervous expressions on their faces when they saw the Black Dragon on her arm. There was one servant that upon seeing her tattoo fled the room and never returned. Jess was unsure what to think from it. The servant was either too scared to be in the same room as her or was going to tell someone, and either way that could cause her a lot of trouble.

The remaining servants scrubbed her body with different colors and textures of soaps. Her arm where the black dragon tattoo was located at stung in pain as the servants scrubbed her. One woman poured almost the entire contents of a bottle into her hair where she then lathered it into a big soapy mess. After having pitchers of water poured on her and the soap rinsed off, they helped her out of the tub and proceeded to dry off her body then place clothes on her. Two women pulled a white linen shift over Jess's head. It had sleeves that ran down her arm almost to her wrists and the shift went down to below her knees. Another woman placed green stockings on her feet that went up to her thighs that were tied on with ribbon. After they had finished dressing her one woman preceded to brush Jess's long blonde hair until it was completely smooth then one of the servant men escorted her to her bedroom and to Jess's embarrassment he folded the sheets down on her bed and offered to tuck her into her sheets.

"Look I know it's your job but I can tuck myself in. I won't tell anyone that you didn't do alright. I would just like to tuck myself in and get some sleep now." Jess told the servant man. "Yes, ma'am." The servant nodded and then excused himself from the room. The bedroom was dimly lit by a slow burning candle that sat on stand next to the bed. Jess blew out the candle, climbed into the giant bed and pulled the sheets on her and soon was asleep.

Jess awoke with a start, jumping out of her bed and to her feet instantly. Her heart was pounding, sweat beaded her face, and she felt like someone was watching her. She scanned the dark room but couldn't see anyone or anything. It was just too dark to see anything. Jess thought it must in the middle of the night. She starred into the darkness trying to make out any shapes but was unable. With her suspicion aroused she felt around for the nearest wall then made her way feeling the walls to where she thought the bedroom door should be. She found the door handle and tried to open it. It didn't open. She tried several more times to open the door with no success. It was locked from the outside. She had been locked in. She knocked loudly on the door, hoping that someone would hear and unlock the door. No response.

Jess listened for any sound outside the door. There was silence for a long moment then she heard something. It was two men whispering discreetly. "What are we going to do?" the first asked. "Be quite you fool! She could still be awake." The other man said harshly. "She might be part of us." The first replied. "And she might not be. We can't take that chance. We will have to finish the plan tomorrow!" The other man hissed and then Jess heard nothing. She listened for a few more minutes but all she heard was silence. Jess hoped that the men had left. There was something wrong going on around here. Guests are not locked in their rooms and who were the two men in the hall and what plan are they talking about? I have to get to Linder. Jess thought to herself. There were no windows in her room and the door was locked. Jess reached her way around the room until she found the candle, she felt around for something to light it. There was nothing useful. There was no way out. Just then she heard a clicking sound coming from the door knob to her bedroom.

Typically she wasn't the type of person to hide but with no visibility and no weapon she decided that hiding would be her best option. She quickly ducked down and slid under the large bed, facing the doorway. The door unlocked and opened.

There stood Marcus holding a lit candle stick in one hand and his sword in the other. "Jess, are you awake?" he whispered as he slowly entered the room, closing the door softly behind him. Jess slid out from under the bed. "What is going on around here?" she asked. "I'm not sure. All I know is that someone really wants us dead." "I suspected something like that, but why?" Jess replied. "I don't know. I had an odd feeling that I was being watched earlier so I decided to investigate. I tried to get out of my room but my door was locked. That was a sure sign that they don't trust us and that we can't trust any of them. I still had my pack with me so I used some rope and climbed out the window. I snuck back into the palace and searched around for anything suspicious.

I found nothing so I came to this hall to check on the rest of you. I check a few of the other rooms on the way here and their doors were locked also. They all required a key; luckily I retrieved the key from a guard that was posted in the hall." "What did you do to him?" Jess asked flatly. "I didn't have a choice. I couldn't fight him. He was much bigger than me and had many more weapons. I am surprised that he didn't hear or see me coming. If I would have fought him that would have caused more trouble for us so I snuck up behind him and snapped his neck. I found a key around his neck and used it to unlock the nearest door. Inside the room I found some man I did not recognize lying dead in his bed. He had been stabbed multiple times. I moved the guard's body into the room and relocked it. That's when I heard two men approaching. I unlocked the door and went back inside the room with the dead men and closed the door and listened. I heard you knock on your door and listened. I heard what the men said about their plan. I waited until they left and came straight here. I don't think anything else will happen tonight but we have to warn the others and make sure they are alright." Marcus explained. "I was thinking the same thing." Jess responded. "Good then let's go." Marcus instructed then led Jess out of the bedroom and into the dark hallway.

The only light in the hallway was the dim flicker of the candle that Marcus held in his hand. They walked to the door next to Jess's which was the room that Erika was in. Marcus unlocked the door and went inside followed by Jess. By the light of the flickering candle they could see that Erika was asleep in the plush bed. "Erika, wake up." Jess said as she shook her best friend from her sleep. Erika opened her eyes, "What?" she groggily asked somewhat loud. Jess leaned in closer to Erika's ear. "We are not amongst friends. Someone locked us all inside our rooms, killed a man down the hall and both Marcus and I heard men talking about a plan that didn't sound very nice. It sounded like they were going to kill us. Erika we have to make sure everyone else is still alive and figure out what to do next." Jess whispered. Erika's eyes grew big as the realization of what Jess had told her sunk in. She untangled her feet from inside her blankets and got out of her bed. She wore the same white shift as Jess except she had black stockings on her feet instead of green. Her shoulder length brown wavy hair flowed around her face. "Let's go." She replied with determination in her tone as she tucked her wavy hair behind her ears. The three of them left Erika's room, crossed the hall and unlocked the closest door.

On the other side of the door stood one of General Jackson's men, Jess didn't remember if this man was Sergeant Green, or Lieutenant Daniels, who were the general's best horse riders or one of the others that joined the general in the palace. He was still wearing his military uniform and looked surprised and angry to see them. There was a candle lit on a stand by the bed. Jess could see that sweat that beaded the man's forehead. He quickly slid a dagger into his belt and his facial expression changed to the look of curiosity.

"What's going on?" he asked while looking between Marcus and the two women. "Someone is trying to kill us. We are checking on everyone in this hall to make sure they are alright and to warn them that we are not in the company of friends." Marcus stated. "Thank you for your concern but I am fine. I am a trained officer, I can protect myself." The man replied then shifted his weight uneasily. Jess watched the man closely.

She saw that his right hand was darker than his left. It was too dark to see exactly what it was but Jess thought it was blood. The man caught her looking. "Well thank you for the warning but I am tired and would like to get some sleep so please leave." He stated briskly as he stared at Jess. "Sorry we bothered you." Erika replied. Jess and Marcus followed Erika out of the room closing the door behind them. "Did you see…?" Jess began to ask but was cut off by Erika's hand covering her mouth. Jess understood and stopped talking. They went to the next door, unlocked it and went in. Inside they found Randy asleep. Erika woke him up, explained what had happened so far, and told him about the odd encounter with the general's horse rider. He joined them in their crusade to warn the others about the two men who plotted to kill them.

Next they found Dumas, then Linder, and then General Jackson. The general listened to what Marcus told him and then after lighting the candle in his room he took it with him and went to retrieve his four men that joined him in the palace. Before he left he told everyone to stay in his bedroom while he retrieved his men. Once they were all together they could discuss what exactly happened to everyone and plan a strategy. Linder put his arm around Jess while they waited for the General to return.

Randy held Erika's hand while they waited. After many long and quiet moments, General Jackson returned with three of his men. One of which was the suspicious man that they had already talked to. He was wearing his dark cloak that covered most of his body and gloves on his hands that hid his hands from sight. General Jackson's expression was one of sadness. "Your suspicion of someone trying to kill us was correct. We were just not quick enough. Lieutenant Daniels is dead. He has been stabbed multiple times in his sleep. Alongside him we found a dead guard with a snapped neck. There are sinister forces against us here. It is not safe to stay here. I know a place where we could protect you better and you all would be safe." General Jackson stated. "Are you sure that's a good idea? I mean, the king and queen think that the answers to their problems are here.

The Northstin Wind and the Prophet have finally come to Tasintall and the king and queen think that they are safely sleeping here in the castle and plan to meet them first thing in the morning. If they leave then what will the king and queen think? What will happen then? You were the one who brought them here and then if you and they mysteriously disappear in the night. That won't look very good on your part. The king and queen might not trust you anymore; they might even take away your rankings. I propose that everyone just stays here for tonight and then see what tomorrow brings. We can take turns sleeping and guarding each other for the remainder of the night. We could all sleep in one room if you think that would be necessary. What do you think General? Do you want to risk losing the trust of the king and queen or do you want to continue with your plan and leave the castle to take them somewhere safer?" The man with the gloves on asked. Jess did not like this man, not one bit. Something about him just made her skin crawl, or maybe that was just the dragon tattoo irritating her again.

The general thought deeply about what the man had said and then replied. "We will stay. I want everyone to gather what belongings you have along with pillows and blankets and everyone will stay in here. Johnson and Smith escort them and keep guard while they collect their things. Sergeant Green I want you to guard this room while I look around the castle for the culprit." General Jackson ordered. "Yes sir." Johnson, Smith and Green replied then set towards their tasks. Sergeant Johnson lit several candles that were hanging on the walls in the hall and handed one to everyone. They all left the generals room and went to their own rooms to gather their belongings, leaving Sergeant Green alone. Jess entered her room, looked around and realized that there wasn't anything that belonged to her in the room. The servants had taken her clothes to wash them right after they took them off her. Anything else that belonged to her was in Linder's pack. She grabbed the pillow off the bed and a blanket and started heading towards the open door when all of sudden the door closed and there in the shadows stood a man. He was blocking the doorway. Jess was trapped.

"Answer this question. Are you with us or them?" the man asked in a gruff voice. Jess tried to see the man's face but he was wearing something dark over his face. The only part Jess could see was the reflection on light coming from his eyes. "Well?" the man asked impatiently but before Jess could ask what he was talking about he continued. "I saw the dragon on your arm. So are you with us or have you betray the master and joined those fools?" he demanded. Jess knew she had to think of something to get herself out this situation. Her arm began stinging, she was losing her concentration. No! I will not surrender! She thought to herself. Just then she knew what she had to do.

"Believe me, I would love to tell you but you are so tired that you can't stay awake to listen to my answer. You are going to sleep right now." She replied while pushing her power out towards him. The man looked confused for an instant and then lost his balance and landed on the floor with a loud thud and was instantly asleep. Linder pushed open the door as much as he could with the man blocking the door from opening all the way. "Jess, are you alright?" he asked as he squeezed in the doorway, stepping over the fallen man. "I'm fine. But I don't think he is going to be when he wakes up." Jess replied as Linder grabbed her hands.

"Is he asleep?" Linder asked astonished. "Yes. I didn't have any weapons and I have control over the dragon inside me right now so I used my power on him and made him go to sleep. Linder, he saw my dragon and was asking if I was on his side or ours. The instant I saw him the dragon tried to take control of me, I kept control but my arm still hurts. I'm worried though because he wasn't the only one who saw it. When I took a bath all the servants there saw it. It scared some and others looked intrigued. I couldn't hide it then, one man even hurried out the bathroom when he saw it. I think it was this man." Jess said as he pointed to the man asleep on the floor.

"What should we do?" she asked. "For starters, no more baths and keep it hidden. Second, you're not leaving my sight any more. I can't protect you if you're not with me. Also, I don't think we can trust anyone besides our friends." Linder replied. "I agree. I don't trust Sergeant Green, each time I'm around him the dragon pulls at my mind and I feel like he is hiding something. He might even be the killer." Jess whispered to Linder. Just then Sergeant Johnson tried to get into the room through the slightly opened door and saw the man on the floor. "What happened here? Is that man asleep?" Johnson asked in astonishment as the man on the floor snored. Johnson stepped over the man and into the room. Jess didn't know how to explain the odd scene. "Magic." Linder replied bluntly. Johnson looked between the sleeping man and Linder and Jess.

"Alright. We should take him to the General. Is it safe to wake him?" he asked. He acted like when the word magic was involved then that was the answer. There was no need for more explanation. "You should make sure he doesn't have any weapons and tie his hands before waking him." Linder stated. Johnson nodded and then searched the man and found two daggers on him that he handed to Linder, then while tying the sleeping man's hands together saw something black on his arm. Johnson pushed the man's sleeve up and there on the sleeping man's arm was a tattoo of a black dragon very similar to the one on Jess's arm. "Black Dragon!" Johnson exclaimed in disgust. "You two are lucky to be alive. Anyone with that mark is evil. They will kill first then ask questions later. What was he doing here?" Sergeant Johnson asked. "He was after Jess. Being the Northstin Wind, she can destroy what he stands for so he came to kill her. Luckily her magic stopped him." Linder explained. Johnson nodded, accepting Linder's reply then attempted to wake the sleeping man. He didn't wake up. Johnson shook the man, yelled in his ear, and getting angrier by the minute even kicked the man in the gut but the man wouldn't rise. Jess bent down next to the man and stopped the magic that was running through his body and told the man to wake up.

Jess saw a slight flicker around the man as the magic left his body and instantly then man woke up and tried to get to his feet, but noticed his arms were tied and then groaned in pain and curled into a ball, his stomach obviously hurting him from where Johnson had kicked him. "What going on? Release me now!" the man shouted. "Release me or you'll pay the price!" he yelled as he regained his composure and got to his feet awkwardly. "Be quiet!" Sergeant Johnson stated as he grabbed the man by the shirt and led the struggling man into the hallway and then into the General's room. Jess saw a look of anger cross Sergeant Green's face as Sergeant Johnson pushed the Black Dragon man passed him into the room. The look seemed to be directed at the prisoner. Jess's arm throbbed as she passed Sergeant Green, making her grab her arm with the opposite hand to try to ease the pain.

Once she entered the room she saw that everyone had returned except the General. They had brought their pillows and blankets to the room along with the few packs that the group had brought with them. Jess realized that she had forgotten her pillow and blanket in her room. Linder escorted her back to her bedroom, refusing the aid of Sergeant Smith. Telling him that he should stay and help watch the Black Dragon. As soon as Linder and Jess were alone in Jess's room he pulled her into his arms and kissed her on the lips. She returned the kiss. "Are you okay?" he asked pulling her closer. "Yeah I'm fine." Jess replied as she took pleasure in the embrace. "Really?" he asked. "Yes really." She replied. "Good. Please tell me when you're suffering though. I will try to help." Linder stated. "I will." Jess replied. Linder put one arm around her waist and pulled her body against his. He leaned in, weaved his other hand into long blonde hair which was braided from top to bottom and passionately kissed her. Afterwards he offered to carry her pillow and blanket. Hand in hand together they went back to the general's room. The General had not returned yet but Johnson, Smith and Green had tied the Black Dragon prisoner to a chair with bed sheets that they had twisted into ropes and had their swords drawn towards him. His sleeved had been pushed up to the top of his arm, giving a good view of the black dragon tattooed on his arm.

Dumas was sitting on the floor in a corner reading a small book labeled The Tale of Two Treasures. He didn't seem to notice anything that was happening in the room. Randy and Erika were sitting next to each other on the large bed, hands embraced together while Marcus stood leaning against the wall near the window. He was watching the three officers and their prisoner. Jess squeezed Linder's hand as they walked past the prisoner and the officers. She could feel the dragon inside her watching through her eyes. Watching and waiting for the perfect time to take control of her mind and body. Her arm stung in pain where the black dragon tattoo was on her skin so she gripped Linder's hand tighter. He looked at her and thought he knew what was happening. They hadn't been in the room more than a minute when Linder placed his arm around her waist and led her out of the room, down the hall and down a set of stairs. The farther away from the room they went the less the dragon pried at her mind and the easier it was to ease the pain and gain control.

"Thank you." Jess told Linder once they were on the main floor of the palace. "You're welcome. I could tell you needed to get away from that room, or was it was it the people?" Linder asked. "The Black Dragon man was really enticing the black dragon inside me. I am also almost sure that Sergeant Green is a Black Dragon. I haven't trusted him from the start and every time I am around him the dragon inside me tries to take control and my arm hurts intensely.

Marcus, Erika and I also caught him with something on his hands and sweat beaded his face when we unlocked his door. He was awake and was acting very suspicious. Then the next time we saw him he had gloves on to cover his hands and he was the one that suggested that we stay here instead of doing what the General suggested at first. I don't trust him at all." Jess concurred. "Neither do I. I felt the same way about him when he suggested that we stay here. I don't think that we are safe here, first an officer is killed and then a guard is killed and you and Marcus heard two men plotting against us and then you were almost killed a few minutes ago because someone knew about the black dragon on your arm.

We need to figure out what to do. You can't go back in that room. I'm afraid that would be too difficult for you and you wouldn't be able to control the dragon from taking control and the pain it would cause you. Also I think that would rouse too many questions. There is no way we are going to sleep the rest of the night. We need to find an empty room to stay in together until morning." Linder proposed. "We will need to tell someone though so that everyone doesn't come looking for us." Jess replied.

Just then General Jackson rounded a corner in the hallway and appeared in front of them holding a small candle in his hand. Jess jumped at the site of him. "Sorry for scaring you. I couldn't help but over hear your conversation. Can you explain something for me though? What is this about you having a black dragon on your arm? I thought only members of the Black Dragons had those." General Jackson inquired suspiciously. "It's a long story but someone was forced to place the dragon on Jess when it was just a small dot. With the power of magic it has and using the magic Jess has its spread and has become a black dragon and is slowly taking control of her mind and eventually her body. It will kill her if we don't find a way to get it off. The dragon has an existence in her mind, it can sense when other black dragons are around and tries to take control of her mind.

It causes her great pain on her arm and in her mind. Dumas is the only other one that knows about it and is searching for a cure. We didn't want to scare the others so we haven't told them about it. We aren't sure how they would react. Jess isn't part of the Black Dragons and never would be but she has been cursed with the mark of black dragons and the living dragon that resides inside her is a constant battle that she is trying to win." Linder explained. The General listened intently. When Linder finished the General looked between Linder and Jess. "I believe you. May I see it?" he asked. Jess rolled up her sleeve to expose the black dragon tattooed on her arm. The General stared at the sight. It was unlike anything he had seen before. He had killed a number of Black Dragon assassins all of which had dragons tattooed either on the faces, bald heads or their arms but none looked as menacing and deadly as the one that was on Jess's arm.

The dragon was as black as midnight and looked as if it were clinging itself to her Jess's skin. It's sharp front talons looked to be dug into her wrist while its long black jaggedly body weaved its way up to her elbow where its spiked tail wrapped around her elbow and ran up to the middle of her upper arm. The dragon's wings were spread outwards wrapping around to the underside of her arm which ended with pointed tips. The dragon's mouth was open with numerous fangs bared and ready to strike. It had black soulless eyes that seemed to suck the light from the world. There were two small red blood stains that were tattooed onto her skin right under the dragon's fangs as if the blood had dropped off the fangs and onto her skin where they join in a puddle.

"What do the blood drops mean?" General Jackson asked as he inspected the terrible creature that invaded her arm. "I have been told that they represent two people that I will kill." Jess replied. "I see. Do you know who those people are?" General Jackson asked calmly. "No. I don't want to kill anyone. But if I have too then it better be while protecting someone else." Jess answered directly. "Well said. I believe the only time killing is alright is when you are protecting the ones you love, even if it means killing someone you thought you trusted." General Jackson confirmed with a hint of regret in his voice.

"Sergeant Green?" Linder asked. "Yes. I had my suspicions about him from the first time I met him. He was not originally one of my men. He was transferred into my squadron about two months ago and I have tried many times but I have not been able to fully trust him. There was always something that bothered me about him. The choices he made, the people he was so eagerly willing to kill, the lack of sympathy, the knowledge he shared with us about the Black Dragons always turned out false and then his actions tonight proved to me that I really could not trust him. He was very adamant about all of you staying here when he knew that you would be safer away from the palace. He went against my judgment. The only reason I went along with his plan so that I would have more time to uncover his true intentions." General Jackson explained.

Jess thought about using her magic to uncover what Sergeant Green's true feelings were but that would that require getting closer to the Black Dragon spy and she didn't know if she would be strong enough to resist the dragon inside her being that close to not one but two Black Dragon spies. The dragon inside her hungered for the hate, rage and evil that existed in the Black Dragon men, which had more power and control over her whenever she was around them. But if she could get Sergeant Green away from the other man she could use her powers to read his emotions and then she could confirm the suspicions about him.

"General, I have an idea. If we could lure Sergeant Green away from everyone else I could use my powers to read his emotions and then I could tell you what his true intentions are." Jess offered. "You could do that?" General Jackson replied hopefully. "Yes." "That would be wonderful. I will order him to come and find you and to bring you back to my bedroom." The General replied. "General, what are you going to do with him if he is a Black Dragon spy?" Linder inquired as he held onto Jess's hand. "Same thing we are going to do with the Black Dragon spy that was disguised as a servant. I believe you have already subdued him." The General remarked. "How did you know?" Jess asked. "Earlier this evening while Jess was taking a bath I saw a servant rush out of the bathing room, I followed him until he entered a room and closed the door behind himself. I listened as two men spoke together in hushed tones. Most of the words were to low and muffled to understand but I was certain the other voice in the room was Sergeant Green's. The only words I could make out were "We will do it after midnight."

I informed the other officers and told them to stay alert. I didn't want to show my suspicions to Sergeant Green so I retired to my bedroom until you all came in to warn me. By that time Sergeant Johnson had already informed me that Sergeant Green had left his bedroom an hour prior and had not returned. When the incident with Lieutenant Daniels and the palace guard happened I knew I was too late. I should have been out there waiting for the killers but I decided to wait for them to come to me. That was the wrong move. After that I knew I had to go looking for the killers.

I left Sergeant Green alone there for a reason. I acted like I was leaving but waited on the edge of the stairs to see what would happen. I had no idea that the Black Dragon spy was still there but once he was apprehended and pushed past Sergeant Green I saw the look of familiarity, and treachery cross his face. Promptly I set off to warn the king and queen about them. Once done I was heading back to the bedrooms to interrogate the prisoner and see if I could somehow prove that Sergeant Green is also part of the Black Dragons. But if you could make him admit or somehow prove that he is a Black Dragon then we can solve this matter resolutely." General Jackson explained. "Yes I can." Jess replied.

"What will happen to them?" Linder requested. "They will be interrogated, imprisoned and then put do death if found to be truly be members of the Black Dragons." General Jackson informed them. "Okay." Linder responded. "I will go and send Sergeant Green and Johnson down to find you that is when you use your powers of him. Get him to prove that he is a Black Dragon then Sergeant Johnson will immediately apprehend him. I trust Sergeant Johnson completely so once this matter is completed than the remainder of the night should be calm then it is yours to do what you please." The General imparted. "Okay. I'm ready." Jess stated as she lowered her sleeve to cover the dragon tattoo on her arm and placed her hand in Linder's once more. The general nodded then left the Jess and Linder alone in the dark hallway. Linder held a small candle in his left hand that flickered slowly while his right hand was nestled into Jess's hand. They decided not to leave the spot they were at until after their encounter with the two sergeants that would be coming to them shortly.

Chapter Thirteen- Interrogation

A few minutes later they heard footsteps coming toward them. Jess took off walking towards the oncoming soldiers. She knew what she needed to do and even though her arm was starting to hurt the closer the soldiers drew near; she was determined to follow through with her plan. Jess had whispered her plan to Linder right after General Jackson had left them alone. Right as Jess saw the soldiers her plan began. "Finally, you found us. Sergeant Green, will you please take me away from this man, he has no respect for women. Do you think that you could show me the way back to the General's room." Jess asked as she wrapped her arm around Sergeant Green's arm. "Jess wait. I didn't mean it" Linder pleaded. "That's too bad. You have hurt me one too many times. Sergeant Green is a much better man than you ever will be. I am going with him." Jess scorned then turned her attention to Sergeant Green. "Please take me away." She asked. "Yes ma'am." He replied with a hint a satisfaction in his voice. "Jess, no! Please stay with me." Linder called out to her. Jess could hear the pain in his voice and hoped that Sergeant Green believed it was real. Jess ignored Linder and let the sergeant lead her away.

Linder caught Sergeant Johnson arm and held him back and whispered to him. "We think Sergeant Green is a Black Dragon, Jess is tricking him and going to use her power on him to find out whether he is or not. We need to stay back but still close enough that we can help her if she needs it." Sergeant Johnson looked into Linder's blue eyes with the brown sunburst in the center and then responded. "Alright." Linder was glad that this man understood and trusted him. They started to follow Jess and Sergeant Green while keeping their distance. Jess stopped walking and leaned in closer to Sergeant Green.

"I have a secret. Can I show it to you?" she asked seductively. "Will I like it? He asked fascinated with her. "I think you will." She replied then ran her fingers down her blouse. "What is it?" he asked as he lusted over her. "This." Jess stated and pushed her right sleeve up to the top of her arm, revealing the black dragon tattooed on her arm. She turned her arm over and over as if showing off the dragon. "Do you like it?" she asked seductively. "You're a Black Dragon." He stated starring at the tattoo on her arm. "Yes. Aren't you? I was certain that you were. I would love it if you were. Tell me that you are." She stated boldly as she pushed her magic outwards and into his body. She instantly felt the hate that raged inside his body, the lust he had for her and the desire to kill. "Well are you a Black Dragon or not?" Jess demanded after a moment of silence, and then pushed more of her powers at him.

Sergeant Green looked straight into her eyes which were only a few inches away from his then replied. "Yes I am but don't announce it. I need the General to believe that I am loyal to his pitiful little army until the time comes when I can destroy him." Sergeant Green admitted and ran his fingers along Jess's arm. "That is wonderful." Jess cooed sadistically and pressed her body into his. Then without warning Jess pulled Sergeant Green's dagger from his belt and stabbed him in the leg with his own dagger then backed away. He screamed in pain and reached for his wound and pulled out the dagger. Just then Linder and Sergeant Johnson rounded the corner. Linder embraced Jess while Johnson took the dagger from Sergeant Green and took a piece of rope from his belt and tied Sergeant Green's hands together. He then pointed the bloody dagger right at Sergeant Green's face. "Walk!" Sergeant Johnson demanded. Sergeant Green had to limp but walked where he was led. Linder hugged Jess and told her that he was very glad that her plan had worked and that he was glad that she was safe and unharmed. Sergeant Johnson led Sergeant Green through the palace back to General Jackson's room. Linder and Jess followed.

The General was waiting with an empty chair and extra rope. "Put him there." He told Sergeant Johnson as they entered the room. The General and Sergeant Johnson tied Sergeant Green to the empty chair as he struggled to get away and yelled profanities and threats at them. Everyone else was still is the same positions that Jess and Linder had left them. Just then the General punched Sergeant Green right in the stomach. "Shut up!" the General demanded. Sergeant Green tried to double over in pain but being tied to the chair prevented him from moving. "He won't tell you anything." The first Black Dragon spy said cockily. "We will never answer your questions." He spat. The dragon inside Jess tried to take control over her mind but she grit her teeth together and fought it. She was not going to lose control. The dragon wanted her mind, and he wanted her body as a vessel to grow into a full size dragon and Jess would not let that happen.

"Where is your master? What are his plans? Answer me." The General demanded at the Black Dragon spy and Sergeant Green. There came no answer. "Where is your base located?" the General demanded. "Where are the people you have taken from us? Where do you keep your prisoners?" The General loudly commanded. He was losing his patients. The last question struck a nerve with Jess. She desperately wanted to know where they had taken her grandma and brother along with everyone else's loved ones. The two prisoners sat stoned faced tied to the chairs not replying. Just then she had an idea for making the prisoner respond.

"Erika and Marcus, could you join me in the hall for a minute?" Jess asked. Linder looked at Jess as she started to pull her hand away. Jess smiled that special smile that she gave only him. The smile that told him that she loved him and that everything was going to be okay. He released her hand and she, Erika and Marcus went out into the hall, taking a lit candle with them.

Once out of earshot from anyone in General Jackson's room, Jess told them that she had a plan to get the Black Dragon prisoners to answer their questions. "What do you have in mind?" Marcus asked inquisitively. "Terrible weather, monstrous creatures and a push of emotions." Jess replied with her mischievous smile.

"Use our magic on them?" Erika asked wearily. "Exactly. Erika will change the weather drastically from one thing to another, Marcus will create illusions of some of the terrible creatures that we have seen and fought, which will hopefully scare them while I push my magic at them to convince them they have to answer our questions or they will get attacked or killed." Jess stated. "I'm in. This sounds like a lot of fun." Marcus replied smiling. "I don't know Jess. That sounds kind of mean." Erika responded. "Maybe but I think it will work. I need answers from them Erika. I need to know where they have taken my grandma and Zander. I need to know where their master is so that we can find him and kill him." Jess stated. "Okay, I'll do it." Erika answered reluctantly.

"Here's what I think we should do. We will all go back into the room and act normal for a few minutes. That's when Erika will start a storm inside the room. Everyone act surprised, like you have nothing to do with it. At the same time Marcus will make a monster, oh a Therion, appear in the room. Make it prowl around the doorway for a minute and roar if you can, then it will act like it's going to attack them. But stop it right before it pounces. I will be pouring fear into them and then I will ask them the questions one more time. They should be so scared for their lives that they will answer. Whether they answer the questions or not make your monster "attack" them then disappear. I want the storm to be so terrible that no one will be able to tell that this monster is an illusion. I want everyone to squirm in fear thinking that the devil creature really is there." Jess stated.

"What about the General? He wouldn't squirm in fear; he would jump up and try to kill the beast." Erika pointed out. "So would Randy, and Johnson." Marcus interjected. "Erika you tell Randy, Marcus you tell Johnson and I will tell the General not to fight it but just to act scared. Whisper it to them so that the prisoners don't hear. We need everyone to seem genuinely scared until after the prisoner answer our questions." Jess replied. "Jess what if they still won't answer our questions?" Erika inquired, and then tucked her wavy brown hair behind her ears.

"Then we leave it up to the General but he said that they will be killed for the crimes they have committed being Black Dragons. This has to work; we have to get them to talk or they will be killed and we will never know where they take their prisoners." Jess admitted. "Alright let's do it." Erika complied. Marcus nodded. "Let's do it."

The three went back into the General's room. Dumas looked up from his book as they entered. He caught Jess's gaze then looked back down at his book. He smiled, closed the book, and pushed it quickly into a small leather bag that Jess didn't recognize then put the bag inside his large black furry cloak that lay on the floor next to where he sat. Jess thought that he just might know what was about to happen. She stood next to Linder, while the others resumed their original positions in the room. The General and Sergeant Jackson were still attempting to get the Black Dragon prisoners to answer their questions. Just then Jess felt a small raindrop hit her on the head. She looked up with a confused expression on her face which was just for show because she knew that soon it would be pouring rain along with whatever else Erika is going to conjure inside the room. Erika whispered something to Randy. Marcus whispered something to Johnson who then whispered something to the General.

The General glanced at Jess for a second then turned his attention back to the Black Dragons. Seconds later another drop of rain and then another hit Jess's head, then the rain started pouring. "What is going on?" The General demanded. His face was red from the frustration of trying to get the Black Dragon prisoners to answer his questions. "Erika, are you doing this?" Jess asked indifferently. "No. I don't know what is going on. It's not me." she replied innocently. Dark clouds grew along the ceiling which spilled down the walls. Fog spread throughout the room while the rain poured out of the dark clouds drenching everyone and everything inside the General's bedroom. Just then the door flew open. Jess thought that Marcus must have moved over there and thrown it open for dramatics.

There came a ferocious roar that ran chills down Jess's spine. Even though she knew it was fake it still scared her. Then the beast from her nightmare came stalking into the room, its large dark furry form loomed in the foggy air. Jess screamed in fear. Everyone scrambled to the far side of the room behind the prisoners that were tied to the chairs. All the men drew their weapons, even though they knew it wasn't real. The massive furry beast slowly moved its way towards the prisoners, sniffing and roaring as it drew near the prisoners. Jess moved out of the group of people and stood between the beast with its glowing red eyes and the Black Dragon prisoners. Facing the Black Dragons she yelled over the sound of the rain and the monster. "Where do you take your prisoners?" she demanded as the rage inside her flared.

"I will never tell you!" Sergeant Green spat. "In the woods the dragons know the way." The first Black Dragon cried. "There are no dragons. Don't lie to me! Where do you take your prisoners?" Jess yelled. "The black dragons on our bodies, they show us were to go. Don't let it kill me." the man pleaded as he looked past Jess towards the Therion. Jess moved from standing in front of him to the side of the chair. All of a sudden the huge Therion bounded right towards the two prisoners. Both prisoners screamed in terror. The beast went right through them and vanished. Erika stopped the storm abruptly. The rain stopped, the clouds and fog disappeared, and the sound of thunder and the roar of the beast vanished. The room was back to normal except for the fact that everything was soaking wet. Water dripped from the bed posts, it dripped from their clothes, and there were small puddles that had formed on the floor that they stepped in. Luckily the sun was starting to rise so the rays of light seeped into the room, giving them the ability to see the room and the people that occupied it. All of a sudden the temperature began to rise, it got hotter and hotter and then a warm wind blew through the air. Soon everyone was drying off. They were still wet but at least water wasn't dripping from their clothes anymore.

Linder offered Jess a blanket and pointed to her white shift that she wore. It had gotten wet and was now see through. Randy did the same for Erika. Jess wrapped the blanket around herself then turned her attention to the prisoners. To Jess's surprise Sergeant Green's eyes changed colors right before her, changing from brown to completely black. His skin seemed to ripple. Before Jess could do or say anything a dagger hit him in the chest. His eyes flickered to their original color and a look of remorse crossed his face and then his head drooped and there came no movement from him. "Don't kill me! Please don't kill me!" the other man cried. Everyone turned their heads to the direction of where the dagger came from. There standing in the open door way stood a man who looked to be in his earlier forties with short brown hair, brown eyes and a small brown beard. He was wearing dark brown trousers, with a tan buckskin blouse that had four buttons at the top of the shirt, two of which were unbuttoned. He wore an animal skin cloak that looked as if he hadn't been properly washed in some time and very dirty brown boots.

"Jusdan?" Erika, Jess, Linder and Marcus all asked at the same time. "No time to explain." He said and pushed his way into the room. He went straight to the dead Sergeant Green, pulled out his dagger from the man's chest and turned to the prisoner. "Is there anything else we need to know about?" he asked the man. "No! The Black Dragons inside will show you the way. Please don't kill me." the man sobbed. "That's what my two children said before you killed them!" Jusdan fumed. "It wasn't me." the man sobbed. "Not you personally but all Black Dragons are the same." Jusdan said and with that he stabbed the prisoner in the heart with his dagger. He pulled his dagger free and wiped it on the man's wet clothes then put it back onto his weapons belt. He started to leave the room but Marcus stopped him. "I'm sorry about your children." Marcus said. Jusdan nodded then left the room. "Well it looks like the night is over, why don't we meet downstairs for breakfast." The General said as if nothing unusual had happened. Dumas un-wrapped his book and carried it with him out of the room as he headed downstairs. Marcus left then Sergeant Johnson. The General looked back at the dead men then thanked Jess for her bravery then left the room.

"We can't go down there wearing these." Jess said to Erika indicating their see through white shifts. "Your right. I have the dress they gave me yesterday I could wear but what about you?" Erika asked. "They took my clothes to wash them so I don't have anything else to wear." Jess replied. "Yes you do. I have clothes in my pack that you could wear. That is as long as you're okay wearing men's clothes." Linder teased. "I think that will be alright." Jess replied smiling. She preferred to wear men's clothes over women's dresses. "Good then let's go get changed and meet downstairs." Erika stated. Jess nodded. Linder grabbed his pack from the floor. "Let's go in a different room." He suggested. Jess looked over at the two dead bodies that were still tied to the chairs. "Yeah." She replied. Randy and Erika left the General's room and went into Erika's room together. Linder took Jess into his room a few doors down the hall. Once inside he closed the door and turned to Jess. "You know you have a knack for making me fall in love with you over and over again." Linder said softly as he pulled her closer to him.

He leaned down and kissed her forehead and then he pressed his lips to hers. She wrapped her arms around his neck and kissed him again. "I wish we were married. I want to love you and fulfill all your desires." Linder said softly to Jess. "In our hearts we're already married." Jess replied as she ran her fingers through his brown hair. "In our hearts we may be but physically we are not. I will not dishonor you." Linder replied removing his hands from her. "Thank you." she replied. "I cannot explain how badly I want to prove my love to you right now but first we are not married yet and second everyone downstairs will be waiting for us and I think they might get suspicious if we don't get down there soon." Linder stated.

"You're probably right." Jess answered then slowly stepped back away from Linder. "Okay I will wait for you outside your door." Linder replied then let go of Jess's hand and retrieved some clothes from inside his pack and handed them to her. She took the clothes and he left the room. She dressed in tan trousers, a long sleeved brown button up blouse which she buttoned all the buttons except the very top one. She still had on the green stockings but she didn't have any shoes to wear. The servants had taken her boots to clean them. Jess wished she had them back now. As soon as she was dressed she opened the door and Linder pulled her into his arms and kissed her lovingly.

Chapter Fourteen- Breakfast with Royalty

When they reached the dining room they found everyone there except Erika and Randy. Amongst their friends were a few faces that Jess didn't recognize. General Jackson directed them to sit down at two empty chairs at the table. Dumas, whom had a small collection of books on the table next to him, along with Marcus, Sergeant Johnson and General Jackson all sat at the table. Next to General Jackson sat a lovely looking woman. The woman looked to be older than General Jackson but had smooth pale brown skin and flowing long dark brown hair. Instantly Jess knew who this was. "You're the queen, aren't you?" Jess asked while trying not to stare at the beautiful woman. "Yes I am. My name is Sierra. How did you know?" the woman replied softly. "You look just like…."Jess started to say but couldn't finish her sentence. Jess started to feel sick. How could she tell the queen that her daughter Adaze was killed by a beast that tore her apart in many pieces?

"Excuse me." Jess said then left the room. Linder quickly followed. "Jess, what's wrong?" he asked when he caught up to her. "The queen." "What about her?" "Even though she is a queen she is a mother too. How can I tell her that her daughter wasn't just killed but torn into pieces and eaten by a monster and that she will never see her daughter again? Linder I can't do that. That's not fair for me to have to tell her that and then ask for control of her entire army. I don't think that will go over very well." Jess implied. "I think I have something that might just help us with that." Linder remarked then he pulled something shiny out of a pocket from his trousers. He held it up so Jess could see what it was. Jess gasped.

It was an exquisite diamond necklace, around the entire necklace diamonds hung by small chains which were connected to the chain that went around the necklace. It was the necklace that Adaze was wearing when she got killed by the Therion. Jess had found Adaze's head with the necklace entangled in its hair and took it with her. Hoping to return it to Adaze's family one day and also hoping that it would help convince them to trust her let her take control of the Northstin Army.

She had put it in her pack but when they went into Jensen city Jess had to leave her pack in the woods and wasn't able to return for it. "How did you get this?" Jess asked astonished that Linder had it with him. "When I got my pack and took the food from yours I found it and thought it might be useful so I took it. I didn't even know that you had it." Linder replied as he handed the necklace to Jess. "Jess you are most determined and bravest woman I have ever met. You have faced many types of terrible creatures including the battle that you face right now with the dragon inside you. I know you can do this. I will be there for you the whole time." Linder offered. "Okay" Jess remarked as she gathered her courage for what laid ahead. Together they went back into the room. As soon as they were seated again Erika and Randy entered the room before Jess could say anything. Randy bowed and greeted the queen and king. The king sat on the other side of the queen. Even though Jess had never met a queen or king before she would not have guessed that this couple was the rulers of a country.

The queen wore a blue blouse with a blue skirt that had dark brown flowers embroidered on it. She had a silver necklace on that held two gems on the end of the chain. One gem was blue that matched her blouse while the other was silver. The king wore the same military outfit as the soldiers which consisted of a bright red military jacket that had two rows of buttons running down the front it, black pants, and a dark green cloak. His cloak was decorated with more stars than Jess had seen on any of the other military men. "Are you alright my dear?" Queen Sierra asked Jess. After a short pause then Jess replied. "Yes I am fine. Thank you but I do have something to tell you." "Go on." The queen insisted.

"It's about the princess Adaze." "Oh, you have word of her. Is she alright? Is she on her way home? She has found you and the prophet and now is she returning home to us?" Queen Sierra enthusiastically asked. Jess looked at the people around the table. Marcus, Randy, and Erika lowered their eyes. Jess caught Linder's eyes and knew she had to tell them the bad news. The King, Queen Sierra, General Jackson and Sergeant Johnson all looked toward Jess, hoping for good news.

"Princess Adaze is dead. She will never be coming home. I'm sorry." Jess stated. "Were you there? Do you know this for certain?" the King inquired. "I was there." Randy interjected looking between Jess and the King.

"We thought we were helping a lost woman find a way out of the forest. It turned out to be a terrible creature called a Therion that takes the form of its last victim. We followed the women unnoticing that she led us right into its territory. She told us that we should make camp there for the night. Some of my men didn't like the idea but most didn't question and started unpacking their sleeping pads. The strange woman had enticed my men with magic. Princess Adaze turned to me for direction since I was the highest ranking officer and she relied on me to help her accomplish our mission. I trusted my men's judgment and decided that we should set up camp there. We all became relaxed, and carefree. The sun was starting to set, and it with it came the cold so I decided to go off into the forest to collect wood for a fire. I had one other man accompany me. As soon as we left the rest of the men, it seemed as if a cloud of fog was lifted from my mind and I could think clearly. That is when the screams started. I glanced at the man I was with, and then we both ran back to the others. It seemed to take an extremely long time to reach the others; I hadn't realized how far we had gone. The sight we returned to was something far worse than any nightmare." Randy said solemnly. "What happened to Adaze?" Queen Sierra asked with sadness and horror creeping into her voice.

"My military instincts took over and I quickly assessed the situation. The other officer I was with went to help someone that had fallen and that was the last time I saw him. There were....." he stumbled over the words. Erika placed her hand on his. "There were bloody body parts strewn all over the area, staining the ground a dark red. The men fought bravely but were no match for the beasts and were ripped apart in moments.

I quickly saw that the princess wasn't there and the men that weren't fighting the terrible beasts were trying to help the wounded. I asked a man that was lying on the ground near the edge of the clearing that was closest to me if he knew where the princess had gone. I assumed the worse. The man told me that one of the other officers grabbed her arm and they ran into the forest together. The man that answered me was wounded bad, knowing I couldn't help him at the moment I started to walk away to help the men fighting the beasts. The man grabbed my ankle and with shallow breathing he told me something that ran shivers down my spine. He said, "The woman is the beast. They are people, anyone. Don't trust anyone. It was a trap." After that his grip went limp and he died.

I knew I had to find the princess but I had to help my men first. I drew my sword and ran to help the men that were fighting the beasts. It was so horrible, most of my men didn't have the skills that I do and were cut down easily. I received many scratches while fighting the first beast. With the help of a couple other men, we killed the first beast. That seemed to make the other beast furious because it became even more savage and went on a rampage and started swinging its deadly claws around, slashing through men as it went. I tried to attack the beast but after losing my sword during the fight with the other beast, all I had left was a dagger. The beast swung its claws at me, I tried to jump out of the way but it got my leg. I lost my dagger when jumping out of the way. I landed on the ground and felt an incredibly sharp pain shoot through my leg.

Knowing I couldn't fight like that and with no weapons I decided the best thing I could do for myself and for those who survived was to runaway. If I hadn't then I would be dead now. I thought that I could go back for any survivors after I took care of my leg and I needed to find the princess and keep her safe. As I left the sounds of men screaming in pain and the terrible ear piercing roar that came from the beasts along with the bloody sight of everything was starting to make me feel sick.

I was able to get away from the gruesome sight and made my way north. I was hoping to find the princess with the officer that took her away. I kept traveling through the night, but no matter how far away I got, I could still hear the painful screams coming from my men. My leg throbbed with pain but I knew I couldn't stop. I kept going until a few hours past morning when my injured leg wouldn't work anymore and exhaustion took over. These people found me, and when trying to help me find the princess and a way out of the forest we encountered another Therion." Randy explained. Jess could see that he was having a hard time explaining the story so she joined in. "As Randy explained Therion's take the form of their last victim. Well the Therion that we encountered looked just like Princess Adaze. It looked, talked and acted just like the princess. Except it wasn't the princess. Therion's use a sort of hypnotic power to lure people near them. Everyone was under its spell except me.

I felt like something wasn't right so I decided to go for a walk and that is when with a little help I found the real princess's head and what remained of her body in a bush. I also found this." Jess stated and held up the necklace that she had taken from the corpse. Queen Sierra gasped then turned her head towards her husband. Jess handed it to the king's open outstretched hand. "Thank you." He replied softly as he took the necklace from her.

"I am truly sorry about your daughter. She was very brave to venture away from home to find someone who she didn't even know existed or where to find them. That was truly a remarkable task. In a way she succeeded. I am the Northstin Wind and I am here to fulfill the prophecy. If it would be alright I would like to have control of the Northstin Army so that I may fulfill the prophecy and avenge her death." Jess proclaimed. "Yes of course. Anything you need will be at your disposal. Just name it." The King replied while trying to comfort his wife. General Jackson cleared his throat. Jess looked over at him. His eyes were red as if he would start crying at any moment.

"I would be honored if you would allow me to be your General in command." He stated and bowed his head. "That would be perfect. Thank you." Jess remarked. Just then a servant came rushing into the dining room. She bowed and apologized for being late. "We will finish discussing this matter after breakfast." The King insisted to Jess then ordered the servant to fetch breakfast for all of them.

No one spoke during breakfast, which consisted of pancakes, bacon and a bowl of oatmeal. They had cold milk to drink. Once everyone was done eating their fill and the dishes were cleaned away. The king rose from his chair. "I have come to a decision." He announced after all of the servants had exited the room. "I have been thinking about everything we have been told about the Black Dragons, the black magic creatures and along with everything that we already knew about the black plague and I have come to a decision regarding your request on taking control of the Northstin Army." The King said to Jess. "We sent many squadrons out into the unknown world to find the one known as the Northstin Wind and the Prophet, because we believe that those people will fulfill the prophecy and destroy the Black Dragons and rid our great city of the blackness that plagues us. I have not known you for more than a few hours but I believe you are who you say you are and I have heard of the many brave deeds that you both have accomplished and hence forth I proclaim Lady Jess and Sir Linder to be co-commanders of the Northstin Army.

Work together and use the army as you wish. But head my warning, if you turn against my kingdom and use the army for evil or to harm any of my citizens then I will be forced to terminate your lives. I also require that my son be your lead general. He has much experience and can offer valuable advice." The king stated. "We graciously accept, except who is your son? I do have a problem with that though because I already said that General Jackson would be the general in command." Jess replied. "I am his son." General Jackson interjected. "You're his son?" Jess asked. "Yes I am. I have the white skin and brown hair like my father while my sister had the brown skin and dark hair like my mother." General Jackson explained. "Oh. Well I accept then." Jess admitted.

"Good. We will have the official ceremony later today. Also I hear that we are in need of another type of ceremony for you and Linder. One involving a priest." The King stated with a sly grin on his face. Jess blushed.

Linder took her hand into his. "We want to wait until we can have all of our families there to celebrate with us." Linder explained. "Well we can send some men for them. They could all be here within a few months. That would give you time to destroy the Black Dragons." Queen Sierra interjected. "I wish it were that easy." Linder replied. Jess and Linder lowered their eyes. "Do you also have loved ones that were killed by the Black Dragons?" the queen asked softly. "Not killed, captured." Jess replied. "Oh I am so sorry." Queen Sierra replied. "We will never stop until we have rescued all those who have been captured and we won't get married until we can have all of our family there." Linder commented. "I respect that and admire your determination. I think that the army is going to be in good hands." The king affirmed as scratched his brown beard.

"What is lost is lost and cannot be brought back so we will remember and cherish what we had and look forward to what the future may bring. Today will be a day of mourning for the fallen princess and the brave soldiers that fought to protect her and gave their lives so that the world will be rid of the black plague. They were wonderful people and deserve a day of respect. Tomorrow morning we shall have a feast and have the ceremony in which I officially proclaim you both as leaders of the Northstin Army. But in the mean time please feel free to explore the city. Meet the people and get to know the soldiers that you will be commanding. If there is anything that you need to buy whether it be provisions and just something for yourself just tell the merchants that the I am paying for it and they will give it to you. I am always good on my word about paying the merchants; if not for them then our city wouldn't strive." The king instructed.

"What about the dead bodies upstairs?" Marcus interjected. "Those were taken care of while we ate breakfast. Does anyone want to explain what really happened to those men? I was only informed that there were two dead bodies that needed disposed of in General Jackson's room." The king imparted. There was silence for a long moment. General Jackson stood. "Those men were Black Dragons. They attempted to murder all of us on that floor; they plotted to kill you, and killed two of our guards. They admitted to being Black Dragons and hence forth were killed for their crimes." General Jackson described. "Are you the one that killed them?" the king asked looking into his son's brown eyes. "No." "But you allowed it to happen?" "Yes Sir. I believed it was the right thing to do." "As do I. Wise decision." The king confirmed obviously proud of his son's decision. "Thank you sir." General Jackson remarked.

"I do have one request. I do not want anyone to know about last night or the idea that there are Black Dragons here in the city. That would cause a panic through the city that is something that we just could not control right now. Everyone is already on edge with the occasional Black Dragon, and the unexplained murders and disappearances. I think it will be better if we don't tell anyone how bad the situation is really becoming." The king insisted. Everyone nodded their heads and agreed not to tell anyone. "Well I think it's time to tell the citizens that Princess Adaze is dead, but she succeeded in finding and bringing the Northstin Wind and Prophet to us." The king stated and rose from his chair. The queen followed and rose from her chair. "I think you are right, husband. Let us mourn our lost daughter today and tomorrow we will celebrate what she has accomplished." Queen Sierra replied and then excused herself from the dining room, but right before she left she instructed Jess to buy herself a dress to wear. "It's not right for women to wear men's clothing. You would be so much more beautiful if you wore a dress." She said and then left the room.

"Well enough talking. Let us proceed in our plans. The market will be opening shortly and I have to gather all the citizens together to make the announcement. Go explore the city, get to know the people, buy what you like, and then return here for dinner which will be served right before sunset. I insist that some of the men from the army accompany you to the city and I will post additional men in and around the palace. We don't want another incident like last night." The king explained. "I will accompany them." General Jackson replied as he stood. "As will I." Sergeant Johnson remarked as he stood. "Good that is settled then. If you would excuse me I have some arrangements I must take care now. Until this evening this is farewell." The king said. General Jackson and Sergeant Johnson bowed. That cued everyone else in and they bowed their heads as well then the king left the room. "Well before we do anything else, can I get my boots back? I can't very well go walk around the city in bare feet and no I won't wear heeled shoes. I would like my boots back." Jess imparted as she stood.

Linder, Randy, Jusdan, Marcus, Erika and Dumas also stood. "I will retrieve your boots and meet you by the main doors." General Jackson replied to Jess. "Sergeant, go and fetch some horses for us. Take them to the main doors until we arrive." General Jackson instructed Sergeant Johnson as they walked to the door. "Yes sir." Sergeant Johnson replied and left the room. General Jackson followed. Dumas had sat quietly through breakfast and the talk with the king and queen and the talk with the general. He stood holding a bundle of books all of which were about prophecies. Without saying a word he walked out the door.

"Is he always like that?" Jusdan asked as he scratched his brown beard. "He is a little odd but he usually will talk your ear off if you give him a chance." Marcus remarked. "I think something from those prophecy books is bothering him and he doesn't want to discuss it." Linder commented. "Well whatever it is, it's his business not ours." Jusdan acknowledged. "Unfortunately I think it is our business. I will try to talk to him later." Linder offered. "Are we going to stand around talking or get going?" Erika asked.

Erika wasn't usually bossy but sometimes her patience would run out and then she would expect everyone to get done what needs to be done instead of batting around the bush, wasting time that could be spent doing something productive. "Yeah let's go." Jess replied. With that everyone dispersed from the dining room. They followed each other until they reached the main door. There they found General Jackson waiting with a pair of clean boots in his hands. He handed them to Jess as soon as she got close. "Thanks, but I don't think these are mine, they're too clean." She replied and smiled. "They are yours." General Jackson replied straightly. "I know, I just can't remember the last time I saw them clean." Jess remarked then sat down on the ground and put her boots on and tied them tight. She was now ready for anything.

Once outside the palace they found eight brown horses standing in a row. Four servants held the reins to all the horses. Dumas and Sergeant Johnson were standing next to the horses. Dumas still had the books in his hands. "I presume you all know how to ride?" the general asked as he mounted the first horse. "Yeah we do." Marcus replied. "Good then pick a horse and mount up." The general instructed as he gripped his reins in his hands. Everyone did as they were told. Dumas was the last one to mount his horse because he tucked the prophecy books into a saddle bag on his horse before he mounted. "Everyone ready?" the general asked as he looked at the group. They all acknowledged then the general instructed them to follow him. Two by two the horse trotted down the road away from the palace. Jess glanced at Dumas who rode a horse behind her. He was being quiet, unusually quiet for his personality. His facial expression had a look of curiosity and worry on it at the same time. She really wanted to talk to him but didn't have the chance yet.

Just then a searing pain pulsed through her arm that seared from her arm through her heart. Her vision was going dark and blurred. She concentrated on her mind. She could see the dragon inside her pacing back and forth growling in anger inside the void of her mind. What had caused this? She had to keep control. Her vision darkened and darkened. Soon she couldn't see anything. She could feel that she was still sitting on her horse but didn't know for how much longer that was going to last. Without her vision and the pain searing her body she was sure she was going to fall off the horse. She tried to focus on the terrible black dragon inside her mind. It looked to be far away but close at the same time.

Space was irrelevant in her mind. "I will never give in." she screamed. Whether the sound was just in her mind or if she was actually screaming she couldn't tell. "I will never stop fighting." She screamed at the dragon. Just then the dragon stopped pacing and starred directly at her. It seemed to be drawing nearer to her. She wanted to run away but inside her mind she didn't have anywhere to run. The dragon grew larger and larger as it came closer. Soon the black dragon with its sharp front talons, black jaggedly body, spiked tail, black pointed wings sprawled openly, black soulless eyes and giant fangs were only a few feet away from her face. She stood her ground.

Chapter Fifteen- Revelation

"You cannot resist me forever. I have control of you, both mind and body. You can never win against me. You will be mine!" said a voice, not from the dragon but from somewhere else in her mind. It was intimidating and demanding. The voice made Jess quiver in fear, yet she held her ground. She knew that she could not show the dragon any of her fear. She looked around past the dragon to see if she could find where the voice had come from. "We are alone. You are always alone. There is no one that can help you. I will take complete control of you and escape this prison." The voice leered. The voice sounded like it was coming from the dragon but its lips didn't move. Maybe because it was already in her mind it didn't have to move its mouth to make noises. "No. I will defeat you." Jess yelled in her mind.

"You stupid girl, you can never defeat me. I am part of you now, until I take complete control and escape from you, you and I are one. There is no way to defeat Me." the dragon leered. Jess listened to what the dragon had said and then an idea came to her. "So, if you are a part of me and you can control me than doesn't that mean I could control you?" Jess asked skeptically. There was a short pause then the dragon replied. "No. That is not possible. You will never be able to control me. I will control you!" the dragon lamented. Jess said nothing but focused her mind on the last thing she remembered seeing before the dragon caused her to black out. She had found a weak point with the dragon and now she wanted out of her own mind and back to reality.

Jess opened her eyes and to her surprise she was still sitting on her horse that was trotting alongside Linder's. Linder was holding Jess's horses reins and had a look of concern on his face. He starred at her trying to figure out if she was alright. He tapped his right arm and pointed to Jess. He was silently asking if the dragon on Jess's arm was the reason for concern. Jess nodded. Linder held out her reins to her. She smiled and took it. She was excited that she was able to concentrate and regain her composure and escape her mind where the black dragon loomed.

Less than thirty minutes later they arrived in the midst of the city. General Jackson led them directly to the market. Citizens bowed when they came into their presence. Remarkably General Jackson greeted each one by name and introduced them to his company. He introduced them as the Northstin Wind's Army. Everyone showed respect to Jess and the others. Women offered to make clothing for all of them and men offered to join them or use their skills to help the Northstin Wind's Army. Such as make armor, weapons, and blacksmith jobs. Some were farmers that offered their crops to the Northstin Wind's Army. General Jackson graciously thanked them all and told them that he would personally come to them if the Northstin Wind Army would need their services. Many citizens asked if they knew where the stolen ones were taken and when they would be returning to their homes.

Fathers, mothers, sisters, and brothers all asked about when their loved ones would be coming home. Everyone that Jess met all believed the prophecy that stated that the Northstin Wind would defeat the Black Dragons, free the stolen ones, and rid the world of the Black plague. Jess was glad they all had confidence in her; she just wished she had a plan to accomplish all of that.

General Jackson calmly explained to each person that today was the Northstin Wind's first day in Tasintall and that they are formulating a plan and would take action shortly to rescue the stolen ones and fulfill the prophecy. Most citizens received the explanation gratefully but others wanted a better explanation of their exact plan. General Jackson tried to explain that he was unsure how long it would take to find the stolen ones, to the first few persistent citizens but when that was unsuccessful he began telling people that they could expect their loved ones home before the fall harvest season is over. That would give them many months to complete the task that lay ahead.

They made their way through the city, meeting many citizens as they went. Linder left the group for a short time and returned carrying a bundle of something wrapped in a burlap bag. Jess eyed him suspiciously but he replied with, "It's just some necessary supplies." That eased Jess's curiosity. General Jackson stopped at many shops, carts, and wooden stands throughout the market. He bought food of many types and ordered that they be delivered to the palace; he bought fabric for his mother and placed it into one of the bags that his horse had attached to the saddle. He offered to have all the men fitted for armor but Marcus and Jusdan were the only one that accepted. Dumas said that he wouldn't need it and Linder politely declined. "What about us?" Jess asked clearly showing that she thought men and women were equals.

"Men need the armor to protect the women so that women don't have to fight." Sergeant Johnson replied earnestly. "I can fight my own battles, thank you." Jess remarked. "I am sure you can. But still men are the proper protectors and take the responsibility of fighting for their women very seriously. Women don't need to fight their own battles, it's just not proper. The men will resolve any issues that a woman may have. Women are too delicate to fight." Sergeant Johnson replied but instantly regretted saying the last part of it from the stare that Jess and Erika were giving him.

"Maybe where you come from its that way but where we come from if you don't stand up and fight your own battles whether you're a male or female then you are shamed. Everyone should be able to fight their own battles. I am not saying that I don't want help from a man but I have fought and survived many battles without one." Jess argued. "Men are stronger and therefore…" Sergeant Johnson began to say but Linder cut him off. "You are both correct. There's no need to argue. Yes men are the protectors of women but some women don't need protecting and those women should only be protected when the man knows for certain the woman really needs his protection." Linder interjected looking between Jess and Sergeant Johnson.

Jess nodded, as did Sergeant Johnson. "I'm sorry. We both have strong opinions on this matter and I should not have argued with you. Do you forgive me?" Sergeant Johnson asked Jess as he reached out his hand toward her. Jess looked at his outstretched hand and then at his brown eyes. She smiled and took his hand. "Yes, of course I will forgive you." "Thank you." He replied and shook Jess's hand in a truce.

For the next few hours the group split into two, General Jackson leading one group and Sergeant Johnson leading the other. They went different directions to explore the city and surrounding areas. Linder, Dumas, Jusdan, and Jess went with General Jackson while Randy, Erika, and Marcus along with two other soldiers went with Sergeant Johnson. While exploring the borders of the city Jess was inexplicably drawn to one section where the city ended and the forest began. The darkness loomed in the trees that grew reaching towards each other, seeming to form a tunnel with its branches. Jess examined the area with her eyes; it seemed to be calling her to go inside. She felt like she needed to go in there for some reason. She dismounted and looked at the forest ahead. General Jackson dismounted also.

Jess took a step of the city dirt road and before she could place her foot on the ground General Jackson pulled her back. She turned to look at him. "That is where the Black Dragons have been seen taking prisoners into. Those who have dared pass this line and take that single step into the forest instantly fall over dead. They just die without any explanation. I could not let you take that step. I'm sorry but you are too important." General Jackson explained as he held onto her shoulders.

She heard his words and wanted to heed his warning but something inside her desperately needed to go there. The dragon whispered in her head that she should heed the general's word. That caught her off guard. Either it would really kill her and then the dragon inside her would die also or there was something in there that the dragon didn't want her to know. Many tidbits of conversations flashed through her mind at that moment. "That is where the Black Dragons have been seen taking prisoners into." "You stupid girl, you can never defeat me. I am part of you now, until I take complete control and escape from you, you and I are one. There is no way to defeat me." "Where do you take your prisoners?" "In the woods the dragons know the way." "The black dragons on our bodies, they show us were to go." General Jackson, the black dragon inside her, and the Black Dragon prisoners that she interrogated gave her the answer she was looking for. Jess gasped and blinked. She knew exactly what she needed to do.

"Did you hear me?" General Jackson asked as if only seconds had passed. "Yeah, thanks." She replied than turned to Linder who had dismounted and stood by General Jackson. She smiled a mischievous smile and wrapped her arms around him. "Jess?" Linder asked curiously as she embraced him. "I love you. Don't go after me." she whispered and then quickly exited the embrace and ran past the general and into the forest.

Once she was at least six feet into the forest she stopped and turned to face the others. She heard them all gasped. "Don't follow me. I will be fine I promise." She demanded. She stood still; arms outstretched, head tilted up and let her consciousness fade away into her mind. There she met the dragon. She knew it would be waiting for her. The dragon was so large and intimating but Jess was getting used to it and she knew that she had to stand her ground and fight. She would not let the dragon take control of her mind and body. She walked right up to the massive and terrifying creature in her mind.

"You know where the prisoners are don't you! You know the way! Show me!" Jess demanded. "You stupid girl, I don't know the way and even if I did I wouldn't help you. I can't believe I got stuck in you. There is no hate, anger or rage in you. There is nothing to fuel me. I just have to sit and wait until you are too weak to fight back until I can take control and destroy you. It's pathetic." The dragon stated in disgust. Jess knew that it could tell her the way to find the stolen ones but wouldn't. It made her angry. Just then a small quite calm voice spoke to her.

"Jessalyn Northstin, you must release your anger. Let it go. It's the only way. But beware of the consequences. Everything has a price. You must be willing to pay that price. If you are willing to pay the price then give him your anger." The voice said. Jess knew that voice. It was the voice of her mother. Her mother had been dead for several years. She thought it might be a trick but she felt comforted at the words and knew that it could not be a trick. "So you want hate and anger, do you? Well I have plenty of hate and anger. I hate that my grandmother was taken by the Black Dragons! I hate that my little brother was taken prisoner by the Black Dragons! I hate Mrs. Morris for betraying my family and cursing me with you! I hate being told that I need protection! I can protect myself! I hate being in charge of an entire army! I hate that everyone is depending on my success to rid the world of your evil kind! I am angry that I can't marry the man love right now; I have to wait and wait and wait because of you! I am angry that my parents died and that I will never see them again! I am angry that I have not gotten to kill more Black Dragons! I am enraged that you think that you will take control over me and destroy me! You are wrong! I will never stop fighting! Now show me the way to the prisoners!" Jess demanded. The black dragon turned its head away from Jess and looked away. "There" the dragon said. Jess turned her attention to where the dragon was looking.

The dark tunnel of trees in the forest where she was standing leered ahead. It went on for a long way, Jess couldn't see the end. "Follow the bones." The dragon instructed. Jess looked at the ground, and to her astonishment there on both sides of the tunnel were bones lining the edges. Many shapes and sizes of bones going on and on right along with the tunnel, farther than her eyes could see. She didn't want to think about where the bones had come from. "Follow the bones." She said to herself then turned her attention to the dragon which was watching her. "How do the prisoners get through the tunnel without being killed?" Jess demanded at the black dragon. It stood over her, fangs bore, trying to intimidate her. "Answer me!" she yelled. "We lead them." The dragon remarked then to Jess's horror the dragon grew in size. It grew at least six feet taller and many feet longer. Jess stumbled back a few steps.

The dragon chuckled a wicked laugh. Jess screamed in pain. It was an agonizing stomach clenching teeth grinding pain that knocked Jess to the ground. "Thank you for your anger. It has served me well." The dragon responded as he grew another few feet taller and wider. She screamed once more than pulled her mind away from the dragon and back to reality.

When she opened her eyes she noticed that she was laying on her back with dark branches leering over her. She could hear a commotion between a few men not far away. She turned her head and saw Jusdan holding Dumas back and General Jackson fighting with Linder to keep him back. She knew that she had to stop them from crossing over into the forest but her head and body hurt so badly. She wasn't sure if she could move. Realizing that she would have to do something or those men would die she slowly and with pain searing through her she sat up and then stood. She saw many bones lining the edges of the tunnel. "Stop! I am fine! Stay there, I'm coming to you." She yelled so they would be able to hear her over their fighting. Her throat felt like someone had tried to strangle her. All the men stopped fighting and watched her as she deliberately took one step after another making her way towards them.

Blood dripped from her head that landed on her shoulder and matted some of her hair. There was blood on her hands, she didn't seem to notice. Once across the line and back onto the city road Linder helped her sit down on the ground and began to examine her. He checked her head, stomach, back, legs and hands. There were no injuries on her. The blood wasn't hers. "Where are you hurt? I have checked all over you and cannot find a single injury. Where did all this blood come from?" Linder asked. "All the people I am going to kill." Jess replied than blinked her eyes. She focused on Linder's blue and brown sunburst eyes. "I know where we have to go now." She said then everything went black.

Chapter Sixteen- Finding the Stolen Ones

When she awoke she was lying on a small bed, much similar to the one at her home that she used to sleep in every night. The small room was dimly lit by a candle flickering in a corner. Linder held her hand as he sat on the floor next to her. He noticed that Jess was wakening. He breathed a sigh of relief. "I thought I had lost you again. You scared me so bad with the incident in the forest and then collapsing into sleep and not waking up. Breann said that your heart was still beating and that you were still alive. I hoped and prayed that she was right but when you didn't wake up after such a long time I began to think that I had lost you." Linder replied. Jess had so many questions that ran through her head. She didn't know which to ask first so she asked all of them at once. "Where are we? Who is Breann? How long was I asleep? What exactly happened in the forest? Where are the others?" She tried to sit up but her head spun and her arm where the dragon tattoo stung in pain.

"Just rest." Linder insisted and helped her lay back down. "We are in General Jackson's home, Breann is his wife, and she has helped take care of you. You have been asleep for two days and half a night. It's around the middle of the night and two days after the incident in the forest." Linder responded. "What happened?" Jess asked her head was groggy. "I was hoping you could tell me. But I will tell what I saw. You gave me a hug, told me that you love me and to not go after you and then you ran into the forest. I thought you were going to die then. You sprawled out your arms and then screamed a terrible scream and fell to the ground. General Jackson held me back from going after you. I fought with him and punched him a few times but he was able to stop me long enough for you to get up. You were covered in blood but told us to stay where we were. You then came to us. I thought you were going to bleed to death. It was almost as much blood as when you got shot in the stomach." Jess cringed at the memory.

"I searched all over you and couldn't find a single wound. You told me that it was the blood of the people that you were going to kill and that you knew where we have to go then you collapsed. We tried to wake you but you wouldn't rouse. General Jackson led us to his home in the city where his wife and children live. They fetched a physician who proclaimed that you were dying and then left. Breann refused to believe that and instructed us to clean you up and she would help nurse you until you awoke. She said that she could hear your heart beating and as long as she could hear that than you were still alive and would have to wake up sometime. Your body was so cold. Breann checked on you a few hours ago and said that it wouldn't be long until you would wake up. I think she might have healing powers, even if she doesn't know it. She will want to know that you are awake. Are you okay for just a minute while I go and get her?" Linder asked. "Yeah I'm fine." Jess replied with a smile. Linder didn't look convinced. "I am really. Well maybe not. I am really hungry though." Jess replied. Linder smiled. "I can fix that." He remarked then was just about to get up and leave the room when Jess stopped him.

"Linder, I do know where we have to go. I know now how to find the people that the Black Dragons stole." Jess stated. "It's not going to be fun and some might die in the process, but I know where we have to go now. I don't know how to rescue them yet but at least we know where to go now" Jess admitted. "That is wonderful. We should discuss this with General Jackson." Linder replied. "Not yet. I want to have a good plan before we talk to him." Jess interjected. "Very well." Linder answered. "Thanks for understanding." She remarked then pushed her sleeve up her arm, exposing the black dragon tattooed there. It looked the same as before except the two red blood drops below the fangs were gone but were replaced by a pool of red blood under the dragon's fangs that covered half of the dragon. It looked as if the dragon were standing in a pool of blood. "This is the reason why I went to sleep and didn't wake up and this is also the way I found out where we must go to find the stolen ones." Jess stated as she stared at the black dragon on her arm. Linder looked the black dragon on her arm than looked up into her eyes. "Fight it Jess. Don't let it take control of you." He stated and then stood and left the room.

Moments later he returned with General Jackson and a woman that was slightly shorter than Jess with light brown hair that was tied into a braid and tossed over one shoulder. She looked as if she had bore many children within a short time, causing her stomach to add extra weight in the center with the rest of her body stayed an average size. She also had blue eyes and small pink lips. "Oh, I'm glad you're awake. My name is Breann." The woman said. "I'm Jess. It's good to meet you. Thanks for taking care of me." "You're welcome; I knew that you weren't dying. Is there anything you want?" Breann asked. "Food" Linder remarked before Jess could answer. "I will see what we have leftover and bring you some." Breann replied. "You don't have to do that." Jess implied. "It's my pleasure." Breann responded then turned and left the room. "How are you feeling?" General Jackson asked. "I am feeling fine. Thank you. Where are the others?" Jess replied. "Everyone is staying at the palace. They are safe there. I have posted some of my best men to guard them. Erika is really worried about you but under my strict orders no one is allowed to leave the palace. Not until you return. I told the king and queen that you had come down with a sickness and could not be moved and I did want to risk anyone else getting contaminated with it so they needed to stay in the palace. I don't think that Erika, or Marcus believed my story but I knew it would be better for them to stay there." General Jackson stated. "Yeah those two would be skeptical. I will go to the palace first thing in the morning. That will ease their worry and curiosity." Jess replied as she sat in the small bed.

"Are you sure you're up to it?" General Jackson inquired. "Yes I'm sure. I will be back to normal by breakfast time." Jess replied as if it wasn't a big deal. General Jackson looked between Jess and Linder for confirmation. Linder nodded in agreement. Breann brought Jess some cold oatmeal with an apple diced and mixed into the bowl along with a glass of water. Jess took it graciously. Breann asked if there was anything else that she needed. Jess replied to her that she would be fine and thanked her for all the help she had given her. Linder said that he was going to stay right next to Jess for the remainder of the night. "You should get some sleep. I think I have my fair share of sleep lately. I won't be able to go back to sleep now. I will be fine. You go and get some sleep." Jess remarked to Breann.

Breann tried to argue but General Jackson told her that Jess was right and led her out of the room saying good night to Jess and Linder on their way out. Jess ate her oatmeal then drank all the water then got out of the bed. "Where are my clothes?" she asked Linder, noticing that she was dressed in a long blue nightdress. "Over there." He pointed to a stack of clothes that had been neatly folded and placed on top of a dresser. "Why do you need them?" he asked curiously. "Because I need to test my theory and make sure that my plan to find the stolen ones will work, and I can't very well go outside in a nightdress." Jess replied as she retrieved the clothes and placed them on the bed. "Where's my boots?" she asked as she searched the dimly lit room with her eyes. Linder bent down and lifted up her boots from the ground right beside where he was standing and handed them to her. "Thank you." She replied and placed them on the bed next to her clothes.

"Close your eyes while I change." She told him. He obliged. She took off her nightdress then quickly dressed herself all the way down to her boots. Once she was ready she told Linder he could open his eyes and then together they quietly made their way out of General Jackson's house. The moon was full and gleaming in the night sky, giving enough light to illuminate the streets. There was a cold chill in the air. The streets were empty except the occasional dog that ran between streets. "Where are we going?" Linder asked quietly. "Back to the forest where the General said the stolen ones are taken." Jess admitted. "Somehow I knew you were going to say that. But why are we going there?" Linder asked as they walked quickly hand in hand down the street. "That's where we have to go to find the stolen ones. I need to make sure that I can lead an army through the tunnel without anyone getting killed. I am sorry but I am going to need you to trust me. I believe that anyone that follows me into the tunnel in the forest will be safe but I want you to try it with just you first." Jess explained. "So I have to be the tester to see if it kills me or if I will survive." Linder replied incredulously.

"I…" Jess began to say but Linder cut her off. "Jess I know you wouldn't let me try it if you didn't believe it was going to work. I am just giving you a hard time." Linder explained smiling. Jess's face relaxed. "Well let's hope that it really works." A voice said from behind them. Jess and Linder turned to find General Jackson coming up behind them. "When my guests sneak out of my house in the middle of the night I get a little suspicious. I knew that you wouldn't be doing something bad but I didn't think it would be something this crazy. But at least now I know some of your plan and as crazy as it sounds let's go and see if it works. If you survived the forest once and are brave enough to try it again than let's go ahead and try it." General Jackson acknowledged. "We're sorry for leaving." Linder apologized. "Don't worry about it." General Jackson replied and shrugged the issues away.

Together they walked through the city until they reached the location near the forest where the trees bowed into each other forming a dark tunnel just beyond the city road in the forest. Jess felt like the forest was calling her into it once more. "What do you need us to do?" Linder asked as he looked at Jess. "Wait here until I tell you to come." Jess instructed. She looked at the pitch black forest that lay ahead of her with its tunnel of tree branches with bones lining the path on the ground. She took a deep breath, released Linder's hand and stepped into the forest. Instantly a sharp pain pierced her arm, she screamed. It made her mad that the dragon would now cause her pain. The instant that she got mad the pain stopped. A thought crossed her mind then was gone. Give him your anger. She was angry. She was angry that she had to be angry for her to be safe here. She saw the look on Linder's worried face. She concentrated on him, she was angry that she had to cause him so much worry about her.

The dragon said that the Black Dragons lead their prisoners into the forest and that's how they stay unharmed. "Linder, I want you to step one foot into the forest." "General, I need you to be prepared to pull him back to you if anything seems to go wrong." Jess instructed. "Jess are you sure this is a good idea? I have seen men die here by just taking one step into that forest." General Jackson asked. "Yes I truly think this will work. Look I'm not dead. Trust me." Jess responded. "Very well." The general answered.

"Linder, if you feel any pain at all get back, okay." Jess stated. He nodded. She moved closer to the line that crossed into the forest. "Linder now slowly take a step towards me." she instructed. Linder placed one foot into the forest. Nothing happened. "Okay move your other foot." Jess said. Holding his breath he moved his other foot into the forest. Jess took his hand. He sharply pulled it away. "Ouch." He said shaking his hand. Jess's arm stung. "So you do have a death wish after all." The dragon's voice said in her head. "Sorry." Jess said to Linder. The dragon had made her angry by not allowing her to touch her future husband. Then a realization struck her. This place is made for people who don't feel love and caring feelings. She must not show affection, only anger and rage to survive here. Linder had moved back into the city limits.

"Try again just don't touch me." she instructed. Linder hesitated while looking at Jess. "You didn't die, and I figured out what I did wrong. You will be fine as long as we don't show any affection. Please trust me." Jess inclined. Linder looked deeply into Jess's blue eyes than putting his trust in her; he took the full step into the forest and stood next to her. Nothing happened. "Where did those bones come from?" Linder asked noticing the bones that lined the tunnel. "They were always there." Jess answered. "I didn't see them back there." Linder remarked. "Only Black Dragons can see them outside of the forest. Once they bring their prisoners into the forest they are able to see them." Jess answered. "What bones are you talking about?" General Jackson asked. "Come see for yourself. You will be safe." Jess offered. "Like Jess said, I didn't die yet. I trust her." Linder responded.

General Jackson took a hesitant step into the forest with one foot and then with the other. Once he realized that nothing bad was happening he took one full step closer to Jess and Linder. "Well that was surprising. My wife would kill me if I had died here." General Jackson remarked. Linder laughed. Jess laughed, which caused a pain to shoot through her tattooed arm all the way into her head. Linder and General Jackson screamed in pain and fell to their knees. Jess ground her teeth. "I hate you!" she yelled. The pain instantly was gone. The two men stood confused and worried and pain free. "What happened? Who do you hate?" Linder asked going to reach for her. "Don't touch me! I felt happiness with General Jackson's joke and with happiness comes pain here. This place is made for the Black Dragons. They don't feel true happiness, only hate, anger, and rage. I have to feel one of those emotions constantly or everyone's life is in danger. So, no physical contact and no jokes. I don't want to cause anyone pain or even death, alright?" Jess informed them as she backed away from Linder.

"I understand." Linder stated and stopped his advance towards her. "Understood. I apologize for the joke." General Jackson replied. "You didn't know. I forgive you. Now I would like to follow this trail for a while and see if we can figure out where it leads. If it takes to long then we will have to turn around and go back and try again another time. Do you want to join me?" Jess asked as she flung her long blonde braid back over her shoulder. "We came this far didn't we. I plan on going with you wherever you go." Linder replied. "I will also go with you." General Jackson replied. "Alright. Onwards we go." Jess indicated and pointed forwards.

The farther they traveled the denser the trees became which caused it to become so dark that they couldn't see their hands in front of their faces. Jess's anger for the dragon faltered and was replaced with fear. Instantly she heard both men scream in pain. Jess looked around but could not see Linder or General Jackson. They sounded near but without any light to see she had no idea of where they were exactly. All she knew is that it was her fault that they were being hurt. She drew her anger back. Why? Why do I always have to be angry to protect them? She thought to herself. "Run! Get out of here! Go back now!" Jess demanded. "Jess what about you?" Linder asked but sounded winded in his breathing. "I will find my own way back just go!" she shouted. "I love you Jess." "I love you too." Jess admitted. Everyone screamed in pain. "Go!" she yelled as she tried to stand after her stomach wrenched in pain. It felt like her stomach was trying to explode from the inside out. She heard laughing. She knew that laugh all too well. It made her angry to hear the laughter.

"Linder, we must go." General Jackson urged. Then Jess heard the sound of the two men running back the way they had come. They had left her alone, in the pitch blackness with only the dragon inside her to keep her company. It was just how Jess wanted it to be. This was the only way to keep them safe. Jess felt the pull on her mind and the sting in her arm that meant the black dragon inside her was trying to get her to confront him inside her mind. "No! I will not give in to you. You will not defeat me!" Jess grit her teeth and continued onward. She traveled what she thought to be almost an hour in the darkness until she saw a small light ahead.

Hoping that she didn't get turned around and end up where she started she continued on towards the light. She was almost to the glowing light when she noticed there was a man standing next to the light, causing her to stop in her tracks. The light was a brightly glowing lantern that hung from a branch on a large willow tree. The man was no ordinary man; he had a black dragon tattooed on his face and wore black pants, a tight fitting black shirt and a blood red cloak hung over his shoulders. Jess couldn't help think that her dragon looked much fiercer than the one tattooed on this man. He had seen her. Instinctively he pulled a long sharp dagger from his waist and aimed it towards her. Jess could see dried blood coating the dagger.

"Well, well, well, are you lost?" the gruff man asked while his eyes darted up and down Jess's body. Jess knew that she was going to have to lie and fake her way past this one. Act just like them. She thought to herself. "No, I'm not lost. My black dragon led me here!" she stated confidently. This in some way was not lying. "You're a Black Dragon? Don't lie to me sweetheart, you know what I do to liars? I cut out their tongue and then cut a single line from their shoulders all the way down their back for every lie they tell me. Some people don't have enough space on their backs for as many lies that they tell me so I proceed to their chests then. It's exhilarating to hear them try to scream without a tongue. So are you lying to me?" the Black Dragon asked. "How dare you say that I'm a liar!" Jess retorted angrily. "I told you that I wasn't a liar and you still don't believe me. How dare you! See, I am not a liar. I am a Black Dragon!" Jess declared and pushed her right sleeve up to her shoulder and pushed her arm towards the Black Dragon man. He looked at it for a long moment.

"I...I'm sorry. I did not mean to call you a liar. Please don't punish me. I was just doing my job. You see sometimes we get people who are lost who make their way out here. Most try to lie to get away but you know the rules. Once they come this far they either join us, or are taken for questioning and either kept for later or disposed like the others. I did not mean to undermine your authority. I will accept any punishment you think appropriate." The Black Dragon insisted dropping to one knee and bowed his head.

"Is that so? Why should I believe you when you didn't believe? Well?" Jess hissed after the man had no response. "I could just kill you but that would be too easy. I think you should suffer. I know. Maybe I should cut off your ears for not listening to me. No, maybe I will carve out your eyes so then you can't see. No, I've got it. I will hurt you where it will hurt the most. I will cut off your manhood. That way you will be mocked forever by both women and men. You will never get to enjoy the pleasures of women ever again. Yes, I think that would be a good punishment." Jess stated.

The man stood and began to beg and cry not to have his manhood cut off. Dropping his dagger to the ground and cupping his most precious area with his hands he cried. "Anything. I will do anything for you, just don't cut it off." He was acting like a little baby in the way he cried, Jess thought to herself. "Very well. I will save your manhood this time if you first give me your dagger, second take me to where the prisoners are and third don't tell anyone else of my presence here. After that you must return here and resume your duty, understood?" Jess commanded authoritatively. "Yes. I understand." The Black Dragon replied submissively then he picked up his dagger of the ground and handed it to Jess. She took the dagger, turned it in her hand admiring it. It was a nice dagger, even though it was covered in dried blood. She thought to herself. She tucked the dagger in between her belt and trousers. "Well which way?" she barked. "This way." He told her and started walking into the dark, leaving the lantern hanging in the tree.

Chapter Seventeen- The Stolen Ones

Jess followed the man as they walked farther away from the tree. The farther they walked the more Jess could hear a sound that she recognized. It was the sound of a waterfall. The sound grew louder the farther they traveled. Just as the last remaining speck of light from the lantern in the tree was visible the Black Dragon stopped. Jess could barely see the massive waterfall up ahead. "This is as far as I go." The Black Dragon shouted over the sound of the waterfall. "Where are the prisoners?" Jess shouted angrily. "Behind the waterfall. Follow the trail that leads behind it. They are in there." The man replied and then ran away before Jess could say anything else. Jess watched him as he ran back towards the willow tree. She looked ahead at the waterfall, it was massive and dark. She felt the cool water spraying her face from where she stood. She followed the trail that ran alongside the river that the water poured into. One slip and she would fall into the angrily churning water. Following the trail she found a cave behind the waterfall. Soaked by the water that splashed her she walked farther into the cave. The cave went back a dozen paces and then turned a corner. She saw a light coming from around the corner. Cautiously she peered around the corner and what she saw made her gasp. A lump formed in her throat.

There was a plethora of people, old, young and in between. There were men and women of all ages along with boys and girls some from ranging from just above the baby stage all the way to almost full grown adults. Some of the people were sitting with the backs against the cave wall; some were leaning against each other while others lie on the ground. Many were asleep but there were some that were awake. All looked as if they hadn't eaten in many days and the cave stunk of human waste and dirty bodies. Most had tattered clothes and dried blood on them. Everyone that she saw look to be beaten and saw what looked to be whip marks on their bodies.

Even the children that Jess could see looked as if they had been whipped and beaten. There were way too many people for Jess to count; if she had to count she would guess at least a couple hundred people. She looked for the end of the cave but the cave seemed to go on for miles. Jess spotted one Black Dragon man standing leaning his back against the cave wall under a lantern that had been hung on a pole that had been hammered into the cave wall. He wore the same attire as the previous Black Dragon and had the same black dragon tattooed on his face. He held a dagger similar to the one that Jess now had on her belt in his hand moving it across the mass of people in the air as if he was ready to throw it at anyone. His eyes darted through the people as if daring anyone to move. Jess had to see if she could find her grandma or brother in the mass of people. But what do to about that Black Dragon? She thought to herself. Gathering her confidence and anger she stepped around the corner.

"Who goes there?" the Black Dragon asked while he pointed his dagger towards Jess as she came closer. "That is none of your business." Jess retorted. "It is my business. I am in charge here, not you! So who do you think you are?" the Black Dragon reprimanded. "You're in charge? Really? Well I think I am in charge here and I need some prisoners that you are going to let me take." Jess declared. "I will indulge you a little. So what makes you think that you're in charge?" the Black Dragon inquired, eyeing her as if deciding to kill her right now or later.

"This does." Jess retorted and shoved her right arm toward the Black Dragon, showing him the black dragon tattooed on her arm. He glanced down at it. His demeanor changed instantly. What is so important about this stupid dragon on my arm? Jess thought to herself. "I'm sorry. I didn't realize. You said that you need some prisoners, go ahead and take your pick. I will break them into submission for you if you wish." The Black Dragon stated and flipped his dagger in the air and caught it by the handle. "That won't be necessary. I have my own ways to break them. But I do expect all of them to cooperate." Jess remarked sternly.

"Oh you shouldn't have any trouble with this lot. Most of them had already been interrogated and have learned obedience from the Master. If any of them give you trouble they will be quickly disposed off, you can guarantee it." The Black Dragon boasted. "Good then I am going to look through all of them and pick the best ones for my mission." Jess responded then turned away from the man.

Jess looked at the faces of the men, women and children all smashed together in the dark, damp, and dreary, not to mention reeking cave as she searched for her grandma and brother. She wished she knew what Loni's husband and Marcus's brother looked like so that she may rescue them along with her family. Jess didn't recognize any of the faces so she moved farther into the cave. She had to look on both sides of the cave and had to weave over and through several people to make her way onwards. "You there, get up and go stand against the wall by the Black Dragon by the lantern." Jess told a man that looked to be in his late twenties who she noticed watching her. The man stood and without saying anything walked away to where she instructed. Jess noticed someone that looked familiar but she wasn't sure. "You there, the women in the back with the blue dress on, go wait by the Black Dragon with that man I just sent. As the women rose and made her way through the throng of people she glanced at Jess. Jess was right; it was who she thought it was. But the look the women gave Jess wasn't the look Jess had expected. It was of disappointment and hatred.

Two down. She thought to herself. She continued onwards farther into the cave stepping over and around people as she went. "I want you and you. Get up and go over there." Jess pointed at a dark skinned teenage boy and an elderly dark skinned man next to him. Jess picked out two teenage girls, two little girls, one little boy, one more teenage boy, one more elderly man, one more middle aged man, and one elderly woman. She was getting anxious; she hadn't found her grandmother or brother and didn't know how much longer she could stay here safely. She reached the end of the cave. There was another lantern hanging like the first at the end of the cave. It dimly illuminated the end of the cave. There curled up sleeping against an elderly woman with badly bruised features laid a boy who Jess recognized.

Jess would recognize that messy blonde hair anywhere and they way he was laying Jess could see the socks that her grandmother had knitted for him right before she had left home. Jess couldn't believe it. It was her brother, Zander. "Wake him up. I am taking him with me." Jess demanded to the old woman. The woman nudged Zander. "Little one, wake up. You have to go with this woman now. It will be alright, just do everything that she says and you will be alright." She told him. Zander looked up towards his enslaver. His face lit up when he saw who stood in front of him.

"Jess!" he shouted excitedly. Jess put a finger to her lips indicating him to be quiet then winked at him. Zander looked confused. "Come here." She demanded, keeping her tone back and actions in a demanding demeanor so that no one would be suspicious of her. Zander walked over to her, fear in his eyes. Jess bent down and whispered in his ear. "Zander, I am playing pretend but I need you to pretend with me. I have to pretend to be mean just like the Black Dragons; I need you to pretend like you are afraid and scared of me okay. You will be safe. I promise." Zander nodded. "Very well then get over there with the others." Jess demanded harshly and shook her head as if disappointed in something. She looked around in hopes to find her grandmother but no luck and she knew that she needed to leave quickly. "Alright." She said scanning the people with her eyes. "You!" Jess stated and pointed to an elderly woman sitting amongst the crowd of people. The woman slowly and awkwardly stood up and made her way to where the others waited. Jess went back to where the Black Dragon stood watching her and the prisoners that she gathered together.

"This will do." Jess scoffed as she looked at the group of thirteen people that she had rounded together in disgust. "Alright, listen up. I am going to take all of you with me. If anyone falls in the river, you will be lost in the waves. If anyone goes to slow, I will kill you. If anyone does anything that I disagree on, you will be tortured or killed, depending on my mood. You will keep up with me and you will do exactly what I tell you to do. Do you all understand?" Jess demanded. There came a few quiet yes ma'am and others nodded. "Good, then follow me." Jess snapped then turned to leave the cave.

Even though she wanted to make sure that everyone was following her she didn't turn around to see if all thirteen people were following her but she could hear the movement behind her. She led them around the corner and out of the cave. The night sky was starting to brighten. Morning was on its way. The cool air was a refreshing welcome from the dank and disgusting air that filled the cave. Jess heard the sound of many of the people breathing deeply inhaling and exhaling the fresh air behind her. She wondered how long they had been in the cave. She led them on the trail past the river and luckily no one fell in and then they continued on to where the Black Dragon waited under the willow tree. Jess thought she should say something to the man to convince him that she could take all these people but couldn't think of anything to say but then she remembered her threat about his manhood. She pulled the dagger from her belt. "Well it looks like I won't need to use this on you tonight or will I?" She said as she turned it around in her hand. The man cupped his hands over his manhood instinctively. "No" he shook his head. "Good." Jess replied and put the dagger back on her belt.

"Keep moving." She yelled at her prisoners. "Which way?" one of the men asked. "That way of course and never speak until I speak to you first." Jess spat at the man. She felt terrible about the way she had to act around these people but surprisingly it was so easy to act terrible. She knew that she couldn't show any nice emotions or the people could be killed because of the magic in the passageway. "You're not terrible. You are perfect." A voice said in her head. She loathed that voice. It came from the black dragon inside her. "Shut up!" she growled. "I didn't say anything." The Black Dragon said still covering his manhood. "Not you!" Jess retorted then led everyone away from the Black Dragon.

Together Jess and the thirteen people traveled without saying anything for almost two hours following the trail made from bones until Jess found the grove of trees that formed a tunnel with its branches. "We are headed there." Jess stated and pointed to where they would go. Linder and General Jackson were not anywhere in sight. Jess really hoped that they had made it back safely. Before she could think of anything else she stopped her thinking and kept her mind on things that made her angry. Such as, how so many people were forcefully taken away from their families, beaten, whipped and forced to be trapped in that cave. How she acted so cruel to these innocent people it made her angry. With only a short distance left before they would be out of the forest Jess saw two men waiting, watching the forest from the city road. Her heart lifted and her anger slipped. There came a collected scream of pain.

"Run to those men! Now!" Jess yelled as she thought about how angry it made her that they were so close and that now she would slip and lose her anger causing all of them to have pain shoot through their bodies. She felt terrible for hurting them but extremely angry and irritated that she had messed up. She stopped moving. Zander stopped too. "Go!" she screamed. Everyone took off running. Someone grabbed Zander's hand and drug him away. The elderly hobbled as fast as they could. She had to be the last one out of the forest or anyone left in the forest would die instantly from the magic. Jess couldn't stand it anymore. She clenched her fists and screamed with all her lungs in frustration. "Why couldn't I find my grandma? Where is she? What did you do with her? Why are all these people beaten and whipped? That's just terrible. They can't help you, their innocent. The Black Dragons won't win. You won't win. You want anger, well you got it! Where can I find Soldum? I will destroy him and all of you!" she ranted then screamed once more as loud as she could. "I will defeat you!"

Linder and General Jackson stopped all the thirteen people that came across the line from the forest into the city and promised them that they were safe and free now. Helping the elderly sit down on the ground to rest and reassuring all of them that they were really safe now. Linder watched Jess as she seemed to have a break down. She screamed and screamed at a force unseen. Once she was done she took a deep breath and had a look of non returnable determination on her face. Linder caught her gaze; she looked at him and sighed. Her eyes closed and she fell to the ground.

When Jess opened her eyes, she found herself face to fang with the black dragon inside her mind. It had grown many feet taller, wider and longer. Jess should have been scared but was more annoyed than anything else to see the dragon. "What do you want?" she asked groggily as if she was just waking up for a long nap. "I see my anger has served you well once more. I guess now you will be taking over my mind completely and then you will escape by ripping out of my body." Jess said nonchalantly as she stood. She wiped the dust off her pants and then faced the dragon which was only inches away from her face. It roared an ear piercing roar. Jess wasn't fazed one bit. She put her pinky finger in one ear, wiggled it around a bit then removed it, as if the roar was just a little itch inside her ear that she could just wipe away. The dragon sneered. "You can act like you're not afraid but I know the truth. You are terrified of me and what I am capable of. I saw your little tantrum, it did you no good. For me on the other hand it just strengthened my powers and control over you. It was quiet amusing though." The dragon reveled.

Jess was tired of his gloating. She pulled her mind back to reality. She opened her eyes and instantly heard many people calling her name. She got up from the forest ground and walked smoothly to where Linder, General Jackson and twelve of the thirteen people that Jess had rescued waited.

They all stopped calling her name as soon as she stood up and began coming towards them. After she stepped out of the forest she was surrounded by people trying to hug and thank her for rescuing them. She graciously accepted their hugs and thank you's. Though confused about it. "How long was I out?" Jess asked. "A few hours. Someone tried to go and rescue you after we explained what you had done for them but with you unconscious the evil magic was in place and it wasn't safe. Unfortunately he died immediately after taking one step into the forest." General Jackson explained solemnly. He pointed to where the dead man lay. "He had one leg still in the city so we were able to drag his body out of the forest. We will give him a proper burial." General Jackson remarked. "Clean him up and put his body on display. I want everyone to look at him. I want to know if anyone knows who he is. I think his family deserves an answer to what happened to him." Jess responded directly. "I will make sure that is done." The general replied.

Linder wrapped his arms around Jess. "You are truly amazing. I missed you." He said to her. "Thank you. I missed you too. I was worried that you and the General didn't make it back safely, but I see now that you did." Jess replied as she embraced his hug.

"Jess?" asked a shy little boy. Jess turned to face the little boy. "Come here Zander." She instructed him and held her arms open. Zander ran into her open arms. She wrapped her arms tightly around him. "I knew I could find you. I told you that you would be safe." She said as she held her little brother close to her. "Mrs. Morris...." Zander began to weep. "I know. But that's behind us now. I will keep you safe from anything or anyone that will try to hurt or take you away, alright." Jess replied protectively. Zander nodded. "Besides that's what big sisters are for. But Zander, I need to know where grandma is. Can you tell me where she is? I need to rescue her just like I rescued you." Jess stated and lifted his chin up so he could look her in the eyes.

His face was dirty and bruised. Someone had hit him at least once on the face. It made Jess angry. "You left and didn't come back. We got a letter from you. It made grandma cry. She told me that the Black Dragons were going to take her away and that I needed to go to Mrs. Morris's until you came and got me. You didn't come Jess. Grandma was taken and when I was at Mrs. Morris's she gave me to a Black Dragon and he gave her a black dot. They took me with other people into the forest. It was scary. They hurt us and made us go into a cave. It was dark and scary. Some people were killed because they didn't do what the Black Dragons said to do.

After a long time they took me and some other people away to the other cave. We had to walk during the nighttime for a long time. My feet and legs got hurt. I was so tired but they made us keeping walking. Then I stayed in that cave until you came and got me. Jess I missed my birthday." He admitted. Jess smiled at the last phrase. "Don't worry. We will have your birthday as soon as we find grandma." Jess replied. "With cake and presents?" Zander asked excitedly. "Yes, with cake and presents." Jess smiled and acknowledged his request then she ruffled his blonde hair.

There was a moment of silence then Zander spoke up. "There was a nice old lady there who helped me not be scared as much. She was like grandma. Her name was Ellen. She knew my name and told me that you would save us. She was the one I was with inside the cave when you came. How come you didn't bring her with you?" A lump grew in Jess's chest. She desperately tried to remember the face of the woman in the cave. The woman had been badly beaten and the lighting in the cave was so dim. Could it have been her grandma or could it have been another elderly woman with the same name as her grandma. Jess thought she was going to be sick. Her head spun. If that was her grandma than why didn't she come with her? What had happened to her and why didn't she tell Zander who she really was? Jess tried to imagine the woman without the swollen lips, black and blue eyes and bloated cheeks. She tried to imagine what the woman would look like without the bloody gash across one side of her face. Jess took a few steps back. "Jess are you okay?" Zander asked concerned for his sister. "Jess, what's wrong?" Linder asked taking her arm. Jess looked into his blue and brown sunburst eyes.

"It was her." She whispered. "Who was?" Linder asked. "It was my grandma. You should have seen what they have done to her. I didn't even recognize her but it was her. She was so badly beaten. I left her there. I left all of them there. Linder we need to go back. We have to go back." She stated, anxiety taking over. Linder watched her closely. She took a deep breath, pushed her anxiety away, brought her anger and determination forward, clenched her fists and narrowed her eyes. "Listen up. This is General Jackson, he is going to take all of you back to his palace where you will be cleaned, dressed, fed and there you will get the proper medical care and rest that all of you need. I need to know if any of you know where the second cave is, if so tell me now, because I plan to rescue each and every person that has been taken from their families. I personally promise to all of you that I will destroy the Black Dragons so that they are no more. No one is going to get hurt or killed anymore by the Black Dragons while I'm here." Jess announced. Clapping arose along with a few cheers.

"I know that the other cave is somewhere in the forest near Hyrum." A woman said. It was the same woman that Jess recognized. She stepped forward out of the crowd. It was Jusdan's younger sister, Ileana, who Jess had met in Taharan. Those days seemed like such a long time ago. The last time Jess saw Ileana she was fleeing to Hyrum to get away from the Black Dragons. When Jess saw her in the cave she thought Ileana would be excited to see her but instead seemed to be disappointed and hateful towards Jess. "I owe you an apology. I thought that you had really been taken over by the black dragon that you wear on your arm. But it turned out that I was wrong. Please accept my apology and hopefully my friendship also." Ileana offered sincerely. "I accept." Jess replied. "The cave is about an hour into the forest near Hyrum. It looks just like Spirit Tunnel. There were many more Black Dragons keeping guard there in and near the cave along with Therion's prowling the forest nearby. I heard them during the night. The cave was twice as big or more than the one you found us in. I couldn't believe how many people were there and that is where they do most their interrogating. In some of the side chambers in the cave, people were tortured and killed." Ileana explained.

"What information were they looking for?" Linder interjected. All the ex prisoners shuffled their feet. Ileana looked between Jess and Linder. "Both of you because you know about the magical talismans and any wizards and also someone known as the Northstin Wind and also a prophet. Most of the people don't know anything about wizards or magic or a Northstin Wind or a prophet. They were tortured for nothing. I did over hear once some of the guards talking about collecting the bait. I assumed they had gotten someone that would lure the wizards, whoever the Northstin Wind and prophet are to where ever they were keeping the bait. I was moved to the other cave shortly after that. Sorry that's all I know." She explained. "I am the Northstin Wind." Jess admitted. "And I am the Prophet." Linder proclaimed. A few gasps came from the crowd.

"Jess, what does that mean?" Zander asked, unsure of what his big sister was talking about. "That means that Linder and I are going to fix everything. No more Black Dragons, no more Curfew Guards or Black Order or whatever they want to be called. No more being scared. We are going to fix all of it." Jess explained. "Good." Zander replied excitedly. "Yes it will be good." Linder said as he put his around Jess's waist. Zander noticed and giggled. Jess smiled but her joy was short lived. She needed to go back to the cave and rescue her grandma and as many more people as she could. "Jess, I know you want to rescue your grandmother as soon as possible but I don't think it's wise to go back there right now. I think that you should get some rest and food before you go back and if we could devise a plan to rescue the rest of the prisoners instead of just a few before you go back than that would be great. What do you think?" Linder asked her. Jess really wanted to get back to the cave and rescue her grandma but she knew that Linder was right. She really did need rest and if they could come up with a plan to rescue all of the remaining prisoner at one time that would be best. "Your right." She told Linder.

"Alright General Jackson I think we are all ready for a hearty breakfast and some rest. Lead the way." Jess told the General. "Everyone follow me. It will take thirty minutes to get to a stable where we can hitch a cart to a horse that can pull the elderly and young ones. After that it will take another thirty minutes or so to get to the palace. Those of you who are capable to help the others please do so and inform me if we need to stop for a rest on the way. Okay let's go." General Jackson instructed waving his hand for everyone to follow him. "What city is this?" someone asked from the group as they started to walk away from the forest. "Tasintall." The General replied. "What about that man?" someone else asked pointing towards the dead man. "I am going to get some my soldiers to collect his body and fulfill Jess's requirements." The General answered then continued walking away from the forest. Jess held Linder's hand on one side and Zander's hand on the other.

Three hours later everyone had made it to the palace safely, eaten a large breakfast, some were bathed and wearing clean clothes while others waited for their turn in the bath room. Servants were sent to the market to buy clothes that would fit everyone and stock up on food for their many visitors. General Jackson had sent out five soldiers with a cart and instructions concerning that man that gave his life to try to save Jess. Jess and Linder explained what had happened in the past few days to Dumas, Marcus, Randy, and Erika, also the king, Queen Sierra. Jusdan, who was very excited to see his sister alive and well, all listened as the past few days events were unfolded.

After Jess and Linder were done, Jusdan explained that the Black Dragons had invaded Kedar's castle and killed his children right in front of him, they took his wife away tried to kill him but he ran into the forest and escaped. "What happened to Kedar?" Marcus asked while the group of them sat at the dining table together. "I'm not sure. He was in a different part of the castle when they attacked. Karlsen Soldum himself came to lay waste to Kedar's castle. I was lucky to get away. I hid in the forest until I came across the griffins. I told them that I needed to find all of you and asked if they could take me to you. I was able to ride them over the Kahidon Mountains.

They brought me all the way here to the outskirts of the city. That's when I listened for your thoughts and found my way to the palace where I saved your lives." Jusdan explained. "You listened to their thoughts?" The King asked suspiciously. "There's no time to explain, just trust us." Jusdan replied. "Magic." Jess interjected. The king nodded, as if that was enough explanation.

"How did the Black Dragons reach Kedar's castle?" Erika asked. "Who is Kedar?" Randy inquired as he held onto one of Erika's hands that were placed on top of the table. "What is a Therion?" The King inquired. "What are griffins?" Sergeant Johnson asked. "Enough. Now is not the time. We need to focus on the matter at hand but to answer your questions quickly. Marcus will you show what they look like. Kedar, a Therion and then a griffin." Jess proposed. "I would love to. I haven't been able to use my power for a few days so it would be my pleasure." Marcus replied then shifted his eyes to an empty spot in the dining room. There out of thin air appeared a man. It was Kedar. He was wearing the same outfit that he had worn the last time Jess had seen him. Dark tan trousers, a very loose and flowing dark green shirt with a leather belt that ran across his stomach. He wore a simple well worn brown cloak with the hood down exposing his shoulder length brown and gray hair that was tied back with a small piece of thread. He held a bowl of soup in his hands. Erika, Jess, and Linder smiled. Kedar was always hungry so to have his illusion holding a bowl of soup portrayed him perfectly.

"This is Kedar Ainsley, Prime Wizard of the Kahidon Mountains, Prophet, and a great friend. He is a great ally to have on your side." Jess informed those in the room who hadn't met Kedar before. "Alright Marcus, show us a Therion." Jess instructed. Kedar's illusion instantly was gone but was replaced by the monstrous creature known as a Therion. Its massive black furry body looked just like the real thing. Even though Jess knew it was fake it still made her nervous. The glowing red eyes of the beast looked at everyone in turn as if they would be its next meal. She described to everyone how terrible Therion's are then had Marcus change the illusion. Lastly Marcus showed everyone what a griffin was. Jess told them a brief description of how the Griffins helped them in the previous months and how great of creatures they were.

"Alright now let's get back to planning how we are going to rescue all the stolen ones and destroy the Black Dragons, along with all the black magic in the world." Jess said firmly. "What do you have in mind?" Erika asked. She could tell that Jess already had a plan devised in her mind. "I have a plan. It's going to involve everyone though. It's going to be difficult but I think if we can get everyone to do exactly what I tell them to do then my plan will go smoothly." Jess remarked. "Okay, what is your plan? That way I can tell you no right now." Erika teased. "Oh, I think you will like your part in my plan. You get to make us all freeze in your winter air and burn us in your summer scorch and blow us away with your ability to create tornados." Jess acknowledged. "Well that does sound like fun." Erika responded.

"What is my part?" Jusdan asked forwardly. "What do you want the army to do?" General Jackson inquired. "Alright, here is my plan and what you all with have to do. Tonight we are going to infiltrate the nearest cave and rescue everyone that is there. Sergeant Johnson your first task is going to get me these items as soon as possible. First I am going to enough black pants, and black shirts that look like the Black Dragons for at least fifteen people. I am also going to need someone who can paint with extreme detail and we are all going to need weapons." Jess instructed. "Yes ma'am." Sergeant Johnson replied. "Alright, I am going to lead all of us in this room plus a handful of soldiers to the cave. We will be dressed in Black Dragon attire with dragons painted on our faces. I have a feeling there are going to be more guards there tonight then there was previously. At first glance I want the Black Dragons to think that we are just another group of them. What they won't expect is that we are going to take them as our prisoners and lead every single one of their prisoners back to this palace. I want enough clothes, blankets, and food ready for when the people arrive. Most or all have been beaten to some extent and will need medical attention as well. We will need ropes and cloth to bind and blind the Black Dragons. We will bring them back here and interrogate them. We have to find out where that other cave is and where I can find Karlsen Soldum, so I can kill him. If they don't cooperate then we will interrogate them their way. If worse come to worse then we will kill them. A few less of them in this world could only be a good thing." Jess stated bluntly.

"I completely agree but what about our powers?" Marcus asked. "That's how all this becomes, well let's call it fun. Marcus I need you to make an illusion of as many of the men that will be with us as you can, placed behind us in the shadows making our group look larger and more intimidating. Erika, your job is going to be very helpful. I want you to cover us in fog when we get close and on the way back the people that we are going to rescue could sure use some warm weather." Jess instructed. "I can do that." Erika acknowledged.

"What do you want me to do?" Jusdan asked. "I want you to use your power to warn us about any unknown enemies if needed but mostly I want you to come because of your extensive weapons knowledge and experience. I hope that we won't have to use force but if we do I want the best man for the job and you are definitely the best person with weapons that I have ever met." Jess acknowledged. "Everyone must be ready to do their part and we will leave at dusk. Any question?" She finished. No one replied.

Chapter 18- Anticipated

Sergeant Johnson returned a few hours later with dozens of servants carrying baskets full of black clothing and weapons for all twenty four people that would be going with Jess to free the stolen ones along with extra blankets, food, bandages, and clothing for the stolen ones once brought to the palace. Along with Sergeant Johnson were a handful of doctors, physicians, surgeons and apothecaries all preparing to help the stolen ones when they arrived. There were also men along with Jess and her companions who over saw the process of preparing the palace for the stolen ones arrival. She was helping move beds from the many extra bedrooms into the great hall where all the stolen would stay together so they could be looked after and cared for all in one room. As she worked her long blonde braid fell over her shoulder and she noticed that something was different.

She examined her braid and found that one small section of her hair was turning darker. It was dark brown now and looked as if it was getting darker as she looked at it. It would be black any moment now. Just great, now my hair is turning black. What's next my heart? She thought inside her mind.

She flipped her braid behind her shoulder and continued to help move the beds, hoping that no one would notice her hair. There came a quiet reply in her head to her question that just made her mad. "Yes it is." The dragon admitted knowingly, Jess shook her head in annoyance and anger. I wasn't talking to you! She silently scolded the black dragon that invaded the space inside her mind. "It's true and you know it. You should just give into me now and save yourself the effort of trying and losing later on. We can accomplish terrible things together but if you keep fighting I will destroy you." The dragon declared. Jess ignored the dragon.

She found Sergeant Johnson near the kitchen directing the kitchen staff for what needed to be done. "Hey can I talk to you for a minute?" Jess asked him. "Yeah sure." He replied and followed her into the hallway. "What can I help you with?" he asked. "I have a favor to ask you." She replied. "What is it?" "Tonight's mission could either be really easy or it could turn into a disaster. There are many things that could go wrong and I want to be reassured that no matter what happens Linder will be safe. I can't protect him against…well myself. The dragon inside me is strong and in that situation it hungers to be released and I can't guarantee anyone's safety. I want you to promise me that you will keep Linder safe and drag him back here if something goes wrong. He will fight and want to stay with me but he needs to be brought here where he will be safe. Can you promise me that?" Jess asked desperately. Sergeant Johnson looked into Jess's blue eyes, he could see the love that she had for Linder was strong, it was the same look that he received from his wife, and then he replied. "I promise I will bring Linder back here if anything goes wrong." "Thank you." Jess replied reassured that Linder would be safe. "You better change your clothes and get ready now. The basket of clothes is in the great hall, along with the weapons that you asked for." He stated. "Okay, thanks. I'll see you later." She answered then turned and left.

Jess found the basket of black clothes alongside a basket with belts and daggers right where Sergeant Johnson said they would be. She picked a pair of black pants that looked as if it would fit her and a black shirt then grabbed a belt and a dagger from the other basket. She carried her arm full of belongings to a bedroom that wasn't being used or torn apart. The room had only a single bed, and a mirror that hung on the wall. There was still enough light shining in from the window that allowed to her see without the use of a candle. There she placed the black clothes on the bed then set the belt and dagger next to them. She sat on the bed, untied her boots and pulled them off. She looked at the black clothes in disgust and wanting at the same time. She knew what these clothes stood for. Hate, anger, killing and darkness are what Jess thought of when she looked at the black clothes but she also felt a dark desire to put them on. She wanted to wear them; she wanted to embrace the hatred that came with them. She needed the anger and hatred to do what the prophecy about her stated she would do. She needed the anger and hatred towards the Black Dragons to help her destroy them and if wearing black clothes is what it took than she would wear them and embrace the darkness to destroy the darkness. She took off her old clothes and let them fall on the floor.

Jess fastened the last button her blank pants and then pulled on her black shirt as she stood alone in an empty bedroom. She checked that her dagger was secure in its sheath that was attached to a belt that she put on next. Once her belt was fasten securely around her waist she looked up and saw her reflection looking back. The black dragon tattooed on her arm seemed to fit perfectly with her new clothes. She looked just like a Black Dragon, which was exactly what she wanted. She saw the one streak of black hair that had appeared hours earlier, it seem to be out of place amongst her long blonde hair. She unbraided her hair and re-braided it tucking the black streak in the middle of her hair so that no one could see it.

As she looked at her reflection in the mirror she pondered on the events that had led her to where she was at now. From the event that started it all. The moment when she and Erika found the red and silver drawstring bag in the forbidden forest near Morganstin and everything that happened after that which led to where she was at now. She shook her head as she looked at herself as she remembered accepting the responsibilities and the impossible task to defeat the Black Dragons and rid the world of black magic. She fingered the gold chain necklace with a small gold hollow heart hanging from the end. She had worn it around her neck since getting it and always felt the heavy responsibility that went with it. The necklace used to give her the power of empathy. She could feel others feelings and manipulate them as well. Making others feel whatever she wanted them to feel. The necklace did her no good now but she still kept it around her neck. She picked up the gold heart that hung at the end of the chain in between her fingers and looked at it for a long moment then put it under her shirt. It didn't matter anymore. She thought to herself. After looking at her new self once more in the mirror she glanced out the window. The sun was starting to set, it would be dusk soon. Changing her thoughts to the upcoming events that the night would bring, she left the room and closed the door behind herself.

She met Linder, General Jackson, and Dumas in the great hall. Linder and General Jackson wore the same attire that she dawned but Dumas still wore his old shaggy black cloak. He was stilling gripping an old prophecy book. "You should get ready." Jess told him. "I'm not going. I am needed here more. Plus I have a bit more research that I need to get done before you return." He replied and patted the book that he held. "Are you sure about staying here?" Jess asked. "Yes I am sure. But I would like to talk to you in private before you go." He imparted. "Okay. Let's do it now." Jess answered. She had noticed that Dumas was acting more peculiar recently and wanted to speak to him alone anyways to see if he had any advice for getting rid of the black dragon on her arm and in her mind. They walked together to an empty room nearby. Once they stopped Jess noticed that Dumas looked as if he could be sick. His head was beaded in sweat and his skin looked pale. "What is it that you want to talk to me about?" Jess asked. Dumas flipped open the book to a certain page and handed the book to her. "This." He stated. Jess read the following prophecy.

"When the time comes that the Northstin Wind believes that they are in control and the task ahead is near, actions taken will be forthcoming and the darkness will prevail. The blood set forth on her arm will appear and grow and the multitudes will parish. Darkness will consume and triumph over the one but in those actions the populace will survive. Embracing the darkness and releasing it will free her from her burden but in doing so will end the world as we know it."

Jess's face went white as she finished reading the prophecy. "Does that mean what I think it means? I am going to… I'm supposed to…" Jess tried to say but stumbled over the words. "I fear so. I have read through this book several times and there is only one other prophecy that mentions this but I haven't figured it out exactly what it means yet and that is why I have to stay here so that when you return I can give you more answers. I truly hope that I am wrong about this one but I cannot see how. I am truly sorry Jess." Dumas replied sympathetically and put his hand on her shoulder. "What am I supposed to do?" Jess asked. "I would recommend not telling anyone about this and to just continue with your plans as if nothing was wrong. By the time you get back I will have more answers so that we can figure this out." Dumas instructed. "What if I don't come back? What if tonight is when it takes place?" Jess asked as she handed the book back to Dumas. "Don't let it be. You are strong, you can fight it. You will make your own destiny not the darkness inside you. Don't let it take control. No matter what the prophecy says I think you should fight it with all your strength until I find out more. If it does happen tonight then I want to tell you that it's been a great pleasure knowing you and that you will not be forgotten." Dumas confided. "Jess, we are ready when you are." Linder called from the hallway. "Okay just a minute." She called back.

"Good luck and I believe you can do this." Dumas said and released his hand from her shoulder. "Thanks. Can you tell Linder that I will be there in a minute?" Jess asked Dumas. "Sure." He replied softly and left the room, leaving Jess alone. Once Dumas was gone she placed her hands on the wall and lowered her head and closed her eyes as she thought about the prophecy that Dumas had just shared with her. People are going to die because of me. I am going to die. The black dragon inside me is going to win. She thought to herself. "I told you so." The black dragon sounded in her mind. The dragon had just crossed the line. She clinched her fists, tightened her jaw, raised her head and opened her hard set eyes. The black dragon tattooed on her arm began stinging. That was the last straw. She would not stand for anymore of it. Her anger ran through every vain in her body. No! She shouted and punched the wall with one fist. "Jess, are you okay?" Linder asked from the doorway. Jess turned around and faced him. "I'm fine. Let's go." She snapped without looking at him then walked out of the room, pushing her way past him. He followed her without saying anything. Nothing mattered anymore except defeating the dragon inside her and the Black Dragons that were ruining her life. Nothing else mattered including Linder. He would just have to wait.

Jess joined the others in the great hall where General Jackson, Sergeant Johnson and fifteen men from the army waited along with Marcus, Randy, Erika, the king and Jusdan all of whom were dressed in black clothes just like hers. "It will be dusk soon. We should be on our way." General Jackson stated. "Then why are we waiting around here, let's go." Jess bluntly replied then walked out of the room and headed for the front door. General Jackson looked at Linder for an explanation. He shrugged. He had no idea what was wrong with Jess but then looked towards Dumas. He was the last one to talk to her; he might know what was wrong. General Jackson instructed everyone to follow Jess and then left the room along with everyone else. Linder grabbed Dumas's arm and once they were the only two in the room Linder asked Dumas what he had said to Jess. Dumas shook his head. "I don't think you really want to know." Dumas replied. "Yes I think I do." Linder remarked still gripping Dumas's arm. Dumas glanced down at the prophecy book that he was holding.

"Linder, you know that prophecies don't always turn out like we think they will." "Yes but what does that have to do with Jess's behavior?" Dumas looked between the book and Linder. "If I show you this, you must promise not to tell Jess that I showed it to you and you must do all that you can to change it." Dumas insisted. "What is it?" Linder asked. Dumas opened the prophecy book to the specific page which held the prophecy that he had shown Jess earlier. "Read this." He said and handed the book to Linder. Linder's eyes darted back and forth between the words as he read it. Once done he dropped the book and without looking back he ran out the door towards Jess.

He found Jess at the lead of all the twenty four people walking down the street with determination in her stride. He took a place walking right next to her but didn't say anything just watched her out of the corner of his eyes. Something has changed inside her, she didn't have the fun loving or mischievous smile and that she always wore. Her sparkling blue eyes were hard set in a cold stare with no compassion in them. Linder noticed that she was clinching her hands into fists by her sides. When they arrived at the forest dusk was upon them. Everyone had talked amongst each other on their way there except for Jess, who didn't say a word. Even when someone asked her a direct question, she acted like she hadn't heard them. When they reached the spot in near the forest that led them out of the city and into the cursed forest Jess stopped and turned to face everyone.

"Now listen up. There will be no talking, joking and having fun of any kind if you want to stay alive. Follow me and when we reach cave take the Black Dragons as prisoners and help get all the stolen ones back to the city. Make sure that a Black Dragon is the last one to leave the forest, and he has to be conscious or the curse will kill you all. Also if I order you to do something you do it. No questions got it." Jess stated. "Yes ma'am." The men from the army replied together. Jess looked at her friends for confirmation. "Yeah we got it." Erika replied. Erika could tell something was wrong with Jess but she trusted her friend so she didn't say anything. Maybe she had to distance herself from everyone to keep everyone safe. Erika thought to herself. She hoped that was all it was. Jess focused her stare on Linder. "I will do anything you say." He responded. "Good. Let's go." She declared and stepped into the forest.

Instantly a variety of skulls and bones appeared on the ground lining both sides of the trail that had a canopy of many tree branches which had grown into each other forming a tunnel. There was a distinct and disgusting smell that wasn't in the air before they stepped into the forest but now saturated the air that they breathed. It smelt like something burning in a fire. Jess didn't recognize exactly what the smell mixed the scent of fire and smoke was. She led the way towards the cave with all twenty three people following her. When she and the others drew near to the tree where Jess had first seen the lone Black Dragon she could feel that something was wrong. She stopped them all at the tree. A lantern hung from branch on the tree but there was no Black Dragons present and there was a piece of parchment stuck into the tree with an arrow. It was very late and dark. The only light there was coming from the lantern.

Jess looked toward the direction of the cave. It was too dark to see and the air was filled with so much smoke that she couldn't see very far even if it was dark. Jess knew something was very wrong. Linder pulled the arrow out of the tree and unfolded the piece of parchment. He read it silently. "Jess it's for you." He said and handed her the parchment. "What does it say?" General Jackson asked. Jess read the words out loud.

To the Black Dragon Woman,

I want to personally congratulate you on your killings this evening. You have killed over one hundred people, not counting those you are with that will add to your number shortly and you didn't have to lift a finger to do it. That is impressive. Unfortunately I still needed some of those people so you have a choice to make now. Either join our cause and be part of the great reign of darkness where your kind belongs or repay me with more people, such as the ones you brought with you or your final option is that you can die right along with the others and then I won't have to worry about you interfering anymore. I will give you until sunrise to make your decision.

From your master, Karlsen Soldum.

"The stolen ones!" Erika stated in horror. "Grab that lantern and follow me!" Jess shouted and took off running towards the cave. She arrived first along with Linder, Marcus, General Jackson, Sergeant Johnson and three of the officers. The terrible smell in the air was resonating from inside the cave. The air was thick with smoke and heat poured out of the cave. She was about to go inside but Linder held her back. "Wait. We don't know what is in there. Wait for the lantern." He told her. Shortly the rest of the company appeared, one man carrying the lantern. He handed it to Jess. Jess held the lantern up to the entrance. It was dark and filled with smoke and the sides of the cave looked to have been scorched. "Erika, cool it down." Jess ordered. Erika turned to the river that ran beside the entrance of the cave. She raised her hands and as she did a large wave of water rose from the river and the waterfall. She pushed her hands towards the cave and the water sprayed into the cave. The cave hissed as the cold water touched the hot rock. Then a cold bitter winter wind blew past Jess and flew into the cave.

"It should be cooled off now." Erika said. Jess didn't reply as she headed into the cave, holding the lantern up to see. Everyone followed. The stench hurt Jess's nose. "Oh no." Erika cried as she saw the awful sight that lay in front of her. Randy quickly pulled her out of the cave. "Jess you shouldn't see this." General Jackson replied. "It's my fault and I have to see if my grandma is amongst all of this. You all check for survivors." She declared without emotion. "Jess there are no survivors." Linder responded and tried to reach out to Jess. She shrugged him away and continued to go farther into the cave.

The last place she saw her grandmother was at the back of the cave. She made her way over the scorched, singed and blackened remains of the people that had been imprisoned there. All of which were soaking wet now from the river water that Erika blasted in there. With Linder, Sergeant Johnson and Jusdan at her side she began searching through the remains for her grandmother. After checking four different people she found her grandmother. There weren't many distinguishable features left but Jess was certain it was her. All Jess could feel was hatred. Hatred that was directed towards Karlsen Soldum and all the other Black Dragons.

After everything she had done to find her grandmother, they killed her. They had used magic fire and lit the cave ablaze with every one of the stolen ones inside it. There were no signs of a struggle for freedom from any of the corpses, there were signs of flash fire but also signs that it didn't burn long and was put out quickly. That is how Jess knew it was made by magic fire. The people wouldn't have known what had hit them until it was too late. There were so many people that could never return to their families, so many people that were killed because of her. Jess knew that she couldn't take her grandmother's body with her so she scooped up her charred remains and gave her one last hug. Jess noticed something hard inside her grandmother's clothes. She reached inside her clothes and pulled out a small square metal box. It was still warm. Jess opened it. Inside the small metal box were her grandmother's ring and a remnant of folded parchment. Jess opened the parchment and read the small words.

"Jessalyn, if you are reading this than you were unable to save me in time. Put that behind you, it is time for you to save yourself now. Wear the ring and do what you must to save yourself and remember I will always be there for you. Love Granny."

Right as Jess read the last word on the paper Jusdan pulled his sword from its sheath. "They are waiting for us. We are surrounded. I would say that are about fifty of them." Jusdan stated as he turned to face the cave entrance. Jess could see the hatred building on his face. She knew who *they* were. They were Black Dragons that had killed Jusdan's children, they were the ones had stolen her brother and beaten him, they were the ones that had killed her grandmother, they were the Black Dragons sent to kill her and every single person that had accompanied her to this cave. *They* were the Black Dragons that she was going to annihilate.

She put the ring on her finger and the box with the parchment into one of her pockets then with determination stood and looked into the eyes of everyone in the cave with her. She knew that some of them would be killed before the night was over. She felt no remorse only a hate driven determination to kill every Black Dragon that stood in her way until she could kill Karlsen Soldum. "Make sure to keep one of them away from me so that they will stay alive and conscious so that you all can make it back safely. Then you can kill him." Jess instructed General Jackson. The general nodded in acknowledgement. She pulled her dagger free from its sheath and headed out of the cave. Linder grabbed her arm. "Jess wait, I..." Linder began saying but Jess stopped him. "Let go of me!" she demanded and pulled her arm away. Linder was speechless. He noticed as she headed toward the entrance of the cave that more of her lovely long blonde hair had turned black. There were at least four large sections of black hair that interweaved them-selves into her braid. Linder didn't think that Jess really wanted him to leave her alone, he was sure it was the black dragon inside her changing her and making her act the way she was acting. He really hoped that the look of hatred that he saw on Jess's face was caused by the black dragon and not her real feelings though.

"It's not all her." Jusdan said to Linder. "What?" Linder asked, caught off guard by Jusdan's comment. Jusdan had been using his power and listening to his thoughts. "She has so much anger and hatred towards the Black Dragons herself, and I don't blame her, but it's not all her. The dragon inside her is manipulating her and she is giving in. She wants revenge and the dragon is feeding on that hate making her revenge seem possible. If we don't help her soon she will be too gone to help at all." Jusdan stated to Linder. "I know." Linder replied and then they both drew their weapons and headed out of the cave with the others.

The sight that waited outside was just as Jusdan predicted. There were almost fifty men dressed in black pants, tight fitting black shirt and blood red cloaks that billowed softly in the gentle breeze. Each and every one of them had black dragons tattooed on their faces. Several held burning torches. The glow of their torches cast an unnatural light making the Black Dragons appear more like beasts than human. They all held various types of malicious weapons, not counting the extra weapons they each had strapped to their person. Linder found the rest of his company waiting armed near the entrance of the cave and he knew that even though all twenty four people with him were skilled in fighting, there would be little chance of survival. He pulled his sword free of its sheath and prepared to fight. One Black Dragon stepped forward. "Which one of you is the Black Dragon woman?" he asked pointing his sword towards the group which Jess stood in.

"I am." Jess replied and stepped forward, dagger in hand. "Jess no." Linder begged and reached his free hand toward her. "Stop." She demanded and flicked his open hand with her dagger, making a small cut on his hand. Instantly blood began dripping off his cut. He tightened his hand into a fist to slow the blood. He was shocked that she actually cut him. The Black Dragon man chuckled at Linder's pain. "Who are you?" Jess demanded, speaking to the Black Dragon. "Are you Karlsen Soldum?" "Indeed I am. You will call me Master." The Black Dragon leader replied. "No I won't." Jess stated as she stared at him. He was not what Jess was expecting. He was in his thirties with flawless features. He had a chiseled jaw, a small dimple on one of his cheeks, and short wavy red hair. He had black eyes that seem to call Jess to them. The other Black Dragons had black eyes as well that were just intimidating but his seem to draw her in. He wore the same clothing as the others, the only difference is that he had a Black Dragon tattooed on one side of his face and as she looked at him she noticed another dragon on his right arm. It looked just like the one she had on her right arm. Then she noticed a third dragon on his other arm that was slightly hidden in the blood red cloak.

"You have three dragons." Jess stated. "No I have five. Each one of them has the same amount of power as your one." Karlsen Soldum responded. "Really?" Jess asked in a non believing tone. Soldum chuckled and then abruptly stopped. "You already know what I'm capable off so stop the games. Have you made your decision yet?" He inquired in an impatient tone. "Now what decision is that?" Jess asked as if she were confused. Soldum raised his hand and instantly a great ball of fire shot across the distance and hit one of the soldiers in their group. He screamed in pain as he burned. Soldum twisted his hand in the air and the fire stopped, along with the screaming. The soldier was dead. He was burnt to a crisp just like the people inside the cave. Just like her grandmother. "Now what is your decision?" Soldum yelled. "I would rather die than join you!" Jess spat. "I can arrange that. But believe me, this is not what I wanted, you could be so great with my help. We could control this wretched world together but if you won't join me than I will free your dragon and cut your heart out myself." Soldum affirmed. Linder put his hand on Jess's shoulder in protection. She felt the urge to push his hand away but before she could act words and images flashed in her mind.

It was all a jumble in her mind. So many familiar faces, so many people telling her what to do. "Believe." Said Erika. "Trust your heart." pleaded Linder. "Embrace the darkness." instructed Dumas. "Kill the dragon." declared Jusdan. "Save yourself." encouraged her grandmother. "Kill Soldum." stated Marcus. "Save us" consoled General Jackson. "Fulfill the prophecy." Kedar remarked. All were underlined with the dragon's voice repeating the same word over and over again. "Die! Die! Die!" Jess's mind raced with the words of the two prophecies about her, the letter from Soldum and her grandmother's last written words to her. She glanced down at the two rings that were on her left hand. One was a gold ring from Linder and the other a silver ring with a single line carved into the metal. The words that her grandmother had written for her sounded in her head. "Wear the ring and save yourself." Jess look at her dagger in her hand. Then an image of a griffin flashed in her mind. Suddenly she knew what she had to do.

"Johnson, now!" she yelled then in a flash she reached her hand back and grabbed Linder's dagger out of its sheath and threw it right at Karlsen Soldum. The dagger hit its target right in the chest. She turned to face Linder as Sergeant Johnson reached for him. "I'm sorry but it's the only way." She said and plunged her own dagger into her heart. "No!" Linder yelled as Jess went limp. He caught her and laid her down onto the forest floor. Jess saw Sergeant Johnson yank Linder away from her dying body. There came the clank of metals as swords hit each other. "Jess!" Erika screamed in panic. Jess saw a bright white light flicker in the sky above her. She closed her eyes and listened to the sound of men screaming as she bled to death on the forest ground. Her last thoughts before death overtook her were… I'm free.

To be continued….

Acknowledgements:

First I want to say a huge thank you to my mother in law for helping me edit and re-edit this book to perfection. It wouldn't be as good as it is without her. Thank you Marilyn!

I also want to thank you the reader for choosing this book and for joining me on this writing adventure. It has been my pleasure to write this story and I hope you have enjoyed it as much as I did writing it.

If you have enjoyed this book or have feedback please make feel free to contact the author at:
kahidonmountains@gmail.com

26781260R00146

Made in the USA
Charleston, SC
18 February 2014